The Secret Journals of Fanticulous Glim
The Gondoliers

BY PAOLO MAZZUCATO

BEPIBOOKS

FOR JULIA & OLIVIA
MY STRONG AND CONFIDENT LITTLE WARRIORS

Contents

Prologue 1

One — the arrival 8

Two — an interruption 36

Three — what came before 38

Four — rising 47

Five — complications 64

Six — a dead end 73

Seven — through the arch 80

Eight — the scenic route 93

Nine — another interruption 102

Ten — waves 104

Eleven — old stories 116

Twelve — something murky 132

Thirteen — a few more 142

Fourteen — wondrous places 153

Fifteen — thickening fog 170

Sixteen — the siren's gift   174

Seventeen — a new morning   187

Eighteen — unspoken tradition   197

Nineteen — work in progress   202

Twenty — the cursed isle   219

Twenty-One — fire and glass   239

Twenty-Two — over the bridge   257

Twenty-Three — a show of force   262

Twenty-Four — a sinking feeling   267

Twenty-Five — outlaws   274

Twenty-Six — paradise   281

Twenty-Seven — low tide   292

Twenty-Eight — help   302

Twenty-Nine — turning the tide   311

Thirty — secrets   335

Epilogue   348

Appendix   350

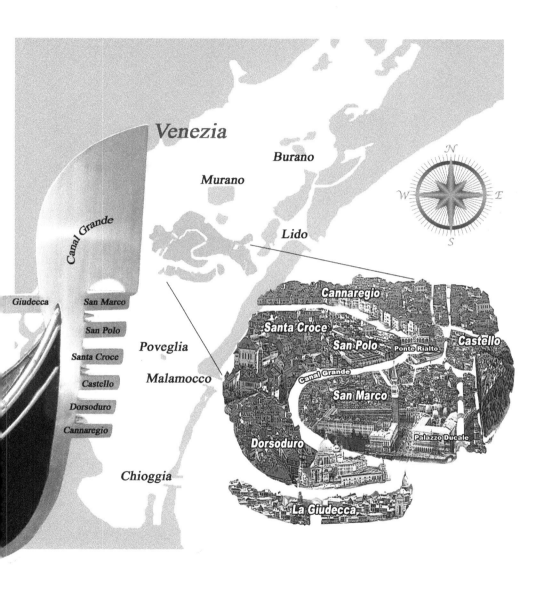

Venezia

Burano

Murano

Lido

Canal Grande

Giudecca   San Marco

San Polo

Santa Croce

Castello

Dorsoduro

Cannaregio

Poveglia

Malamocco

Chioggia

Cannaregio

Santa Croce

San Polo   Ponte Rialto   Castello

Canal Grande

San Marco

Dorsoduro

Palazzo Ducale

La Giudecca

N
W   E
S

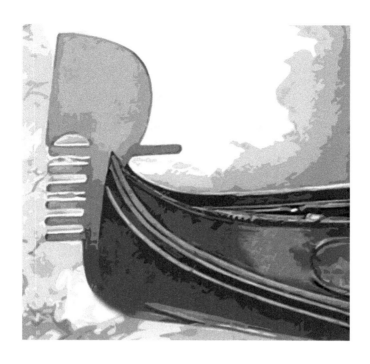

PROLOGUE

"Hello, *Buongiorno*. Welcome to *Venezia*, the city where hope springs eternal."

The old, white-haired gondolier says this to you as he looks down from his perch at the rear of his shiny, black gondola. You smile, of course. I mean, why wouldn't you? You're on vacation, strolling along a picturesque walkway beside an ancient canal through one of the most fabled cities in all of Italy. You've seen all of the top attractions—toured the *Palazzo Ducale,* the Ducal Palace, where once the noble *Doges* ruled over all of Venice; You've climbed to the top of the famous *campanile* in St. Mark's Square and stood beside the *Quadriga*, the four enormous bronze horses of Constantinople from the balcony of St. Mark's Basilica; You've even watched the two Moors, the giant statues on the roof of the clock tower, as they swing their hammers to chime the hours. You've seen Venice...right?

And yet, you can't help feeling, as you watch the old gondolier in his traditional striped shirt and straw hat, and notice his wizened gaze, that maybe, just maybe, there is something more to know...to understand about this place. There is a story, not yet told, seeping from the mossy, stone walls and whispered in the evening air—a timeworn tale of mystery or magic, or both. Venice has a secret, and you know that if you open your mind and search deep enough you might discover more than you imagined.

"Come. Come aboard." The gondolier motions you toward the plush, red velvet seat in his gondola. He smiles warmly. His voice is comforting with perhaps a wink of impishness that reminds you of a playful song or a lullaby saved back in some distant memory of your childhood. "Sit," he says. "Lighten your load for a bit, and I will take you on a wonderful ride, an extraordinary journey beyond everything you see and know."

You step to the edge of the walkway, captivated in the moment. Glancing curiously at the gondolier, you pause, as if just now seeing him for the first time. Somehow, despite his white hair and rugged hands that look as rough as the open sea, he suddenly doesn't seem nearly as old as you first thought he was. There's a youthful gleam in his eyes and a sturdy strength in his posture that makes him look both ancient and childlike at once. His expression is old and wise but...young and hopeful as well, like a grandfather seeing the world anew through his grandchild's eyes. He beckons to you again, and you find yourself wondering... Maybe nothing is as simple as it first seems.

And there's something about the invitation that you can't pass up. Whether it's the way the late afternoon sun is glistening on the water, or the faint hint of an old Italian melody drifting in the air, or perhaps just simply the way the gondolier's outstretched hand is welcoming you into his world, a place afloat between the past and present where reality seems that it might melt away and make anything possible, you nod and step off the stone walkway and into the gently bobbing embrace of Venice.

"Good. You sit right there," he says as you take your seat. "Make yourself comfortable. This is the most fantastic gondola ride in all of Venice—beautiful, relaxing, full of history..." He shoves off, pushing the gondola away from any chance that you might change your mind. "...and not too expensive." He chuckles to himself, and you suddenly wonder if you've just been had. "Trust me," he reassures. "You will enjoy."

The gondolier gently sweeps the long oar of the gondola back and forth as you glide onward past old baroque-styled houses, Gothic palaces, Romanesque and Byzantine buildings—rugged, stone ramparts scented with salt air and steeped in briny water that surround you like the ancient walls of an abandoned labyrinth.

But far from abandoned, the waterway is filled with sound and movement—motorboats puttering past, water taxis ferrying fancy tourists to their hotels. People's voices drift by and mingle with the din of sidewalk merchants and pedestrian traffic that flows over bridges and steps along the stone-paved promenades beside the canal.

And as elegant gondolas gracefully skim across the water's surface, you see them—the gondoliers. Each has a face etched with what you can only describe as a knowing expression, a silent and subtle nod of greeting to you and your guide as you pass.

"What you see, all around, is a city of invention," your gondolier explains. "Built on marshy islands within the Venetian lagoon over 14 centuries ago, Venice rose up from an idea, a hope that the people who came here believed, that they could make something special out of this place and create an extraordinary world. Of course, Venice has had its share of problems—high tides, floods, erosion and even just the settling of the city's muddy foundation. Truthfully, it is a wonder the city did not crumble and sink years ago."

The gondolier chuckles again. You...not as amused.

"But do not worry," he continues. "Venice will not fall while hope survives. Hope is a powerful thing. It can keep many dreams afloat, *eh*? It is what flows through the air, through the water. It is what gives the city its...magic."

Just then, your gondola pushes past the rough, stone corner of a building, emerging from the maze of narrow waterways into a wider...more impressive canal. It's the Grand Canal, the main passage through Venice, gently winding through the heart of the city, its curves mirrored in the sweeping shape of each gondola's bow iron, or *ferro*, with the six comb-like teeth representing the six *sestieri* districts of Venice. From the largest, *Cannaregio* and *Castello* along the north waterfront, to *Dorso Duro* along the south, they are joined by the narrow *calli*, walkways, alleyways, canals and bridges that wander and turn their way inward to the central *sestieri* of *Santa Croce, San*

Marco and *San Polo* along the Grand Canal. There, the reddening sunlight washes the roof and arches of the celebrated *Rialto* Bridge in a glow and gleams on the marble and gold accented façade of the *Cà D'Oro,* and the other palaces that line the water's edge.

"It is beautiful, no?" your gondolier smiles.

Just then, to your right, a battered, flat-bottom barge passes. A weathered fisherman, cleaning his catch, slaps his cutting board over the side of his vessel, dumping a boardful of fish guts back into the canal.

"*Ei!*" your gondolier howls. "What's a matter with you? I got a tourist here."

The fisherman looks up with a scowl, his eyes practically hidden beneath two enormously bushy eyebrows with a life of their own. He grumbles to himself before continuing on his way.

Your gondolier puts his smile back on. "So sorry. Not everyone appreciates the charm and beauty of Venice."

And with that, the gondolier pauses. He stills his oar for a moment, glances up the canal then back down in the other direction as if to ensure that no one is within earshot of what will soon follow. You look up at him, curiously, sensing in his silence that something more is about to be revealed, something that will change everything you thought you knew about this place, something unexpected. And your gondolier, his eyes bright with the promise of that unexpected something about to unfold, catches your look and leans in close.

"But there is something...charming, you know—something that swirls unseen through the day and night and protects the city from harm. A kind of enchantment that, if you believe... well..." He sweeps his oar back and forth a few times as he angles the gondola into the flow of boat traffic. Then he begins. "Let me tell you a story of a time long ago—a memory of a fanciful world now forgotten, when Venice, this city we have all come to know and love...was almost destroyed."

CHAPTER ONE — THE ARRIVAL

You might think that the 'beginning' is the perfect place to start a story. But sometimes, a story does not become a story until much later, not until a particular person on a particular day drifts into the tale and stirs the water. Then, like ripples on the surface, the story is revealed and you see that it began much earlier than you ever thought it did.

It was roughly the turn of the century, 1902 to be exact, when the waters of the Venetian lagoon were 'rippled' by a new arrival. A young traveler, no more than 15, dressed in baggy

trousers, a faded mariner's jacket and cap, and a battered pair
of old, leather shoes with tattered laces, waited anxiously near
the bow of a steam-powered *vaporetto*—a water bus that ferried passengers to and from their stops along the canal. At first
glance, there didn't seem to be anything extraordinary about
this particular passenger, something that would make you say,
"Hey, I wonder who that is," or "Hey, I bet that person right
there is going to change the course of Venetian history." In fact,
by all appearances, you might have thought that this young
person would soon be lost in the flow of the ordinary, wading
through life slowly and unremarkably, barely making a ripple
at all. But in that, you would have been mistaken.

The boat captain, his sea-worn face rimmed by an untidy,
grey beard, stared out suspiciously from behind a pair of thick,
round goggles at the 'unremarkable' youngster on his boat.
From his perch at the helm of his *vaporetto*, he had seen many
new arrivals in Venice, and this one, he thought, looked like
just another young boy wandering through with no real direction. So it seemed odd to him that, for some reason, he felt a
peculiar need to reach out and offer some guidance or a word
of wisdom before they docked. He squinted through his goggles and looked closer.

The boy wore his dusty cap low on his forehead, had a weathered copy of Jules Verne's *20,000 Leagues Under the Sea* tucked under his arm, and a battered suitcase tagged with travel labels from around the world at his side. In one hand, he had a stale crust of bread, all that remained of an earlier meal; in his other, a few coins left over from having skimped on that meal. He pocketed the coins and finished the bread, fidgeting nervously, ready and anxious for whatever might await him on shore.

The captain leaned over the ship's wheel, considering with a curious scowl. There was something different about this new arrival, but he couldn't quite fathom what it was. He wiped his goggles clear and turned his attention back to his work, steering his *vaporetto* handily past the vague shapes of other boats that slipped by like phantoms through the mid-February mist on the lagoon. His curiosity would keep for now.

The other passengers—a dozen or so Venetian locals making their way home at day's end—waited patiently as the boat chugged along through St. Mark's Basin on its way to its destination, the landing at the *Riva Degli Schiavoni* near St. Mark's Square.

CHAPTER ONE

Now, the *Riva Degli Schiavoni*, you see, was the main promenade on the south-facing waterfront of Venice proper, the place of arrival for most everyone and everything coming to the city. Built on sediment and silt dredged from the lagoon's basin in the ninth century, it stretched wide like an open embrace, from the *molo*, the main pier of the Ducal Palace, all the way to the picturesque *rio Ca' di Dio* canal. It bustled with the lively flow of fishermen, merchants and locals, and was the first impression of Venice for those arriving from beyond. Looking out over the lagoon toward the Adriatic, it reminded all who came that Venice and the sea were intertwined and inescapably bound to each other.

The captain scanned the hazy shoreline with a routine gaze as he veered inward, throttling back to adjust his *vaporetto's* bearing and speed. Standing at the helm, he too seemed bound to this place—like the boats and water, a part of Venice itself. As he nosed the bow of his boat toward where he knew the dock would soon appear in the mist, he paused, suddenly spotting his young passenger staring up at him curiously from beneath the brim of his cap.

And that's when the captain noticed. The 'boy'—who had till then seemed like 'nothing particularly extraordinary,' was not a boy at all. Traveling incognito, her face smudged with dirt and yet luminous, eyes bright with the glimmer of adventure, the traveler was in fact a young girl, and the tag on her suitcase said her name was Fantina.

Wait a minute now, I am sure you are saying to yourself. You are thinking that I should have told you right away that the young traveler was a girl. That by letting you believe, as the captain did, that Fantina was a boy, I was misleading you a bit, *eh?* But consider instead what you now may choose to embrace—that you must always be open to the unexpected, and not everything is as it first may seem.

Of course, you are probably also wondering how it is that a girl of 15 would be out on her own? Though her rough and tumble exterior might suggest to you that she was perfectly at home on the road, 1902 was hardly a carefree time without peril to be wandering the world. It was a dangerous time. Why, only just two years before, the king of Italy, Umberto I, had been murdered for some sinister reason it was said. There were pirates on the high seas, bandits on the low roads, and travelers in Venice had recounted tales of being set upon by a band of mysterious brigands that prowled the dark alleyways at night.

The new century had barely begun and there was already such uncertainty. People didn't know whether they should cling to the past or trust in the future. The old ways of doing things seemed quaint when considered under the bright light of progress. With steam power moving people about faster, and inventions like Guglielmo Marconi's telegraphic radio transmitter connecting people across oceans, the mysteries of the wide world were fading. And many, if not most of the local Venetians had begun to see their city through a fog of...trepidation and in a darker, less hopeful light.

But Fantina was different. Where some people saw uncertainty, she saw possibility. To her, the new century wasn't a fearsome place where change threatened everything that was; it was just the crest of a wave connected to the swell behind it as it rode forward into the future. She smiled as they approached the shore, eager to venture out into this new place.

She had a vague recollection of Venice, but wasn't sure if it was from an actual memory or from one of the many stories her father had told her during their travels together. If she closed her eyes, she could still see her father as he had been, bold and spirited, pointing out the stars and constellations to her as they navigated the world. And she heard his voice, hoarse with what seemed like centuries of exposure to the wind and salt air, and yet, gentle and comforting to a little girl who somehow understood that her future was completely boundless in his care.

And somewhere, deep within, she remembered the story he had invented for her—a playful, little nursery rhyme that he would recount each time they set out on a new voyage. He would leap to the bow, trim the jib and foresail and explain that '...to find what is golden, the journey must start, with an open mind and a worthy heart.' Fantina would laugh and listen as he continued the tale of mystery and mermaids, ghosts and drag-ons—verse after verse of fanciful ideas that would always end with starry skies and hidden treasure.

So now, leaning into the breeze at the bow of the *vaporetto*, Fantina imagined herself a great explorer in search of fortune and glory. Though her father was no longer with her, Fantina could still feel his embrace in the ocean spray and his voice in the wind reminding her that 'the search is always worth the trip, but only if the thing you are looking for is worth the search.'

She crinkled her nose and raised a dubious eyebrow, realiz-ing that she wasn't at all sure what her father had meant by that. The 'thing' she was looking for wasn't complicated, she thought, as she glanced at her threadbare jacket and scuffed shoes. With a little hard work, fortune would definitely smile on her, and how could that not be worth it? But was that the 'thing' her father was talking about? She had always figured there would be time enough later to ask, and she had always meant to...but she hadn't.

Fantina turned to look out over the bow as the *vaporetto* slowed. Anticipation, like a wave, flowed to meet her. She nodded to herself, excited, but in the same moment, a bit confused. Nothing in her mind was completely clear about this place, and like the shoreline now appearing gradually through the mist, her notion of Venice was hazy.

And yet, it all seemed familiar, more than just a vague impression from a half-remembered story. It was the place she had been longing to see, from even before her father's passing. The thought of '*Venezia,*' which had always brought a smile to her father's face, was now the idea that had drawn Fantina in, as if with a sense that for her, Venice wasn't just a destination...it was her destiny.

The boat captain shifted his goggles up onto his furrowed forehead abruptly as his *vaporetto* belched a final puff of steam and smoke and glided to the quay. He glanced at Fantina with a wary look, certain now that he should dole out some insight gathered from his many years at the helm, navigating life. "*Attenzione a l'acqua,*" he bellowed in a gruff voice as he looped a mooring tether around a sturdy, wooden pylon. "Be careful of the water."

But it was too late. Fantina had already tucked her book into her suitcase and leapt from the bow of the boat onto the stone walkway of the landing and...SPLASH, now found herself in five inches of water.

A little unexpected, *eh?* But don't worry. As I was mentioning before, the sea had always been both the blessing and the curse of Venice. Back in the 6th century, it provided safety for refugees fleeing Lombard invaders from the north of Italy. They settled small communities offshore on the marshy and mostly uninhabited islands of the lagoon and, in time, banded together to dominate seaborne trade between the West and Far East. By the 9th century, they had formed the city of Venice.

Massive wooden pylons were sunk deeply into the muddy lagoon bottom to control the shifting sediment and support the foundations of the growing city, but no matter what was done, the land beneath the homes, palaces, churches and cathedrals of Venice would never be solid. Venice would always be settling...sinking. And the tide, rising and falling, would always add to both the charm of Venice and...its dampness.

Fantina looked up from her soaked shoes as the *vaporetto* captain shook his head and rubbed his beard with a surly grin. "In *Venezia*," he cautioned, "you must always look before leap, *eh?*"

Fantina crinkled her nose, considering, then shrugged. "Maybe," she mused in her bright and mischievous voice. "Or you can dive in and hope for the best."

The captain squinted uncertainly at Fantina. She was definitely an odd one, he thought. He then lowered a short gangway onto the dock. The other passengers, evidently not surprised in the least by the flooded landing, disembarked donning the latest in latex rubber boots, and continued on their way.

There was a dapper gent with stylish, buckled galoshes, and a petite lady in waders that matched her handy waterproof mantle. Overshoes, gumboots...some plain, some fancy, Fantina admired the ingeniously practical footwear as they passed—a clever and new century solution to a soggy problem. "What will they think up next?" she beamed.

Fantina gazed about in awe as she splashed along the walkway of the flooded *Riva Degli Schiavoni.* The tile pavers of the promenade glistened beneath her feet, and the brisk, salty air tingled her nose as she eagerly took in the sights and sounds around her. People flowed past in every direction, intent and purposeful, but with their eyes focused on their feet, careful not to step carelessly and hazard a slip. They didn't seem to appreciate their grand and astonishing surroundings as they marched along on their way, Fantina thought to herself.

The building to Fantina's right was a stunning palace façade of intricate archways and pink, patterned stone that shimmered in the sun. Before her, two, giant granite columns capped with enormous statues towered overhead. But it wasn't just the impressive architecture that caught Fantina's interest. In her eyes, Venice was alive with innovation and fanciful inventions of the mechanical age. Beyond the steamboats and water taxis that criss-crossed through the basin, Fantina was delighted by even the simplest of novelties.

A fruit vendor, packing up for the day, loaded a few wooden crates onto the back of his acquatrike—a pedal-powered tricycle of sorts with paddle wheels to propel it over the flooded walkway. It spattered past a shopkeeper clearing water from his *merciaio* haberdashery storefront with a gear-driven, hand-cranked water pump. Fantina smiled, intrigued by it all.

"Scarpe d'Acqua!" a young street vendor called out enthusiastically. *"Die Wasser Schuhe...Chaussures d'Eau."* He was a handsome, young boy, maybe a year or two shy of being taken seriously as a full-fledged Venetian merchant, but not for lack of flair. He worked the promenade with charm and hustle, trying to lure customers with his multi-lingual sales pitch for his floating, banana-shaped, water-walking footwear displayed on his waterlogged vendor cart. Uninterested locals continued past without stopping as he slipped the mini pontoons onto his feet, fastening them with a twist of a brass wing nut. Just then, Fantina popped up behind him.

"What's that?"

The boy, startled by Fantina's sudden appearance, spun about, nearly losing his footing. He took a moment to steady himself and straighten up, then turned to Fantina as he regained his salesman's grin. "These are Da Vinci water shoes," he pitched, "the latest in turn of the century togwear."

"Fanticulous," Fantina smiled as she stooped to study the design a little closer.

The boy sized up his potential customer, looking her over, not fooled for a moment by her drab disguise. It would take more than travel-worn clothing, and a shabby, old suitcase to throw him off his mark or hide her dazzling eyes...her radiant smile...her— "Uh...yes," he sputtered self-consciously as he stopped his mind from wandering. "They are...wait a minute. What?"

Fantina straightened up. "Fanticulous," she repeated. "Fantastic, with just a little bit of ridiculous thrown in."

The boy considered. "Ah, thank you...I think. Is that good?"

"Absolutely. All great ideas need a little of both. And Venice is the source of all things fanticulous." Fantina took a moment to scan the scene—tourists and locals bustling about, a crowd gathering in the little square, the *Piazzetta San Marco,* before the pink-stoned building, the Ducal Palace. It was all so full of life.

The boy stared at Fantina. Her enthusiasm was refreshing. Most of the people he encountered along the promenade these days kept their eyes downturned as they hurried along, preoccupied more with the dank world at their feet than the world of possibility before and above them. They were missing two thirds of the world by his calculation. "Have you been here before?" he asked.

"Not entirely sure," Fantina reflected. "Parts seem familiar, but not in an absolute kind of way, more of a vague, deep-down, forgotten memory way. Does that make sense?" Before the boy could reply, she continued. "Then again, my father told me all about Venice, so it could be that I'm just remembering what he told me, right? Anyhow, either way, so far...I like it." The boy hesitated, dazed in the whirlwind of words. Fantina took a step closer and leaned in furtively. "I'm an explorer, see? And here is where I'll make my mark."

"What mark?"

"Fortune and glory," Fantina said.

"You don't say?"

"I do say. I have ideas, and some start up funds." She jingled her frugally saved coins in her pocket. "Unfortunately I work alone, and I don't need any help, otherwise I might've been able to use someone like you." Fantina tossed the boy a quick smile as she sloshed on past him.

The boy, caught off-guard by the smile, felt for that moment like he was floating on air. Then he realized, of course, that he was actually floating on water, and his feet were slipping out from under him. He landed on his bottom with a splash.

Fantina eyed his water shoes. "Very clever," she called back to him, "but a little wobbly."

The boy sat up on the flooded walkway, enchanted despite his soggy bottom. "Maybe another time, then."

"Maybe," she smiled.

The boy watched Fantina wistfully as she disappeared into the crowd. "Hope springs eternal," he sighed.

It was an often-repeated motto in Venice, the city where 'hope springs eternal.' If Fantina had heard the boy say it just then, she might have turned back curiously, because of the memory it would have stirred.

From as early as Fantina was old enough to recall, her father had woven that sentiment into every bedtime fairy tale he told when he tucked her in for the night in whatever place their travels had taken them. Along the shores of Copenhagen, hope sprang eternal for a starry-eyed mermaid who aspired to a life above the waves. A magic lamp and a genie in middle-Asia gave hope to a would-be prince, and a hopeful, curious girl in the English countryside followed a white rabbit down a rabbit hole in search of adventure.

Hope was the common thread in every story for her father, and especially in the many wondrous tales he had told her about Venice. But here, in this place, Fantina felt that hope wasn't just the thread of an idea. As tangible as the wind and water, the people, the buildings in the piazzas...it somehow felt like something more.

The Ducal Palace, once the noble residence of the *Doges* that ruled over Venice until 1797, was still an impressive sight. The late afternoon sun shone through the intricately patterned cornice rimming the perimeter wall, making it look like the palace itself was crowned in delicate lace.

The crowd gathering in the *Piazzetta San Marco* edged forward toward a raised platform before the ornate façade of the palace. On the platform, the mayor of Venice, Filippo Grimani, a short, fastidious man with close-cropped hair and a well-groomed, handlebar mustache, was preparing to address the people. Donning long coattails and knee-high galoshes, he was a bit of an odd duck, the type of man who seemed unsure in his position of leadership but determined to prove his worth. He was flanked by two other skittish city officials and an escort of gallantly uniformed, sword-toting Venetian police, the *carabinieri*.

"As our city steps into this new century of progress," the mayor began in a tenuously wavering tone, "we must leave the past behind, and look to the future." He looked up, tugging the tip of his right mustache nervously, as if trying to gauge the crowd's reaction. A few people nodded and murmured approval, but most remained silent, their eyes focused on the water at their feet—their third of the world.

Fantina paused at the edge of the *piazzetta* as she pulled a tattered map of the city from her pocket. Scanning the square and the narrow walkways that branched away in every direction, she turned the map about, trying to get her bearings. She sighed. If the maze of walkways, narrow *calli* and passages throughout Venice was confusing under normal circumstances, under five inches of water it was incomprehensible. She took a step toward a passing gentleman with a grim, under-the-weather look on his face. "Excuse me, where is the church of *San Lorenzo?*" she asked, a bit bewildered. The gentleman continued on without noticing her, settling into the crowd gathered before the platform.

Fantina lowered her map, watching curiously, then edged a bit closer. She wondered what the gathering was all about and craned her neck to see through the crowd.

The *carabinieri* escort was the first thing that caught her eye. Standing tall and still as statues, they flanked either side of the platform, each with a sheathed *cinquedea* short sword on his belt. With the mayor's talk of leaving the past behind and embracing the future, they almost seemed out of place, Fantina thought. The *cinquedea*, named for its 'five-finger' width at the hilt, was little more than a fancy dagger, and the *carabiniere* stately uniforms with epaulets and shiny, brass buttons were a bit old fashioned as well. But even though Fantina presumed their presence was mostly just ceremonial, the show of force made her uneasy all the same.

The mayor continued, his wavering voice struggling to sound decisive. "For hundreds of years, Venice has suffered from the watery hand that grips us. It slaps at our shores, muddies our foundations, and rises to flood our streets and *piazzas*. So, it is with great appreciation for his efforts to save Venice from the rising tides, that we recognize a man touched with greatness, *Signore* Massimo Malvagio, and bestow on him the title, 'Protector of Venice.'"

Scattered applause rose through the crowd as a tall, well-dressed gentleman stepped forward on the platform. Fantina angled herself for a better view. Massimo Malvagio was a lean but imposing man with sharp, angular features jutting out from beneath a stiff shirt collar and long, black coat that made him seem even more so. He towered over the comparatively diminutive mayor as he looked out over the people with an appreciative smile and a wave that could only be described as...aristocratic. He was, in fact, descended from a family of ancestral nobility. His great grandfather, it was said (mostly by Malvagio himself), had resisted Napoleon's conquest of Venice in 1797, and Malvagio's own father (again, according to Malvagio) fought alongside the rebel hero, Daniele Manin, in 1848 to free Venice from the Hapsburg Empire. People were generally impressed by the Malvagio family history (at least as it had been relayed to them), and Malvagio enjoyed the reputation that came with it.

The mayor rose to the tips of his rubber boots to pin a handsome, bronze service medallion onto Malvagio's left breast pocket. He strained to reach. Malvagio might have helped by bowing forward a bit, but that would have required him to lower himself, which was something that Malvagio was loath to do. So he stood patiently and perfectly erect while the mayor managed, as best he could, to pin him. Then, Malvagio took center stage with perfectly practiced humility and spoke in a stiff and haughty voice.

"Thank you. Thank you all from my heart for your kindness and generous support." Fantina studied Malvagio as he raised his hands to silence the cheers from the crowd. He looked quite pleased with himself, she thought, and from the applause, the crowd seemed to love him too. And why not? If *Signore* Malvagio was the 'Protector of Venice,' he must really love this place—its unique beauty, its charm...the enchanting essence of this city in the heart of the lagoon...

"The sea is our enemy," Malvagio declared. Fantina cocked her head curiously. She wasn't sure how you could love Venice and hate the sea, but she'd give him the benefit of her doubt. After all, she just got here. What could she know?

Malvagio continued. "My father, the loyal right hand man of the heroic Daniele Manin who delivered Venice from the tyranny of the Hapsburgs..." he paused to allow for the requisite nods of respect and approval, "...always told me that one day Venice would call upon the Malvagio family again, to rescue it from the ravages of the sea. And I assure you, when my 'Gatekeeper Project' is complete, the Venice problem will be solved."

Led by the mayor, and his *carabinieri*, the crowd chimed in with a wave of enthusiastic applause. Fantina scanned their faces in an attempt to glean a little more information. She wasn't sure what this 'Gatekeeper Project' was, but everyone seemed to be on board with it. Everyone, that is, except for one woman.

She was a short, elderly lady, her silver hair pulled back neatly into a tight bun bobbing just above a lace scarf bunched casually around her neck. In a rose-embroidered dress and garden-themed rain poncho, the woman seemed more colorful than the rest of the crowd, and stood apart from them on the stepped base of a marble column where the flooded *piazzetta* couldn't reach her fancily flowered dress shoes. She looked unconvinced by the public pronouncements of the…'Protector of Venice.' In fact, if Fantina had to guess, she would have said that the old woman didn't trust *Signore* Malvagio at all.

The old woman spotted Fantina watching her, and nodded a friendly and...hopeful greeting. She glanced at the flooded *piazzetta*, then at her fancy shoes with a concerned expression. Evidently, the woman was stranded on the one place in the *piazzetta* where her feet could stay dry, and she was looking for someone with a solution to keep them that way.

Fantina stepped closer. "You look like you need some help," she said.

The woman looked up briskly, her eyes twinkling with gratitude tinged in a touch of surprise that seemed to percolate with her every word. "Oh, look at that. You saw me after all. Not many people these days see anything beyond their own shoes."

"Oh, well," Fantina shrugged, "in my case, it's too late for my own shoes." She lifted her soaked foot up from the flooded *piazzetta* then splashed it back down again. "But you looked like you were hoping for someone to—"

The woman shifted abruptly. Fantina stopped short. "Interesting," the woman said with an inquisitive expression. "You thought I looked hopeful?"

Fantina crinkled her nose, considering. "You weren't?"

"Oh, yes, I was. I am. I always will be. What about you?" The woman looked curiously at Fantina, but not in an unsettling way. There was something warm and amiable in her eyes that put Fantina at ease.

Fantina found herself thinking back to her father's stories again, and wondering if she dared to be as hopeful as they were. Why not? She just wanted a little fortune and glory after all, not magic lamps, fairy tales or wonderlands. Fantina nodded and looked about optimistically. "I was told that this is the place for great ideas."

The old woman considered Fantina with an uncertain glance, then carefully scanned the flooded *piazzetta* left and right as if on the lookout for the 'great ideas.' She looked again at her shoes and shrugged. "Well, maybe so, but I see none so far."

Fantina crinkled her nose again then narrowed her eyes, thinking deeply. It was her 'inventing look,' and what this situation needed was an invention. Then, her eyes lit up. She had it —the spark of an idea. "Don't go anywhere, I'll be right back," she said.

The old woman moved to the edge of her dry step and leaned forward with interest to watch as Fantina retraced her soggy steps back across the *piazzetta* the way she had come. First, Fantina grabbed an old fruit crate left behind by the acquatrike vendor; then she dug into her start up funds to haggle with the haberdasher for his hand-cranked water pump; finally, she stepped up to the young Da Vinci shoe salesman.

"I want two," Fantina said as she handed over the few coins she had left. "Two shoes that is. One pair."

The boy nearly lost his balance again, surprised by Fantina's second sudden appearance and even more surprised, it seemed, by the prospect of an actual sale. "You do?" he said. "I mean, of course, you do. Let me see if I have something in your size."

"No need, I'll take these," Fantina said as she reached forward and grabbed the two largest pontoons on the boy's cart. "Thanks." She left in a whirlwind, splashing away across the promenade. The boy watched her go, a heap of coins in hand and a baffled look on his face.

The old woman widened her eyes, intrigued, as Fantina sloshed to a halt and deposited her armful of gear before her. "Well, you certainly are a curious one." she said.

"Oh...you have no idea." Fantina smiled and flipped open a pouch on her belt to reveal a handy, portable tool kit. Then, in a flurry of mechanical innovation, Fantina began assembling pieces.

Minutes later, the old woman was stepping onto a makeshift catamaran-canoe-water-scooter of sorts—the fruit crate fastened between the pontoon shoes and propelled by the hand pump. It wasn't fancy, Fantina thought as she snapped her tool pouch shut, but it would do under the peculiarly damp circumstances.

"Very good," the old woman smiled as she pumped the controls and started forward. She pointed toward a small side street at the other end of the main *piazza*. "*San Lorenzo*...is that way," she offered.

Fantina looked, then turned back gratefully. "Thank you."

The old woman nodded and paused beside Fantina. She touched her gently on the cheek and looked deeply into her eyes. "You have a good heart, and Venice welcomes you."

Perhaps it was just a reflection of the setting sun, but for a moment, Fantina's eyes almost seemed to glimmer. The old woman considered, then tossed an odd look up toward the sky. "There is something about this one," she mused.

Fantina followed the woman's glance but saw nothing other than a flock of pigeons fluttering along the rooftops of Venice. When she looked down again, the woman was already sputtering away on her scooter down a flooded alleyway.

Fantina smiled. She had just arrived and already felt swept up in the excitement and the possibilities of Venice. "Making my mark," she mused. "Fortune and—"

Fantina stopped short as a vendor wheeled past with a cart of roasted chestnuts. The warm, smoky aroma drifted past her nose, suddenly reminding Fantina of her meager meal earlier in the day. She checked her empty pocket where her 'start-up-funds' had once jingled. This first invention had set her 'fortune' back a bit, or, in truth, all the way back to broke.

She eyed the chestnut cart hungrily, trying to brush off the craving she now had along with the fact that she hadn't a single coin left to—

Fantina paused, a thought brightening her face. She reached up to her neck and pulled a fine, golden-rope chain from beneath her shirt. Attached to it was a small, round pendant—a coin actually. Though it seemed old and worn, with markings that had all but faded completely from view, it was still quite shiny, an untarnished ingot of gold that somehow seemed warm and hopeful in Fantina's hand. Fantina had been wearing it around her neck for as long as she could remember. Her father had told her to keep it close and that someday it might prove useful to have. Fantina thought of it as her emergency, get-out-of-serious-trouble coin.

Fantina glanced back at the chestnuts again as the vendor stopped to bag a steaming scoopful for a smiling customer. As temptingly appetizing as they looked, Fantina was pretty sure her father wouldn't have considered getting a tasty snack a serious emergency, so, with a wistful sigh, she tucked her pendant back inside her collar, grabbed her suitcase and slogged onward across the *piazza*.

From high above, the flow of people moving along the flooded pavement seemed like petals swirling in a current. They streamed and circled toward their destinations unaware of anything above or beyond the ordinary. But even though they didn't know it yet, they, like Fantina, were part of the story that would soon ripple outward from this particular day.

Four, ominous shadows fell over them and the *piazza* from above—from the balcony over the towering, arched entrance to

St. Mark's Basilica. There, the bronze *Quadriga* horses stood regally on their stone pedestals, the late afternoon sun glowing on their sturdy backs, their front hooves raised as if ready to march on command.

And the enormous bell atop the majestic clock tower, adjacent to the basilica, rang out—resounding peals echoing over the rooftops as the two, imposing and mechanically animated bronze Moors swung their giant hammers to chime the five o'clock hour.

Pigeons stirred from their perches on the Moors' outstretched arms and fluttered off, a few coming to rest on the stone ledge just below the roofline, where another statue stood sentry—the iconic symbol of all Venice—the regal winged lion of Saint Mark the Evangelist.

Gracefully chiseled in stone, its mane flowed down over its broad shoulders where two mighty wings, intricately detailed with sculpted feathers, rose from its back. The noble face, polished smooth with time, stared out from its ledge at the skyline of the city with a curiously lifelike expression, both majestic and intimidating at once.

And in that moment, as the late afternoon sun began to redden in the sky, it seemed like more than just a simple statue or ancient architectural detail on the clock tower. It was...an atten-tive presence watching over the *piazza* and Fantina below.

Chapter Two — An Interruption

"So, you see what I was saying to you before," your old gondolier explains, interrupting his tale. "Now you are wondering about the lion with the wings, and rightly so. Because the lion of *San Marco* is very important to the story. You thought that the beginning of this story was the beginning, but it happens to be the middle, and the beginning, I can tell you now, is many years before the middle because it is, of course, the beginning when everything you have just heard really began."

The gondolier pauses, studying your expression. You look confused. "Let me go back for a bit, and tell you what came before, how this all came about and led to the day that Fantina arrived. We may drift out a little further, but be patient and do not worry. This gondola ride, if you listen, will certainly bring you home again."

The gondola glides onward, as if being swept along now in a gentle, unseen current. The sun reddens over the rooftops and shimmers on the water, and your gondolier sweeps his oar back and forth, and continues...

CHAPTER THREE — WHAT CAME BEFORE

A bright, red and gold flag emblazoned with the winged lion of *San Marco* flapped sharply in a seaward breeze. Down below, a hardy crew of military mariners led by a short, square-chinned commander, Venetian Admiral Vettor Pisani, trimmed sail as their heavy galley plowed the tide heading toward Chioggia along the coast of Italy. It was a time of bold adventure, a time of glorious conquest. It was a time of war.

In 1380, Venice and its rival, the city of Genoa, were locked in their fourth war, this time over control of *Tenedos*, a small Greek island in the Aegean Sea. Now, why the two most

38

powerful maritime city-states of the time would raise such a fuss over a tiny little island so far away from either of them might seem extraordinary, but then again, this story is not about ordinary things.

For now, suffice it to say, the Venetians and Genoese had been at odds for over one hundred years, presumably over everything from who would dominate the trade routes to the East to...who made the best *Fettucine al Pesto*. No, really...they never seemed to agree or resolve anything. But this time things would be different. This time, Venice had something that would turn the tide and change the story once and for all. This time, they had the terrible Chinese dragon of Marco Polo.

You see, in 1271, when the great adventurer, Marco Polo, was just seventeen years old, he had traveled east to China with his father, Niccolò, and his uncle, Maffeo. There, as guests of the great Emperor Kublai Khan, they had seen many wonders and received many marvelous gifts. Some say that when he re-turned to Venice some 25 years later, Marco brought back a world of astonishing possibilities and untold riches. And that, you see, is where this story really begins. For even just a rumor of a secret treasure is enough to spark curiosity and desire in the hearts of many.

In any event, it was here, during the Battle of Chioggia, that the Genoese fleet would meet its final fate. They had left their ports along the quiet coast of the Ligurian Sea, sailed all the way around the Italian peninsula into the Adriatic, to battle with Venice and take for themselves whatever treasure and secrets they might discover. But now, trapped in the shallows just south of the Venetian lagoon, they were about to face...

"What is that?" The first officer aboard one of the Genoese ships squinted nervously out over the water toward the Venetian fleet. The Genoese Admiral Pietro Doria, a weary old salt with a thin tuft of silver hair flapping in the breeze, took a dispirited breath then warily raised his dented spyglass to his eye.

"It is...the dragon," he sighed defeatedly, then handed the spyglass to his first officer. The first officer, a wiry, and agitated young man, blinked uncertainly as he raised the spyglass to his own eye and peered out across the shallows.

Aboard the Venetian galley, Admiral Pisani signaled to his crewmen as a large, bronze cannon was wheeled to an opening in the side bulwark of the ship. Prepped and ready, the long barrel was intricately ornate, etched with a scale-like pattern. It rode on limbs fashioned into great iron claws grasping the trunnions beneath it. The chase of the barrel narrowed like a slender neck and opened to a fierce, gaping jaw at the cannon's muzzle. It was, by any account, an intimidating sight to see, especially from the deck of a ship at which it was aimed. "Send them back to Genoa," Pisani thundered.

With that, the short fuse crackled, not so much like the Chinese firecracker from which it had evolved, but more like the hiss of a ferocious reptile waking from a century of slumber. The cannon exploded with a roar and a flash of flame, and fire raced out over the water toward the Genoese ships like a charging beast zeroing in on its prey.

Now, history books tell that the Genoese were defeated that day. They say that the Venetians and their never-before-seen ship-borne cannons won the battle and destroyed the enemy's fleet. That is the 'ordinary' tale that is told. But here is where we leave the ordinary behind, because the truth is much more...*fanticulous.*

The Genoese first mate lowered his spyglass, his mouth nervously agape. "Dragon," he repeated in an anxious whisper stifled by the enormous knot now caught in his throat. For racing toward his ship across the water's surface, a billowing mass of smoke and fire was changing shape, swirling wildly till it sprang forth to reveal its true form—a fiery, red, Chinese dragon, scales glistening, mouth ravenous.

It tore through the forecastle bulwark of the Genoese ship as Admiral Doria and his first officer dove aside. Crewmen fled in a panic as the dragon spiralled up the foremast setting it ablaze.

"Abandon ship. Hope is lost," Doria shouted as he and his first officer leapt from the burning deck to the waters below.

Across the water, Admiral Pisani smiled. A cheer rose up from the deck of the Venetian galley, eventually joined by similar cheers from every galley in the fleet. The day and the battle would belong to Venice.

So, as I said, Genoa was defeated. A peace treaty was struck at Turin through the mediation of Amadeus VI, the 'Green Count' of Savoy, and the Genoese returned home empty-handed and utterly beaten.

But what history can never explain is the true reason for Genoa's ruin. It was something more subtle than cannons or gunpowder, and had less to do with fact, than it did with what some might call fancy. It was something much more elusive, however, than simply a dragon. What had defeated the Genoese was the loss of hope. The magic that had unlocked the spirit of their city had faded and turned to stone.

Magic...treasure...the dragon...these were all part of a fantastic story that had spread since Marco Polo's return years ago. It told of how Kublai Khan had opened the well-guarded doors of his imperial palace's most secret chamber, and gifted a treasure beyond all imagination.

Marco, his father and uncle, had sailed from the East in fourteen fully fitted out 'junks,' Chinese sailing vessels, but somewhere along the route, or perhaps upon their return, the treasure was lost...or hidden, as was the secret of its final resting place.

Then, in 1298, Marco was captured in the Battle of Curzola during the second war between Venice and Genoa, and in a Genoese prison, he shared the tale of his adventures with his cellmate, an able and tireless writer named Rustichello.

Stories of a 'cursed isle,' 'banished fires,' 'dragon's bone,' 'paradise' and 'starry skies,' filled the pages of a journal, and stirred the curiosity of all who heard them. Some laughed them off as exaggerated tales or outright fabrications, while others pondered if the stories might actually be true.

Were the wealth and wonder brought back from the court of Kublai Khan real? The idea became a whisper, and the whisper a rumor that took hold like a craving in the minds of prison guards as they scurried away like rats into the night.

So, the notion of a secret treasure persisted over five centuries, and while no one could say for certain if the rumor was true, many wondered...and were tempted to find out.

In 1797, Napoleon Bonaparte of France conquered the *Repubblica Serenissima di Venezia,* as it was called, and carried off various works of art. But the French found no secrets. The Austrian Hapsburg Empire held Venice for years after, but learned nothing new. Finally, after years of being claimed by one side or another, Venice was formally annexed by the Kingdom of Italy in 1866. King Umberto I and Queen Margherita *di Savoia* had heard murmurs of stories, and were eager to see what 'eternal' secret Venice might offer them.

They attended the first Grand Exposition of Venice in 1894, where art, artifacts, relics and mementos from distant corners of the globe were on exhibit in what was billed as a 'Celebration of the Great Names of Italian Exploration.'

An old portrait of Amerigo Vespucci stood watch over a glass case in which his *Mondus Novus* (New World) letter from

1503 was displayed. Beside it, a bust of Christopher Columbus stared out over the captain's journal from his 1492 voyage across the Atlantic. Matteucci's Egyptian Expedition letters, Caboto's maps from his journey to Newfoundland...and finally, tucked away under glass at the far end of the great hall, was an old leather-bound journal, *Il Milione*—the adventures of Marco Polo.

The king was certain that the journal was the key to finding Polo's treasure, and so he had come to Venice to claim it.

But that night, after all the guests had left and the exhibit space was dark, a mysterious visitor arrived, determined to steal the secret for himself. He moved like a shadow through the great hall and paused before the glass case enclosing Marco Polo's journal. Suddenly, a silver-tipped walking stick came crashing down on the glass, sending shards exploding across the marble floor. Two gloved hands reached into the shattered case, seized the journal and in an instant, disappeared with it back into the night.

The King was incensed and swore he would hunt down the thief. Nothing would stop him from getting the journal back... except maybe death. Umberto I was assassinated in 1900, and the quest to find *il Milione* quickly faded away into a vague memory and rumor once again.

No one could say who had stolen the journal, or where it had been taken, but soon, along the ancient trade route from the Far East—the route that most believed Marco Polo had traveled on his way home from China centuries before—reports of mysterious events began to surface.

The landscape was ravaged. A shadowy crew, working in the dead of night, would descend upon a town and strip it bare, excavating for some unknown purpose and with no mercy. Entire villages were razed to the ground then abandoned as the crew moved on to their next site. They were searching for something, and the man with the silver-tipped walking stick was obsessed with finding it. And obsession can lead to terrible things, unless someone rises up to stand against it.

CHAPTER FOUR — RISING

Fantina stepped briskly along a damp, stone walkway, turning her map clockwise then counter-clockwise as she did her best to find her way through the maze of canals. A brisk breeze whistled through like a melody, flittering over the water and past rugged walls, and Fantina paused for a moment atop a small bridge to listen.

She looked up and blinked her eyes, enjoying the dwindling rays of the late afternoon sun, still high enough overhead to penetrate the narrow passageways below. It was quite an enchanting place, she thought, and she wondered why anyone would ever leave Venice behind.

She looked about—a modest *palazzo* to her right, a small *piazza* to her left. Fantina wasn't entirely certain of her course, but she was confident enough to continue.

Before she did, however, she pulled a crinkled letter from the folds of her map. It was a single page that she had received the month after her father had passed away—a letter from Venice from her *Zio* Giovanni, or Uncle Gio as she knew him.

Fantina didn't actually remember much of Uncle Gio, if anything at all. From the stories her father had told, however, she imagined he was a wise and very important person in Venice, a master restoration craftsman hired by the mayor him-self, without whom the city would 'instantly and completely collapse and cease to exist.' Okay, so maybe her father had ex-aggerated a bit, but still, Fantina was sure that Uncle Gio would be amazing...or pretty sure. At least she hoped he would be. Since her father was gone now, and her mother had passed away years earlier, Uncle Gio was the only 'family' she had left.

Of course, she did wonder why it was that in all her travels with her father around the world, they had never made their way to Venice, even just to pass through for a visit. There had always been just one more place to go, to explore, and while Fantina had always enjoyed the adventures, she had often felt a bit adrift on the sea, not belonging to any one place. Uncle Gio's letter, though, was quite clear: 'Venice is home, and you are welcome any time.'

Fantina paused, her face brightening for a moment at the notion. She kept telling herself that she'd come to Venice to find 'fortune and glory,' but maybe, she thought, she was searching for a little bit more. She looked back the way she had come, then tucked the letter into her pocket and continued on.

The Church of *San Lorenzo* had been built, destroyed and re-built at least three times. Incredible, but true. It burned to the ground in the great fire of 1106, back when many buildings in Venice were still made of wood, and before the furnaces of the glassblowing artisans were relocated by decree to the outlying island of *Murano*. But even though the church was rebuilt in stone and had been standing since the 16th century, in Venice, being closed for restoration seemed to be the norm for many places including *San Lorenzo*.

Fantina checked her map again curiously when she arrived at the small courtyard before the church. It was a narrow, cramped *piazzetta*, made even smaller by the enormous sections of wooden scaffolding that rose up against the plain, brick façade. Sandbag barricades snaked along the canal's edge and surrounded the front steps of the church where the now receding floodwaters had left a moist sheen that faintly reflected the fading light.

It wasn't the fancy and ornate church Fantina had imagined it would be when she had set out to find her Uncle Gio, but this was it—where she would settle, for a while at least.

Fantina stepped in through the large wooden doors of the church and looked up in awe. The walls were alive with painted frescoes at various stages of restoration—scenes of patron saints and other figures from Venetian history; elegant *bissone* longboats in the Grand Canal; a 13th century gathering welcoming a trio of merchant ships at the quay... Some were faded and practically lost, almost invisible on the flaking, plaster walls, while others seemed to have survived through time but were caked in soot from centuries of neglect.

Fantina wandered silently across the uneven, stone-tiled floor, careful to avoid the sections where shallow trenches had been dug into the church foundation to shore up spots that were sagging...or sinking. The church seemed scarred by time, like whatever restoration was underway couldn't possibly keep step with the forces at work against it. Fantina sighed. Seeing the slow decay of *San Lorenzo* made her think how all of Venice might be in similar danger, and it made her sad.

A sudden noise broke the silence. Fantina stepped around the side of the ornate altar into a secondary space, the front half of the nave that was flanked on all sides by towering, wooden scaffolds reaching up toward the ceiling.

"Fantina?"

Fantina looked up. Light, streaming in from an open window at the base of the vaulted ceiling, rimmed a figure standing on the top tier of a scaffold. He was a somewhat disheveled old man with a bushy mustache and an expression that seemed weathered by both time and dusty work. His eyes, however, were sharp and focused, even a bit hard perhaps, but not from being cross by nature, more likely from being alone most of the time. Fantina squinted.

"Uncle Gio?"

The man furrowed his brow, eying Fantina in her traveling outfit curiously, like he wasn't entirely convinced she could possibly be who he knew she was. Fantina pulled the letter that Uncle Gio had sent from her pocket and continued, "I worked my way across on an ocean steamer, fifteen days on the Minnetonka—funny name for a boat, but I guess a boat can be named anything. Anyhow, I crossed the Channel, Dover to

Calais, then hitched a ride from Paris. I got sidetracked a bit in Geneva, but who wouldn't, right? The chocolate there is just, well…yum—"

Uncle Gio raised his hand to silence her. Bright, plucky and full of spunk…she was definitely Fantina, he deduced. Her father had written often over the years, chronicling their journey together, and Uncle Gio felt as if he practically knew the girl already. Her appearance, however, had thrown him a bit off balance. He remembered, of course, his letter and the invitation, but somehow now that Fantina was standing before him, he wondered if he would be up to the task. He was always ready for a new project, but…he restored churches, fresco paintings, art in need of a careful cleaning. The 'project' before him suddenly seemed like it would be a bit more perplexing. "Do you always talk so much?" he asked.

Fantina shrugged. "So much? I wouldn't say that. I mean, I talk as much as needed to get my point across. Papà called me 'loquacious' which I kind of liked, but he did mention you might not. 'Uncle Giovanni is a man of few words,' he used to say. You don't mind if I call you 'uncle,' do you? I know you're not really my uncle, but Papà—"

Uncle Gio raised his other hand. Fantina stopped. Very perplexing, he thought. "Your father was like a brother to me,"

Uncle Gio said. "'Uncle' is fine." He stepped closer to the edge of the scaffold, peering down. "So...let me have a look at you." Fantina set her suitcase on the floor and stood up straight. Uncle Gio looked confused. "You look like a boy."

Fantina considered her appearance, then quickly pulled off her dusty cap. A bob of chestnut hair tumbled out. It was only a slight improvement. She explained, "These are my traveling togs. You know...blend in and stay out of trouble."

"Trouble? Yes, I heard something about that from your time at the orphanage. You and 'trouble' are good friends it seems."

Fantina hesitated. She had only been at the 'New England Home for Little Wanderers' in Boston for a couple of weeks before her predilection for inventing had resulted in what she considered a relatively minor incident.

"They kicked you out?" Uncle Gio confirmed.

Fantina tried a positive spin. "Actually, I wanted to travel, and I'm sure the story you heard was blown up way out of proportion."

"Blown up. Yes, that was the story."

Fantina considered, "Okay, but in fairness, they needed a new kitchen in that place anyway."

Uncle Gio eyed Fantina skeptically, as he stepped toward the edge of the scaffold. He slid his foot into a loop at the end of a rope attached to a pulley and counterweight, and held on as he stepped off the edge. The pulley spun, the counterweight rose, and Uncle Gio descended slowly to the church floor.

"Very Verne," Fantina smiled.

"A what?" Uncle Gio looked at her oddly.

"Jules Verne. He's a writer. Fantasy...fiction? He writes these amazing stories—"

Uncle Gio interrupted with another raised hand. She was talking too much again. "Never mind. You do not have to explain everything," he grumbled. He hooked his rope 'elevator' onto the bottom of the scaffold and wiped his sooty hands with a rag, as he got a better look at Fantina. He indicated the smudge on her cheek. "You have a little...dirt." Fantina considered, then quickly grabbed Uncle Gio's hand rag and wiped her face. Unfortunately, now her face had a sooty smudge on both cheeks.

"How's that?"

Uncle Gio smiled awkwardly, "Uh...much better," he fibbed. Uncle Gio suddenly paused and leaned close, staring intently into Fantina's eyes. "I see something of your father bouncing around in there. You have that same, odd look about you—like someone who wants to believe more than what she sees."

Fantina smiled. She had heard that before—well, the first part about having her father's 'odd look,' especially in those moments when she and her father were caught up in the excitement of planning another trip and adventure. They had that same spark and glimmer, but it had been quite a while since anyone had reminded her. She was happy at the idea that her father was still with her in some little way.

"That pain in the neck," Uncle Gio completed his thought. "He was trouble too." Uncle Gio stepped abruptly past Fantina, motioning for her to follow.

Fantina hesitated a moment. Uncle Gio, like the church he was rehabilitating, seemed a bit worn down and rough along the edges—like a painting that had dimmed over time. He might need a little work too, she thought. Fantina grabbed her suitcase uncertainly and hurried after him.

The walls of fresco paintings, murky and awaiting restoration, looked down on them as Uncle Gio led Fantina through the church. Fantina studied them as she passed, each one depicting what she imagined was an intriguing story. Uncle Gio explained. "Our family has been in charge of restoring Venice for generations—fighting the salt air, high tides...the flood waters. I learned from my father who learned from his father. I would not say I am the best in all of Venice, but—"

"But you are, aren't you," Fantina smiled. "Don't be modest, you can tell me. Papà said you were. The city would crumble without you. He said you save the stories of Venice from being forgotten."

Uncle Gio raised his hand...too much again. Fantina stopped talking with a twinge of compunction, but Uncle Gio saw something more in her expression. He could see that however tough and independent Fantina had seemed at first glance, she was looking to him now the way he imagined she might have looked to her father if he had been here with her—like she needed a helpful word or two to guide her along in a strange new place. Uncle Gio considered, then gave it a shot.

"Fantina, in life it is sometimes better to be a little...quiet, *eh?*"

Fantina crinkled her nose.

Uncle Gio tried again. "You see, the best gondolier does not make a splash when he rows. He does his best, smooth and steady, careful not to disturb the water. A big splash makes a big wave, and a big wave is a big trouble. You tip the boat, and then maybe everyone gets wet." Uncle Gio nodded, impressed by his pearl of wisdom. Maybe he was up to the task, after all. He looked to Fantina.

Fantina stared at him blankly, a dubious eyebrow raised. "Um, okay? That's...good to know." Fantina stepped onward gingerly. Uncle Gio reassessed his parenting skills with a baffled sigh.

Fantina paused by a particularly stunning mural— a golden sunset over a *piazza*, pigeons perched as if watching something in the empty sky above the Venetian lagoon—beautiful despite being dingy with time.

Uncle Gio stepped up beside Fantina, heartened by her appreciation of the imagery. He wondered, though, if she was truly ready to understand...all of it. He knew that there were things he needed to explain to her. He had promised her father he would, but he wasn't quite sure how to begin. "There is something special about Venice," Uncle Gio said finally. "We always thought your father would stay or someday return, but...he met your mother, and then you came along." Uncle Gio trailed off, his eyes distant, fixed on the memory. "You were just a little one in your father's arms when you left."

Fantina hesitated. A hazy image of that day, long ago, had popped into her mind. She could see her parents...and a boat sailing to sea...Venice growing small in the background and vague figures with unfamiliar faces waving from the shore. But she wasn't sure if it was real. It just felt like part of a fantastic tale. She looked to Uncle Gio expectantly. If anyone could help her make sense of all the pieces of stories she remembered from her childhood, it would be him. He knew the answers to the many questions Fantina had. "Why?" she wondered out loud.

Uncle Gio rubbed his chin. "Your father left Venice behind...he changed his life, because he wanted you to see beyond. He wanted to show you the world."

Fantina waited, sensing there was more that Uncle Gio wanted to say, but nothing came.

Uncle Gio saw Fantina staring up at him hopefully and withdrew a step uncomfortably with a shrug. "Families always complicate things, *eh?*" he said reverting to his brusquer tone. He turned back to the mural to wipe a smudge with his finger.

Fantina studied Uncle Gio curiously. As eager as she was to get answers, she realized that maybe she would have to take it slower, so they could get to know each other comfortably... gradually... Of course, that wasn't exactly her style. "So, you never got married? Any children?" she blurted out.

"I do not like children," Uncle Gio stated flatly before reconsidering his abrupt response. "I mean, I do not need anyone to take care—"

Fantina backpedaled quickly. "Of course not. Need? Me neither. The last thing I want is an anchor holding me back. I have things to do, places to go. I'll probably head out again, soon…probably."

Uncle Gio noted Fantina's stoic expression. He sighed to himself. He had been alone with his paintings and portraits for quite some time, and he realized that when it came to dealing with real people, he was a bit out of practice. He would have to try harder. "What I meant…it is not that I do not want you to—" He paused, and softened his tone. "I am just not used to having anyone around." He pulled a clean handkerchief from his pocket and gently wiped the soot from Fantina's cheeks. "That is not to say I could not get used to it. I just mean it might take some time."

Fantina took the handkerchief tentatively from Uncle Gio to finish wiping her cheek. She considered. It might be easier for everyone if she just moved on. She could find what she was looking for anywhere, right? Or was she looking for a little bit of something more?

"I suppose I could stay a bit," Fantina said finally. "Maybe I could help out around here, you know, for a while."

Uncle Gio nodded like an agreement had been struck. He turned toward the dingy fresco and wiped some more soot away with his finger. "Restoration is a slow and difficult process. I could show you. The dirt is like layers of years gone by. Sometimes I cannot even see the image beneath all this."

Suddenly, Fantina's eyes lit up. She tossed her suitcase to the ground and flipped it open. Inside, beside her book, was an assortment of odd contraptions and homemade gadgets. Uncle Gio shot her a peculiar glance. "What is all this?"

"Papà always used to say, 'Travel light. Only bring what's important.'" Fantina pulled a curious-looking gizmo from the bottom of her suitcase—a hand-cranked, gear-driven, electric dynamo connected to a cathode ray generator that looked a bit like a cross between a flashlight, microscope and an egg beater. Uncle Gio stared blankly.

"Ah, well, it is a good thing you brought one of those, then." He paused, a confused expression across his face. "What exactly is...one of those?"

"It's my latest," Fantina explained. She held it up for Uncle Gio to see. "I call it an 'electro ray-o-scope.'" Uncle Gio raised a skeptical eyebrow. Fantina continued. "This tube sends out something called X-rays and when you crank it up—" Fantina spun a lever, gears turned, a magnifying glass snapped out into position. She stood and held her device up to the murky image on the wall.

"Wait." Uncle Gio looked concerned. "This is not the… blowing up thing, *eh?* It is safe?"

"Of course," Fantina assured him. "As far as I know," she added, less certain. Fantina hit a switch on the device. A faint cone-shaped beam of light glowed against the wall as a low electric hum swelled. Uncle Gio took a cautious step back, lowering his hands to shield his…vital organs.

The light intensified and then, suddenly, the sooty painting on the wall seemed to fade, and another image beneath the surface appeared within the cone of light. Pigeons morphed into painted images of *fate*—mythological faeries with feathered wings. And, revealed in the previously empty sky above the lagoon, was the winged lion of *San Marco*, teeth bared, locked in combat with another flying beast, this one with the head, wings and talons of an eagle and body of a lion—the griffin of Genoa. Fantina smiled in wonder. "Fanticulous."

Uncle Gio stepped forward and grabbed Fantina's ray-o-scope. The cone of light faded as the device whirred to a halt. Fantina turned to Uncle Gio with wide eyes. "Did you see that? There's a painting under that painting."

"Yes," Uncle Gio explained quickly. "Old art on old walls sometimes gets 'over-painted' with something new. It happens quite often in old churches and buildings, restoration, renovation…" Uncle Gio pointed to the sooty, less fantastical mural. "You like this one?"

Fantina smiled enthusiastically, raising her ray-o-scope toward the image again. "Yes, but the old one—"

"It is a fairy tale, from the past," Uncle Gio intercepted. "Old stories of old Venice. It is complicated."

Fantina considered, a memory stirring in her mind. "But I know that one. Papà used to tell me about the lion that protected Venice. And a treasure—"

"Yes, yes, but you must be tired, *eh?*" Uncle Gio gathered up Fantina's suitcase and hurried out through the church entrance.

Fantina glanced up at the mural again. The sunset over the *piazza* and lagoon on the wall's surface was beautiful, but the image beneath was the one that called to her now. She could almost hear the story itself, like a whisper getting clearer as it woke from somewhere in the past. Fantina hesitated. The memory was still hazy. She turned and followed Uncle Gio outside.

The glow from the late afternoon sun was beginning to fade in the sky above, as Uncle Gio turned on the step outside *San Lorenzo*. He pointed toward a walkway south of the church as he pulled a house key from his pocket and handed it to Fantina.

"It is the first house after the bridge. There is a room for you up in the attic. Not much, but it has a little view."

Fantina nodded. "So I should stay?"

Uncle Gio paused. He realized now that he may not have come off as congenially as he thought he had. His weathered expression softened as he handed Fantina her suitcase.

"Yes. You stay. We will see how it goes."

"And I'll try not to be...a 'pain in the neck.'"

Uncle Gio half cringed, recognizing his own words. He stepped closer to explain. "Fantina, you are family. And family is always a little pain in the neck. That is what makes them family." Uncle Gio smiled, pleased with that pearl of wisdom, then turned with a nod and headed back inside the church. "I will see you back at the house later. No trouble, *eh?*"

Fantina took a deep breath as she turned toward the walkway to Uncle Gio's home. "No trouble," she thought. That's what she wanted too—a quiet place to settle in for a while, with no more complications.

CHAPTER FIVE — COMPLICATIONS

Uncle Gio's house was a tall, slender building sandwiched tightly between two shorter homes facing a narrow canal spanned by a small pedestrian bridge. The lower part of the outer wall, still damp from the recent high waters, glistened in the fading light and, to Fantina, made the house seem enchanted by some shimmering glow. She turned the key in the front door lock. It creaked loudly like she was unlocking the entrance to something ancient, a place that time had passed by and left behind—a forgotten secret locked away in a hidden corner of a backwater canal.

The door swung open and Fantina stepped inside. She paused in the dim light, squinting uncertainly and wondering if this place would be a comfortable change of pace after all her wandering and time spent in makeshift lodgings, from leaky cargo holds to rickety boxcars and rumbling trucks. Then again, the cozy bed and well-tended order of the orphanage hadn't really suited her either. Maybe, here too, she just wouldn't truly belong. Fantina leaned in as her eyes adjusted to the room.

Now, to say that Uncle Gio's sense of home decor was 'eclectic,' would be to suggest that he actually had a sense of home decor. The room was more of a mix-and-match jumble of old pieces of furniture, makeshift shelves of ancient books and art stacked against the walls and filling every blank wall space and spare corner. A small kitchen area near the back was cluttered with the tools of Uncle Gio's trade—art brushes, paints and cleaning supplies. A small kitchen table was covered with stacks of manuscripts and even more books. It was crowded, messy...completely disorganized. Fantina nodded, a smile creeping across her lips as she scanned the space. To her, it looked wonderful.

Fantina set her suitcase down by an ornate, wrought iron, circular staircase that led to the floors and attic above, and wandered deeper into the room. The paintings, like the church murals she had seen in *San Lorenzo*, depicted scenes of Venetian history—timeworn images of people and places, real...or legendary.

Fantina suddenly stopped. In a back corner of the room she spotted an odd, ink drawing in a gilded, bamboo frame—odd because it seemed out of place amongst the other paintings of ships, gondolas...and water. This drawing was fire. Red flames swirled against a plain background, encircling an intricately drawn lizard-like creature, long, slender and shrouded in smoke and shadow.

Fantina stepped closer, as if the image were not entirely unfamiliar to her. Like the winged lion of *San Marco* that she had remembered from her father's stories, this dragon was part of a story too, one she had completely forgotten until this moment, and even now, a story that wasn't entirely clear in her mind. "Dragon's bone," Fantina whispered to herself. She closed her eyes, trying to remember more, but it was too vague a recollection, too distant. She sighed, clutched her suitcase and spiralled up the stairs.

The attic space of Uncle Gio's home was as 'eclectic,' as the rooms below, with art and history stacked in piles along the old brick walls. The steeply sloped ceiling was open to the ancient rafters of the roof, and it looked like there might even be a bird's nest or two somewhere up near the peak.

Rough, wooden, floor planks and a few worn tapestries attempted to make the space cozier than the brisk temperature would allow, but Fantina saw plenty of blankets folded at the edge of a narrow mattress near the wall, so she wasn't concerned. It looked quite comfortable to her.

Fantina stepped in through the low doorway and dropped her suitcase onto the mattress. A plume of dust exploded into the air around the suitcase and swirled through the room catching the last rays of sunlight as they streamed in through the broken slats of a large, shuttered window.

Fantina popped open the latches of her suitcase, threw open the lid and placed her book on her pillow for later. She then reached in past her collection of gizmos and mechanical contraptions to find a small, silver frame. It was old and tarnished, an oval shape worked with a simple maritime motif—an anchor-rope detail coiled around a faded black and white photograph of a man.

He was handsome and bright with a bit of a roguish smile, and his eyes had that same quality—a spark or glimmer—that

Uncle Gio had earlier noted in Fantina's own. "Well, Papà," Fantina whispered, "I made it here. What do you think?"

Fatina stared at the picture for a moment. She knew she would get no answer, but she wanted to believe that her father would be happy for her. She considered his smile. While he was probably about the same age as Uncle Gio, there was a youthful vitality in his expression, as if despite his years, the adventure of traveling the world or something within had kept him young at heart.

Fantina set the frame onto an oaken chest of drawers coated in a thick layer of dust, then stepped to the shuttered window. She pushed the window open, out onto a small balcony, and the warm light washed over her face. It was a stunning view—the rooftops of Venice outlined by the reddening sky, the streets below cast in an enchanting glow. "Not bad," Fantina smiled.

Just then, off to one side, perched on the edge of the terracotta tiled roof, a white pigeon turned toward Fantina. It cocked its head, cooing curiously, as if genuinely interested in what Fantina might say or do. They stared at each other for a moment, then the pigeon turned back out toward the setting sun. Fantina turned as well, just as the last rays of sunset faded behind silhouetted chimneys.

Then, in that moment when the sun blinked beyond the horizon, an almost imperceptible golden pulse swept out across the city like a gentle, glowing wave—a fine mist of flickering stardust that rose up from the streets and into the night sky. Fantina rubbed her eyes uncertainly. "What was that?" she wondered out loud. She looked back across the roofline, as if half expecting the pigeon to answer her question, but the pigeon wasn't there anymore. It had moved up along the terracotta tiles to a stone chimney and glanced at Fantina one last time before disappearing behind it.

Fantina wasn't sure why, unless it was because of the odd way the pigeon had looked at her, but she was overcome with curiosity, and before she realized what she was doing, she had climbed over the balcony railing and was edging her way along the roof tiles toward the chimney and the faint cooing sound beyond. Then suddenly...silence. Fantina hesitated for a moment, then leaned forward to peak around the edge of the chimney.

And there she saw the white pigeon. Except that now, it wasn't a pigeon anymore. A tiny *fata*, a faerie, with delicate, white-feathered wings and wearing a dainty, feather dress, looked up at Fantina, startled. Fantina, just as surprised, jumped back. A tile beneath her foot came loose, and before she could catch her balance, she found herself tumbling toward the edge of the roof.

The faerie darted away into the sky, but paused mid-air as if reconsidering. She wasn't a particularly bold or heroic faerie. In fact, in these uncertain times, she had often remained in her pigeon form throughout the night, afraid she might startle some unsuspecting passer-by and add, even if only incrementally, to the sense of apprehension and fear that seemed to be growing in Venice these days. But now, in this instant, something had changed in her, and she felt a twinge of courage, and a willingness to take a chance... There was something about this one.

The faerie turned back, locking eyes with Fantina in the moment before Fantina and her stunned expression disappeared over the edge.

Spurred to action, the faerie soared back cooing loudly, swooping down toward the small bridge over the canal.

Two curiously vigilant frogs, as if answering her call, jumped up onto the edge of the canal and spotted Fantina falling from the rooftop above. They nodded to each other. And then...they leapt.

Fantina clutched wildly at the air as she fell helplessly toward the cobbled walkway. Though still astounded at the sight of the faerie, she knew that in her reality, she would be striking the hard ground any second. But then, her reality was about to change.

The two frogs, in mid-leap, suddenly transformed. The flickering stardust glow swept over them as their nimble bodies stretched, and they became two short but gangly, young men in rubbery diving suits and scuba goggles. Their faces retained a distinctly amphibian look, their skin still a wet, translucent green, but they had grown to somewhat human proportions, or at least those of an awkwardly lanky teen. They reached out with their webbed hands and caught Fantina and brought her safely to the ground where they deposited her gently on the walkway.

Fantina, wide-eyed, took a quick step back as the two frogmen regrouped, crouching together at the edge of the canal. "Who...what are you?" she asked, unsure if frog people would even be able to understand or answer her.

The two frogmen looked at each other strangely as if considering an appropriate response. "Ribbit," they croaked in unison before leaping away back into the canal.

Fantina rushed to the water's edge, trying to spot her rescuers as they swam away, now mere shadows beneath the surface. She scrambled up onto the bridge, scanning the dark water. "Wait. Come back!" Fantina hesitated only a moment before charging off after them along the walkway beside the canal.

The white-feathered faerie, perched on a mooring post and hidden in shadow, watched with concern as Fantina disappeared into the night. What kind of trouble had she started? And to what kind of trouble was the girl now heading? She was sure she had done the right thing by calling for help—that was her job on the patrol after all, but now she wondered if she needed to report back and call for more...substantial help. She took a moment to catch her breath, then opened her wings and took off in the opposite direction.

Chapter Six — A Dead End

Fantina hurried along a dark walkway racing after the fleeting shadows in the water. The clouded moon, waning above, left the evening unnervingly dark, she thought, and the tune played by the breeze that she had heard earlier seemed more like an ominous chord of foreboding now. A distant splash stopped her in her tracks. She spun about to catch the reflection of a vaguely amphibian silhouette cast by the moonlight against a glistening, stone wall, but as she chased it down an alleyway it faded in a mist. Suddenly, she stopped short, teetering at the edge of another canal...a dead end.

This is crazy, she thought. I'm just seeing things.

A rustling noise caught Fantina's attention. She looked up. The shadow of a large rat scurried along the top of a dank and mildewed, brick wall then disappeared. A foul odor, like vapor rising off stagnant water, suddenly wafted past and Fantina hesitated. She felt a wave of uneasiness that chased out whatever wonder she might have had from the strange and mysterious moments that had happened earlier. The memory of faeries and frogs was already fading as if it were trying to hide itself back in an ordinary night, but Fantina sensed that there was something more than 'ordinary' lurking in the shadows of the alleyway. She looked about somewhat nervously and realized she had no idea where she was. In the dark, in the maze of narrow streets, Fantina was lost.

She turned to start back the way she had come when suddenly, at the other end of the alley, a young, stubble-faced stranger strode past. Cloaked in shadow, his pointed features rimmed by the moonlight, he paused as he spotted Fantina then doubled back to the mouth of the alley.

Fantina stopped. She couldn't see the stranger in the dim light, but something about the way he moved put her on edge. She glanced back, looking for another way out, but there was none. Fantina edged closer, trying to step as far as she could to one side to get past the stranger. But then, a second figure appeared at the alley's entrance, blocking her way.

Startled, Fantina jumped back. As she did, her gold pendant swung out from beneath her jacket, glinting as it caught a ray of moonlight. The two strangers turned together, fixing their dark and beady, black eyes on it. Fantina took a step back, quickly tucking the chain and pendant back inside her shirt collar.

She'd been in worse fixes, she thought. She knew that being on her own meant relying on herself, and beyond the stories her father had shared with her, she had also learned from him how to stand her ground—be confident, be strong, be his 'little warrior' (or, if all else failed, how to fake it until the opportunity to run away presented itself). She raised her fists and assumed a persuasive, fighting stance. "Okay, it's a fight you want? Two against one?" she quipped. Just then, a third brigand joined the other two. Fantina, noticeably less confident, hesitated. "Or maybe we could just talk it over."

The band of brigands huddled close, as if to discuss their plan of attack, but as they began chattering to each other, Fantina stared at them oddly. Something was not right. She leaned in curiously, then froze as they turned to face her, their noses twitching, pointy teeth gleaming, their unmistakable rat faces harsh in the night.

Fantina gasped. Like the frogmen who had startled and then saved her earlier, these rat-men were just as shocking, though clearly not here to help. Matted, black fur surrounded their grimy faces and paws, their hunched bodies clothed in dirty, beggared attire. Fantina retreated a few steps, nearly falling into the canal behind her. She regained her balance and turned back to face them. She was unnerved...maybe even unhinged she thought—but definitely trapped with nowhere to run.

Just then, the white-feathered faerie appeared, swooping in from the canal behind Fantina. She hovered over Fantina's shoulder, cooing loudly and shaking her fist at the rat-men in a way that remarkably looked almost threatening.

Fantina stared, a bit puzzled—giant rats and a furious faerie...? It seemed a bit peculiar. She closed her eyes and shook her head to clear it, but when she looked again, they were all still there. Fantina crinkled her nose with a shrug. She wasn't sure what to believe.

Suddenly, the rat-men froze in their tracks. Their black eyes grew large with dread; their whiskers and limbs stiffened in terror.

Fantina looked from them to the delicate faerie over her shoulder, then back again with a bewildered expression. Impossible, Fantina thought. Why would three, fearsome, giant rats be afraid of one, dainty, little— The answer came to her in the form of a low growl rumbling in the night.

The rat-men were looking past the faerie, up toward the roofline behind Fantina, where a looming shape reflected in their glassy eyes was perched. Fantina followed their gaze, and then she froze as well.

Poised on the rooftop above, silhouetted against the night sky, was the large shape of a lion ready to pounce. Fantina's eyes went wide, as if recognizing an image from a long forgotten dream. The rat-men, visibly panicked, began to back away.

Then, the lion rose, two majestic wings extending wide from its back. It leapt from the rooftop with a resounding roar and soared downward to the alley as the rat-men turned and scattered.

Fantina, terrified and awestruck at the same time, watched as the rat-men, moments before disappearing into the shadows, changed shape, shrinking down as they scurried away like rats in the night. The winged lion swiped a great paw at the last of the fleeing rodents as he landed, chasing them off with a final growl and shaking the very pavement of the alleyway beneath him. Then, when the night went quiet again, he turned to face Fantina.

Fantina stood motionless, teetering at the edge of the walkway, her eyes glued on the fierce beast before her, as if hoping that standing still would somehow make her invisible. The lion stared. Fantina cringed. It didn't.

Fantina's dread faded, however, and became something more like uneasy bewilderment as the lion stepped closer into the dim moonlight. His face, ringed in a flowing, golden mane, was definitely fearsome, but he seemed noble and kind, both powerful and gentle at the same time. Fantina stared at him uncertainly. She wasn't quite sure what to make of him.

"You should not wander the streets of Venice alone at night," the lion said to her in a deep and comforting voice. "These are dangerous times."

Fantina shook her head. Yeah, she was definitely seeing...and hearing things. "You're...a talking lion," she stated plainly as if still trying to convince herself.

"Leonardo, but you may call me Leo."

"Right," Fantina hesitated, still unnerved. "Because... you're Leo...a lion...with wings...who talks."

Leo stared at Fantina curiously, then looked to the faerie with a confused expression as if to ask for help in communicating with this odd creature. He had faced many challenges through history—battled the Griffin of Genoa, the Hapsburg Eagle, even the gargoyles of Notre Dame—but never, he thought to himself, had he ever encountered anything as perplexing as this...a teenage girl.

Just then, Fantina spotted an old fishing boat puttering past in the canal behind her. She quickly leapt from the walkway onto the boat's bow, then continued leaping from the boat onto the walkway across the narrow canal. She was off and running before the old fisherman in the boat even realized what had happened.

Leo looked impressed. Perplexing perhaps, but the girl was resourceful and spirited. He motioned to the faerie with a nod. "Keep an eye on her, Bianca." The faerie cooed softly then took off and fluttered away after Fantina. Leo watched, a knowing look in his eyes, as Fantina turned a distant corner and disappeared.

CHAPTER SEVEN — THROUGH THE ARCH

Fantina ran desperately along the dark walkway, her head spinning. Had she bumped it, she wondered? She remembered falling...yes, that was it. She must have bumped her head when she fell off the roof, right before the two frogs...the rats, and a flying— Fantina stopped herself. No, it couldn't be. It was the Lion of *San Marco*, from the stories her father had once told her, the stories in the old paintings on the walls of the church. Other images began flooding her mind as well—the golden pulse rising up over Venice; glowing mist; a fiery dragon swirling in a starry sky... But they were just stories, right?

She turned left then right, down another alleyway...but now, the passage seemed to be closing in on her, the cold, stone walls arching over her as if trying to meet above and plunge the street and Fantina into darkness. She was dizzy from everything that had happened, and she was losing herself in the labyrinth of Venice.

The sound of voices and laughter called out to her, and she turned. At the end of an alley, a low archway and a flickering light beyond looked like the mouth of a tunnel. It wasn't so far away, but as she stood there, it seemed to be shrinking away from her. Fantina ran. She dove for the light and ducked through the archway when suddenly...

A ball of fire burst into the night sky. Fantina jumped back, faces passing her in a blur. She was in the middle of a crowd, a *piazza* alive with people—a man with white rabbit ears, a woman masked in peacock feathers, a tall, lanky fire-eater, with a devilish mustache and goatee, blowing flames into the night.

It was the Venetian *Carnevale,* the annual celebration held during the weeks leading up to *Martedì Grasso,* the 'Fat Tuesday' festival. Revelers in elaborate costumes and paper maché masks with beaked noses, lace ruffles and feathered crowns, swarmed around Fantina as she stumbled forward uncertainly.

Acrobats in fluttering outfits flipped from suspended silk cords, while street performers dressed as motley fools and checkered harlequins tumbled past.

Fantina was hemmed in and dazed, like a boat caught in a swirling current and spun about by the flow of faces. She was unsure now which were real and which she might have simply conjured from her imagination. Blank eyes, painted smiles… they were all unnerving to her now.

She spun about and came face-to-face with a ferocious lion —a golden face with bristled fur. Fantina gasped and leapt backward, but then relaxed as the lion passed. It was just another *Carnevale* reveler in a furry mask. Fantina shook her head clear. "Just stories," she repeated to herself.

"Hello," a voice suddenly interrupted.

Fantina turned. A mysterious figure, cloaked in a flowing robe, a beaded soothsayer turban and a lace mask, stared at Fantina from behind a table of tarot cards.

"Are you still lost?" the figure smiled. She removed her mask to reveal her familiar face. It was the old woman from earlier, the one with the flowered shoes in the flooded *piazza*.

Fantina sighed with relief as she recognized the woman. "It's you—"

"Contessa," the woman offered. "But...you can call me Tessa the Mystical Oracle of the Venetian Lagoon." She looked to Fantina for a reaction.

Fantina eyed her uncertainly.

"*Beh*, never mind. I'm still working on the name."

Fantina glanced about curiously. "What is all this?" she asked.

"*Carnevale*," Contessa announced with a flourish. "Starting tonight and up until the mayor's masked ball next week, you can be anyone and anything you wish for a while."

She pointed to a short, jolly man in a brocaded jester's outfit, amusing the crowd with a juggling act and laughing skittishly as if on the verge of losing control. He huffed as he sprung back and forth, trying desperately to keep his juggling pins from crashing to the ground. "That is my cousin, Giuseppe," Contessa explained with a slight roll of her eyes. "He runs the oldest citywide gondola service in Venice, so usually, he is a bit over-worked and a little jumpy. But tonight..." she considered, then shrugged, "well...still kind of jumpy, *eh*? For *Carnevale*, we call him Jester Joe." Contessa caught his attention with a tiny wave. Joe noticed and acknowledged Contessa with a quick, jittery nod before missing a catch and dropping a pin onto his head. Fantina chuckled.

Contessa then pointed to an athletic and nimble woman further up in the *piazza*. Long, dark hair flowed almost to her waist as she swung, in a type of aerial ballet, from silk cords strung overhead. Sheer fabric, trailing from her arms like wings, fluttered behind her as she bounded up and back. "That is his wife, Eva, the wind dancer. She is...how should I say...the more graceful half of the duo."

Fantina considered the colorful display as tumblers vaulted past, minstrels sang and thespians entertained the costumed crowd. Everything seemed so exciting. *Carnevale* was like a circus and costume party where it seemed anything could happen. She sighed and held her forehead, a bit relieved, almost certain now that the peculiar events of before had all been part of the pageantry, and that she had simply gotten caught up in the spectacle of the moment.

Just then, the lanky fire-eater twirled his flame-tipped staff before his face and ignited an arc of fire spouted from his mouth. A chorus of 'oohs' and 'ahhs' rose in the night.

"And that," Contessa continued, pointing to the fire-eater, "is my nephew Cosimo." She leaned in close toward Fantina. "So very serious."

With his thin mustache and goatee trimming his lean face, and intense, deep-set eyes on either side of his sharp, prominent nose, Cosimo seemed as heated and scorched a personali-ty as Eva seemed breezy and Jester Joe down to earth. He was dressed in black from head to toe, with a beaded vest that shimmered in the flickering firelight. As the *Carnevale* crowd applauded his act, he bent his lanky frame and took a courtly bow.

Fantina watched him curiously. "Just Cosimo?" she asked. Fantina thought it seemed a rather plain name for such a flashy *Carnevale* character. "How about Torch Man or...Flame Boy?" Fantina wasn't sure if Cosimo overheard, but he suddenly gulped back a flame and singed his goatee.

Contessa chuckled. "Flame Boy. That is funny." Cosimo straightened up with a severe look on his face, made doubly so by his now-smouldering beard. Contessa shrugged. "I told you, so serious, *eh*? Better we just call him Cosimo." Fantina nodded.

With that, Contessa motioned to Fantina and spread her deck of tarot cards across her table. "Come, let me read your future."

Fantina edged closer. "You're a fortune-teller?"

Contessa reflected playfully, "Yes, absolutely. I make a 'fortune telling' tourists their destiny." She chuckled, amused by her turn of phrase. "It is a joke." Fantina stared at her blankly. Contessa shrugged and rolled her eyes. "*Beh*, never mind."

Contessa flipped a few cards as Fantina leaned in to get a better look. Contessa paused and closed her eyes as if deep in thought. "Your name is…" She hesitated.

Fantina waited. Contessa opened a single eye expectantly. Fantina nodded and filled in the blank. "Fantina?"

Contessa opened her eyes with a confident grin. "Yes. Your name is Fantina. That is correct."

Fantina raised a skeptical eyebrow. "Wow, you're good."

"*Ei*, I am just getting started," Contessa countered defensively. She turned a few cards and pointed to them. "So, I see here that you have just arrived in Venice after a long journey."

Fantina crinkled her nose, catching on to the game. "You saw my suitcase earlier."

"Sssstt," Contessa hushed her. "You are hoping to prove yourself, and you are...looking for something." Fantina bobbed her head side to side. Okay, that was peculiarly accurate, but...a lucky guess, she thought.

Contessa suddenly opened her eyes wide, as if struck by an otherworldly revelation. "Fortune and glory," she said definitively.

Fantina stopped short. Now that was uncanny. She sup-posed a guess might have come up with that bit too, but what were the chances. She took a step closer. Contessa continued, quickening her patter to stir some excitement.

"But I sense that there is something about you—something different. Like the path you are on will soon reveal a wonderful surprise, something you never even suspected was possible for you, *eh?* Sometimes it takes a while, but then destiny strikes like a bolt of lightning, you see?" Contessa pointed to the card combination with interest.

Fantina leaned a bit closer, intrigued. For a moment she wondered if Contessa could truly know something about her— the hope that had brought her to Venice, that thing for which she longed...

"Look! Look at this," Contessa crowed enthusiastically, "I see your true love approaching." Fantina frowned and stood back. Then again, maybe not.

Contessa looked up. "Ah, Enzo, there you are. Come talk to this lovely, young girl."

Fantina turned. Stepping through the crowd toward her, carrying a small wooden box, was another familiar face. Enzo, the young 'Da Vinci Shoe' vendor from earlier that day, stopped short as he saw Fantina. He looked both surprised and flustered, like perhaps he had been thinking about her ever since their chance meeting and was sure he'd be more prepared and more debonair if ever they met again. "You," he blurted out in a decidedly non-debonair manner.

Fantina looked suspiciously from Enzo, to Contessa, to Contessa's cards. "I see you've been talking about me."

Enzo smiled sheepishly. "No, I...might have mentioned you...in passing, but—" he fumbled, then pointed accusingly at Contessa. "My grandmother is always trying to match me up with every pretty girl that comes along."

Contessa quickly nudged Fantina with a wink. "Did you hear that? He called you 'pretty.'"

"He did, didn't he," Fantina played along with a grin.

Enzo back-pedalled. "No, what I said—"

"We heard what you said," Contessa interrupted.

"No, what I meant to say—"

"You meant to say I'm *not* pretty?" Fantina broke in.

"No, I... What I was trying…" Enzo stopped for a breath, and shot Contessa a confounded look.

"What…" Contessa shrugged as she reshuffled her deck. "I see what I see. It is a gift," she explained. Fantina chuckled. Enzo loosened his shirt collar awkwardly.

Contessa pointed to the box in Enzo's hands, beckoning him over with enthusiasm. "Is that what I think it is?" Enzo placed the box on Contessa's table and pulled out a curious device. It was a spherical orb on an axis suspended between two points on an ornate, bronze, base plate fitted with gears and a lever. Contessa smiled and nudged Fantina again. "You will like Enzo. He is what we call a gizmologist, you see?"

"A what?" Fantina inquired.

"Gizmologist. Always coming up with new ideas...inventions."

"Really," Fantina looked impressed. Enzo managed a modest shrug.

Contessa leaned in with her pitch. "He has his own boat... He loves to read..."

"*Nonna!*" Enzo tried to interrupt.

"Of course he needs to get out more. Always tinkering around at home with his tools."

"*NONNA!*" Enzo shot Contessa an urgent look. Contessa nodded, and yielded.

"Okay, okay. I am just trying to help." Contessa tossed Fantina a side glance. "Some people really need a bolt of lightning to jump start their destiny." Contessa pushed aside her cards and positioned Enzo's new gizmo in the center of her table.

"This should rake in some tourists. A magic crystal ball." She turned to Fantina and leaned in conspiratorially. "Go ahead, ask something. Maybe about romance?"

Fantina chuckled. Enzo rolled his eyes and stepped forward. "Here is a question," he offered. "Will my *Nonna* Contessa ever stop embarrassing me?"

Contessa considered the query with a frown, then pulled the lever on the side of the device. Gears turned, the orb began to spin. Inside the orb, words and phrases spun by in the opposite direction. Then, the device whirred to a halt and locked into position. Contessa leaned over the orb glancing inside to divine the answer. "The chances are slim to none," she read. "Well, there it is."

Enzo sighed. Contessa sidled up to Fantina, "So, where are you staying?"

Fantina turned uncertainly, looking back through the crowd. "I'm staying at my...over by the...uh...I'm not sure about anything anymore. I've seen some strange things tonight."

Just then, Cosimo, the fire-eater, stepped up beside Enzo, a humorless expression and a whiff of smoke still trailing from the tip of his goatee. Contessa nodded. "Strange, yes. I agree." She nudged Fantina with a wink. "Flame Boy."

Cosimo stared at Fantina. "Who is this?" he asked curiously in a raspy, fire-tinged voice.

"Enzo's new girlfriend," Contessa chimed in quickly. Enzo and Fantina were about to object when Contessa continued. "Enzo, you will help her get home safely. Near the church of *San Lorenzo,* I think. You should be a good boy and do this. Do you not agree, Cosimo?" Cosimo hesitated just long enough for Contessa to continue uninterrupted. "He will take you in his gondola," she said as she leaned in close to Fantina. "Very romantic." Enzo, mouth agape, tried to get a word out, but wasn't fast enough. "Enzo, what is the matter? You look befuddled. Are you befuddled? Do not be. I see what I see."

Enzo turned to Cosimo for support, but Cosimo knew better than to argue with Contessa's 'gift.' Enzo shrugged defeatedly. "Are you ready to go?" he sighed. "I know I am."

Fantina nodded, "Lead the way."

Enzo motioned forward and led Fantina away through the crowd. Contessa called after them with some final instructions. "You should take the scenic route. Venice at night can be a magical place."

Enzo groaned. Fantina glanced back curiously over her shoulder, "Magical?" she wondered. She scanned the *piazza* as if searching one last time for some proof of what she thought she had seen earlier, but despite all the colorful and unusual costumes and people, there was nothing, she decided, out of the ordinary. She turned and followed after Enzo.

Contessa watched Fantina and Enzo as they disappeared in the crowd, then looked up to Cosimo. She licked her thumb and forefinger and doused his smouldering goatee. "What do you think? There is something about her, no?"

Cosimo stretched out his lanky frame to look out skeptically over the *piazza*. He wasn't the type to speculate about what might be. He put his trust in the things he knew, things as they were and always had been. He shrugged, unconvinced. "What do you mean, something…"

"Something special," Contessa nodded. She reached down and pulled the lever on her crystal ball contraption. Gears turned; the orb spun. She leaned in to view the answer: "Absolutely."

Chapter Eight — The scenic route

A grumpy, old, masked man in a red suit and black mantle strode into view on the balcony of the Ducal Palace. Only, it wasn't the real palace, and it wasn't a real man. It was a costumed marionette on an ornate puppet stage set up in the *giardinetti reali*, the royal gardens, a narrow park planted with small trees and groomed shrubberies between the *Piazzetta San Marco* and the Grand Canal.

The show was in mid-story, and the finely detailed marionettes—the old man in red, a young lady in blue with a flounced skirt, and a mischievous gent in a colorful, jacquard

93

outfit, harlequin mask and a floppy hat—paraded across the painted scenery to the delight of the gathered audience of both young and old. Fantina slowed as she and Enzo passed the show, eyeing it with curiosity.

Enzo watched her. Ever since he had first seen her that afternoon on the *Riva Degli Schiavoni*, he felt as though there were more to her than her wandering story and dusty travel clothes. And it wasn't just her enchanting smile or spellbinding eyes that had affected him, although, in truth, they had done that. He felt...different around her, like she would understand things, appreciate new ideas and be able to see the world the way he did...with hope.

Just then, the lady marionette slapped the man in red across the face. Fantina laughed.

"They are the classic characters of *Carnevale*," Enzo explained.

"It looks like fun," Fantina mused. "Who is that?"

"Ah, well…" Enzo paused and pointed. "*Colombina*, in the blue dress, has a secret, and *Pantalone*, the devious, old man in red wants to steal it from her, of course."

"Of course," Fantina nodded, edging closer. The colorful marionette in the harlequin mask then stepped up to confront *Pantalone*, swinging his trusty billy club.

Enzo pointed. "But *Arlecchino,* brave and always true to *Colombina*, arrives to defend her and…" Enzo hesitated.

Fantina turned to him. "What?"

"I am not sure I remember what happens in this story. I think *Colombina* gets carried off, but *Arlecchino* rescues her and knocks *Pantalone* into the lagoon...or something."

Fantina raised an eyebrow. "Or something?"

"Sunk, drowned, swallowed by the sea," Enzo clarified. "You know, a happy ending."

On stage, the *Arlecchino* marionette pummeled *Pantalone* with his club till *Pantalone* collapsed out of view. An offstage splash sent a small spray of water out onto the front row of the audience. Adults ducked. Children cheered. Enzo laughed with a snort.

Fantina eyed Enzo curiously. He was a bit odd, she thought, but, in all honesty, she had always been more at ease with what people considered 'odd.' Her father had seen to that. As they traveled the world together, from port to port, continent to continent, he would take her beyond the ordinary city sites and sounds to the places where people shared their stories and whispered of wondrous happenings that most people would very well consider odd. 'Look with more than just your eyes,' her father had told her, 'beyond what everyone sees, or you may miss that one thing in life that is most important.' Fantina paused, crinkling her nose. She really wished now that she had asked for some clarification about that 'one thing.'

"Are you all right?" Enzo asked as he stepped up before Fantina.

Fantina quickly uncrinkled her nose self-consciously. Her mind had wandered, and she wondered how long Enzo had been staring at her. "Yes," she said quickly, tossing a last glance toward the puppet stage. "Good show. Which way? This way?" Fantina turned abruptly and crossed onward. Enzo eyed her strangely. She was a bit odd, he thought.

Fantina walked along the moonlit quay up onto a small bridge over the narrow *Rio di Palazzo* canal. The water shimmered and swirled as Gondolas skimmed silently over its surface, and Fantina paused to take in the view. It was all so enchanting, and dreamlike, she thought. No wonder she was seeing things…and getting distracted. She frowned. She hadn't come to Venice to get distracted. She had ideas and start up funds and— Fantina paused, remembering her empty pockets. Oh, right, she sighed.

Enzo smiled as he stepped up beside Fantina.

"What?" Fantina asked.

Enzo pointed a little further up the canal where an elegant, gleaming, white stone bridge, enclosed on all sides, connected two buildings over the water like a suspended, elevated tunnel.

"You sighed," Enzo explained, "and that is *il Ponte Dei Sospiri*, the Bridge of Sighs."

Fantina glanced at the bridge. It was quite beautiful and mysterious with its arched roof and intricate stone screens covering its two, small windows. "The Bridge of Sighs," Fantina repeated to herself. "Well that's charming."

"Yes," Enzo said distractedly before he caught himself. "Actually, no."

"No?"

"It is the bridge from the Ducal Palace to the prison on the other side," Enzo explained. He pointed to the two windows in the stone walls of the bridge. "Through those openings, condemned prisoners would catch their last sight of their beloved Venice as they were marched to their dark cells and their doom, forever. And so, they sighed."

Fantina's face froze. Her smile faded. "Seriously?"

Enzo thought it through, then nodded. "That is how the story goes."

"Well then...not so charming, at all." Fantina shook her head rethinking her initial impression. Now, on second glance, the bridge looked a bit intimidating against the night sky, cold and foreboding. The two stone-screened windows stared back at her, almost fatefully, and Fantina began to wonder if anything in Venice was as it first seemed.

Fantina and Enzo stepped toward a row of gondolas bobbing in the water along the quay. The boat tethers, tightly bound to their mooring posts, creaked with the tide. Enzo studied Fantina, watching the boats. She seemed...at home, he thought, here among the gondolas, but he wondered if it would seem too presumptuous for him to say so. "Do you think you might stay for a while?" Enzo finally asked.

Fantina hesitated, unsure if what she had heard was just a question or if it had sounded like a request.

"You know, to find your 'fortune and glory.'" Enzo continued. "I could show you around if you need—"

"Oh no," Fantina cut in awkwardly. "Thanks but…I'm used to being on my own."

Enzo considered. "Strange," he murmured.

Fantina paused. "You think I'm strange?"

"No, not you," Enzo clarified. "Being 'on your own' is strange...to me. I mean, I have always been part of...well, one big family really."

Fantina's expression softened, savoring the thought for a brief moment before she noticed Enzo watching her. She quickly put her stoic face back on. "Well that's just...weird. It sounds inconvenient. Someone always telling you what to do…"

"Stay out of trouble!" Enzo nodded.

"Telling you to be careful…"

"Do not scratch the gondola!" Enzo recalled.

"Looking out for you…"

"And do not blow up the lab again!" Enzo recollected.

Fantina stopped short, as if only just hearing Enzo's asides. "What?" she asked.

Enzo hesitated, "What? Oh...never mind." He stopped. "Here we are."

Fantina looked up. Before her was an elegant gondola with a shiny, black, lacquered finish, brass fittings and gilded trim. She nodded, impressed. "That's your boat?"

Enzo eyed the fancy gondola briefly, then shifted his gaze to a gondola docked a little further down. "Uh...not quite." Fantina followed Enzo's glance to a smaller, battered, old gondola that had definitely seen better days. The boat creaked decrepitly as Enzo stepped on and offered Fantina a hand. "It is a hand-me-down, but I have done some work on it."

Fantina eyed the gondola uncertainly, then stepped aboard. A piece of trim along the edge broke off in her hand as she steadied herself. "Oops."

Enzo took the piece from her. "It is a work in progress," he explained. He tossed the trim aside as he untethered the boat from its mooring post and shoved off. From a small compartment near the gondola's seat, he pulled out a small, mechanical music box and gave it a quick wind before stepping up onto the rear stoop. Gears spun, the music cylinder turned and a plucky rendition of the folk tune 'Carnival of Venice' began playing as Enzo swept the gondola toward a narrow canal. "And on the scenic route, you get the deluxe package complete with music," he said.

Fantina sat back in the gondola seat, watching Enzo. Okay, so he was odd, but oddly charming too, she thought. She was surprised to find herself wondering if her father would have liked him—not in the 'boy-taking-my-daughter-on-a-romantic-gondola-ride' way, but as a father hoping she would come across good people as she navigated her way through life. Fantina smiled.

Enzo noticed the smile, and, momentarily mesmerized, inadvertently sideswiped the elegant gondola docked at the pier as they passed. He cringed. Fantina raised an eyebrow.

"Maybe we should just walk. Might be safer."

Enzo adjusted course. "No, no, that was just...all good. You are perfectly safe."

"I meant, safer for the boat," Fantina joked as the gondola rocked precariously in the canal. Enzo glanced at Fantina, clearly flustered as he steadied the gondola. He didn't quite understand it, but there was something... He had never been so distracted by anyone before. It was as if, from the moment he had first seen her, Venice had somehow become...brighter. And though Fantina looked dusty, travel-worn and weary as she sat there against the frayed, velvet gondola cushion, Enzo had a sense that she was, as his *Nonna* Contessa had noted when she 'saw what she saw,' extraordinary.

CHAPTER NINE — ANOTHER INTERRUPTION

"So, you are enjoying the ride, *eh?*" your gondolier says to you as you glide gently around another bend in the Grand Canal. The sun is low now and glistening on the water's surface. Passing boats seem to drift on air, wisps of cloud in the orange sky above reflected beneath them, and you wonder where you are heading.

"The story so far, like the Grand Canal, is quiet and calm," the gondolier says, "—a little mystery perhaps swirling around the bend, but, all in all, a tranquil journey with only a few ripples. But do not be fooled. Every journey must take a turn at some point—beyond a dark corner, into a narrow canal...to that place where adventure is met by sinister intentions. And that is where the ripples become waves."

CHAPTER TEN — WAVES

The Venetian lagoon surrounds Venice like a vast moat protecting a fortified castle—a barrier that centuries earlier kept those who would do the city harm at bay. The lagoon, however, is also the road into the city, and access to that road is controlled at three points along the shore, the inlets from the Adriatic Sea at *Chioggia*, *Malamocco* and *Lido*. I am telling this to you now because you will soon understand how these three gateways into Venice, and the city's willingness to turn them over to a certain, unscrupulous individual, nearly cost the city its very existence.

That individual, as you may have surmised by now, was none other than the newly honored 'Protector of Venice,' *Signore* Massimo Malvagio. He had returned to Venice a few years prior with a grand idea to control the tide that constantly threatened and regularly flooded the city. He proposed the construction of a trio of steam-powered sea walls that could be raised and lowered at each of the lagoon inlets to maintain the water level at whatever height was desired. It was a radical idea back then at the turn of the century, but it was exactly the kind of 'modern progress' that Mayor Grimani loved. At the mayor's urging, the Venice city council had eagerly embraced Malvagio's 'Gatekeeper Project,' and allocated the necessary funds to build it, without question. After all, the Malvagio family's reputation for coming to the city's aid in the past was well known (or at least, well recounted). Why wouldn't they trust Massimo Malvagio to save Venice?

Malvagio stood at the edge of an old, stone terrace, attached to a watchtower on the shores of the *Lido* inlet. It was part of an ancient, noble residence that looked more like a desolate and disused fortification than it did a home, with moss covered walls that seemed held together by strands of tangled ivy.

It had been at the forefront of the Venetian resistance against the French in 1797 when Malvagio's grandfather had defended— well, so the story went. In truth, Malvagio had purchased the property (along with its pedigree) less than a decade ago and had skillfully and repeatedly spun the story of his family's bravery and nobility into the local history which, left unchallenged, was eventually accepted as fact.

Now, having convinced the Venetian elite of his noble intentions, Malvagio could operate with no interference as he worked to achieve his secret, and much more sinister goal.

Malvagio considered the work at hand. Down below, at the *Lido* inlet, the primary gap through which the Adriatic Sea flowed in and out of the lagoon, a shadowy crew of roughnecks toiled under the dim moonlight. Steam-powered machines with massive, metal arms and cables drawn over squealing pulleys, hissed as large panels of steel were lowered into the water. Malvagio nodded, pleased with the progress, then turned and entered his residence through a crumbling archway.

Inside, was a vast gathering hall, which time ago might have been quite grand. Beneath the towering, vaulted ceilings buttressed by marble columns and elaborate stained-glass windows, were the remains of a once great house. Its former grandiosity, in fact, had been one of the main attractions for

Malvagio when he bought it. Malvagio knew that, in addition to the prime and requisite location at the *Lido* inlet, the stature of the residence was as important, for his purposes, as its actual condition. City officials had been properly impressed.

The house was now, dark, damp and run-down. Faded frescoes were marred by mud and moisture seeping in through cracks in the plaster, chunks of the ceiling were missing, and glass in the tall, panelled windows was broken.

At the center of the space, laid out across a low table, was a detailed, miniature model of Venice and the surrounding lagoon. The *piazzas* and palaces, alleyways and houses, constructed to exacting architectural detail, made the city into an oddly pristine version of itself, perfectly neat, unsullied and untouched by time—a beautiful copy of Venice...but without the charm.

Kneeling before the model, like a toddler playing with an elaborate diorama, was a peculiar, old man with a jovial face rimmed by a wisp of white hair peeking out from beneath a well-worn captain's cap. He pushed a tiny, toy steamboat through the water-filled miniature lagoon, acting out his own, mini-adventure with childlike delight. "Chugga, chugga, chugga, chugga—" Suddenly, the pointed end of a silver-tipped walking stick came crashing down atop his boat, sinking it. The old man looked up. Malvagio stood over him, not amused.

"Primo," Malvagio bristled, "do not play with my city."

The old man, Primo, lowered his head penitently. "Ah, okay, sorry boss." Primo gave his sunken steamboat a final, dejected glance before taking a step back from the model. He was a simple man who, while older than his employer, was definitely younger at heart. A bit of a jack-of-all-trades, Primo had been working for the Malvagio family for some time—a gardener and chef to Malvagio's late father, and now, Massimo Malvagio's personal assistant in all schemes large and small. And while Primo understood that he was not always privy to the precise details and full scope of his employer's grand plans, he did believe that someday soon his faultless loyalty to the Malvagio family would be rewarded.

Primo checked his old pocket watch. "Would you like a late dinner, boss. I made my speciality—*Fettucine al Pesto*, the best in Italy."

Malvagio ignored Primo, pacing around the table and model, surveying his domain, inspecting the three areas of the lagoon that he had roped off with string—the inlets at *Chioggia, Malamocco* and *Lido.*

Primo, lost in his own thoughts, continued. "Well, it is better than what they serve in Genoa anyhow. They say they invented it there, but I use an old family recipe, see? The secret is all in the fresh basil and—"

"Venice has a secret," Malvagio interrupted. "A pearl in an oyster that I need to find."

Primo shook his head. "No, no, I no do oysters. They are *schifo,*" he said, sticking out his tongue disgustedly. "But my *linguini* with clams is pretty good."

"Primo!" Malvagio snapped. "I am talking about solving a mystery."

Primo stared blankly. "A what?"

"A treasure hunt with a hidden prize—"

Primo looked back at the model, then nodded, eager to agree. "Oh, I see, yes, like a game, it is like...he hid it, and we seek it. We should call it 'Hide and Go Seek.'"

"Primo…" Malvagio interrupted.

"No, you are right...that does not quite describe it. It is more like he tricked us and we are looking for it blind. I got it. 'Blind-man's-bluff,' *eh?*"

"Primo!" Malvagio tried again.

"No, no, not blind, more like we are blindfolded." Primo tipped his cap down over his eyes and reached out toward Malvagio. "Looking for this treasure of, what is his name, Marco…"

"Polo,"

"Marco…"

"Polo."

"Marco…" Primo bumped into Malvagio and tipped his cap up. "Hey, look, I found you. It is a good game, no?"

Malvagio suddenly exploded forward, drawing a long, razor-sharp blade from within his walking stick in one, fluid sweep and holding it to Primo's throat. His eyes, cold and dark, froze Primo in his place.

"Uh…well, never mind." Primo swallowed hard.

Malvagio held his glare for a moment, then stepped away to a broken window, resheathing his sword and looking out over the lagoon with cold disdain. His loathing seemed to be etched on his face, and he carried his contempt in his every step. He stared, across the dark water at the lights of Venice glinting on the surface of St. Mark's Basin, and sneered.

"I really hate the water," Malvagio said somberly. "Years ago Venice was a great city, ruled by families of wealth and power. Now…it is a sinking swamp town run by idiots." Malvagio turned back.

Primo was on his knees again by the model, floating a small rubber duck in the lagoon. "Quack, quack…"

"PRIMO!"

Primo jumped and sank his duck. "Right, no playing. I was just…not playing at all." He backed away in terror and planted himself quickly on a dilapidated chair.

"This city is doomed," Malvagio said with cold, calculated certainty. "Without someone of vision, Venice will never be great again. And I, Massimo Malvagio, have a vision. I will take Venice back and usher in a new century of progress. It is only a matter of time now."

Primo rose with equal certainty. "And I will help. I am your right hand man, *eh?*" Primo looked to Malvagio for validation, but got none.

Malvagio crossed away and stopped near a rotted fireplace mantel, where a white rat with piercing red eyes sat watching. Malvagio stroked the rodent with a finger, babbling playfully, "Who is my good girl?" The rat squeaked for her master, then clawed her way from the mantle down to a carved, wooden podium lit by moonlight streaming in through the cracked window. On the podium, was an old, leather-bound journal…the stolen journal of Marco Polo.

Malvagio opened the cover. The leather was creased and brittle, the yellowed pages crinkled with age. Malvagio's eyes burned with unsatisfied greed then grew distant as he remembered, "My father never believed I would succeed. When I told him that I would be the one to find the treasure of Marco Polo, he laughed at me. He said I did not have what it took."

Malvagio turned to a marked chapter—the account of Polo's return to Venice in 1295. A sketch of a Chinese sailing vessel was surrounded by scribbled notes and text. Malvagio grinned. "But my father did not know I would have this." He ran his hand over the page, as if hoping to glean some secret information from it, but then his eyes dimmed. He knew that those secrets were still out of his reach. "I have to find it," he told himself. "I have dug up everything along the path, and spent most of my family's fortune searching for this treasure."

Primo stepped forward gingerly. "Actually, boss, you have spent all of it. You are broke. And once the mayor realizes your 'Gatekeeper Project' has nothing to do with saving Venice from floods, the money you get from the city will stop too."

Malvagio slammed the journal shut. Primo jumped and retreated to a safe distance. "Then again," Primo reasoned, "maybe there is nothing left to find. Maybe this Marco Polo fellow spent everything. He retired, bought a house, a little boat. And then there is family. You know how that is. As soon as you make a little money, it is gimme, gimme, gimme. He had a wife, a daughter... probably bought a lot of shoes—"

Malvagio eyed Primo coldly, advancing on him. Primo kept his distance retreating to the other side of the city model as Malvagio fumed. "Fourteen imperial ships from the Chinese Emperor, full of gold, jewels...more wealth than he could have spent in ten lifetimes…"

Primo shook his head timidly in disagreement. "You have no idea how many shoes a woman and a girl are capable of buying." Primo gulped nervously. He could see from Malvagio's icy expression that his point, while perhaps valid, was of no interest. He tried a different angle. "Besides, most people who hide a treasure…they leave a map, no?"

Malvagio raised the journal triumphantly. "We have this."

Primo looked unconvinced, "That is a book."

"*Il Milione*, the journal of Marco Polo."

Primo sighed wearily. "But, we have been looking for eight years now, boss. All over the place, thousands of miles along the trade route from the East. We never found anything."

"Because we were looking in the wrong place." Malvagio held the journal firmly and looked out the broken window toward the lights of Venice in the distance. "It has been here all along, waiting for me to find it."

Primo shrugged. "Maybe that is just a story—a fairy tale for children."

Malvagio opened the journal again, flipping through its pages confidently. "No, it is a map."

"But it no even have pictures. A map needs a picture and a big 'X' to mark the spot," Primo insisted.

"The story is the map." Malvagio ran his finger over the text. "But you cannot find the clues if you do not know how to read."

"I can read," Primo chimed in defensively. He thought about it then added, "...for the most part, I mean. Okay, I am better with the picture books. A picture can really tell a story, *eh?*"

Malvagio frowned. If he didn't find something soon, he would fail, just as his father had believed he would. And that, more than anything, was what Malvagio could not let happen. He would not let his ambition fall to ruin like…the walls around his purchased pedigree. Malvagio surveyed his shabby great hall, where the faded frescoes swirled before him like so many tales of long ago. Suddenly, he paused, Primo's words echoing in his mind… 'A picture can really tell a story…' Malvagio smiled. "You are right, Primo."

"I...I am?" Primo looked confused.

Malvagio closed the journal and touched the wall before him. "I need someone who reads more than words, someone who knows…the old stories of Venice."

CHAPTER ELEVEN — OLD STORIES

Uncle Gio gently rubbed a dingy image on the wall of *San Lorenzo* with a damp cloth. The picture beneath slowly revealed itself—a young Venetian mariner standing beside a 14th century *Doge*, a handshake cementing some now forgotten accord. Uncle Gio paused, studying the image as if trying to recall the story behind it. He nodded to himself. Of course he remembered.

In fact, since Fantina's arrival, memories of the past and details that he had promised Fantina's father to pass on to her had come flooding back. There were things that she should know, truths about Venice that her father had woven into the stories he had told her throughout her childhood. Now, Uncle Gio supposed, Fantina was old enough to see beyond the ordinary, and he would have to figure out how to reveal the extraordinary to her. There was so much he had to share...but not all at once.

Up above near the open window at the base of the vaulted ceiling, Bianca, now re-disguised as a white pigeon, fluttered in and perched herself atop the scaffold. She watched Uncle Gio. In fact, she had been watching him for some time. The first time he had spotted her up in the rafters of his attic where she had made her home, she thought he might grab a broom to chase her out, but he hadn't. He had smiled and tipped his hat —a gallant gesture as if he were greeting a true lady, as if he were somehow aware of the world that existed beyond the evening glow of Venice. So Bianca had watched and wondered if through the painted stories that he restored throughout the city, Uncle Gio had come to know more than what most could ever imagine.

"Uncle Gio?" Fantina stepped in through the church doors and crossed over toward the scaffolding.

Uncle Gio turned, squinting in the dim light. "Ah, Fantina. You found your room? Did you settle in?"

"Well, yes," Fantina explained, "but I got a little side-tracked." She looked back as Enzo entered, greeting Uncle Gio with a somewhat skittish wave.

Uncle Gio eyed him suspiciously. "Sidetrack, *eh?*"

Enzo opened his mouth to explain, but Fantina charged ahead. "I got lost following these…frogmen, but then there were these rats who were actually…and someone dressed like a lion…" Fantina hesitated, questioning her memory. She spotted Bianca above, and pointed excitedly. "And she was a faerie." Uncle Gio looked up to Bianca. Bianca cooed. Uncle Gio then turned to Enzo with an accusing stare.

Enzo gulped, raising his hands before him. "I just brought her home."

Uncle Gio set down his cleaning cloth and squared up to Fantina. "There are things you have to understand, Fantina. And if you are going to stay here with me, you need to listen."

"She is staying?" Enzo perked up. Uncle Gio shot him another suspicious look. Enzo retreated a step. "I mean, not that I will be seeing her again…ever." Uncle Gio nodded. Enzo smiled awkwardly.

Fantina paused, replaying the evening's events in her head. Something inside was telling her now that it had been more than just imagination. Her hazy memories were suddenly less so. She looked up, eyes wide. "It's Papà's story. It's real." Enzo looked to Uncle Gio curiously.

Uncle Gio wiped his hands and stepped over to Fantina. "Venice is not so simple to see clearly. It is like a painting on the wall…many hidden layers to consider."

Fantina glanced at the fresco mural near the door, remembering the over-painted scene she had discovered earlier of Leo battling in the sky over Venice. Hidden layers? What secrets were out there waiting for her to find. She turned back to Uncle Gio, her mind spinning and full of questions, but before she could get the first one out, Uncle Gio continued.

"That is enough for now. We will have a talk later." Uncle Gio shot Enzo a cautionary look. "No more sidetracks, *eh?*" He then took Fantina urgently by the shoulder. "You cannot be out so late at night. Not here in Venice. What are you, looking for trouble?" Fantina shook her head. She never went looking for trouble, she thought. It just seemed to happen around her.

Just then, an evening breeze whistled past the open church doors, and a figure stepped in from the dark outside. It was Malvagio, and he grinned. "Well, we are all looking for something, are we not?"

Just then, Primo shuffled forward as well and stood beside Malvagio. He sighed, "In our case, looking and looking, and looking…" Malvagio silenced Primo with a stern glare.

Uncle Gio eyed them in the dim light, cautiously. "*Signore* Malvagio, I am sorry, but the church is closed."

Malvagio smirked and stepped forward, Primo following. Behind them, a half dozen of Malvagio's shadowy crew members, masked in the shadows, edged their way in as well.

Uncle Gio scanned the church uneasily and gently nudged Fantina toward Enzo. "You need to leave," he mumbled. "Both of you."

Malvagio crossed slowly toward Uncle Gio, speaking as if from a memorized text. "To find what is golden, the journey must start, with an open mind and a worthy heart."

Enzo looked confused. Fantina hesitated, a memory stirring, and then springing forth. "Wait. I know that. That's—"

"—an interesting little nursery rhyme," Uncle Gio interrupted. "That is all it is."

Malvagio eyed Fantina curiously, wondering briefly who she was and what she had meant by her interruption. Uncle Gio, assessing the threat as Malvagio's menacing crew circled in, promptly cleared his throat, drawing Malvagio's attention back to him. "What is it that you need?"

"A restoration of history," Malvagio explained. "I heard you are the best."

"He is," Fantina agreed.

"No," Uncle Gio corrected quickly. "I am actually not so good, second rate really." He stepped forward, pushing Fantina behind him, while drawing attention to the church frescoes. "None of this makes any sense to me. I just clean it up a little. I am afraid I cannot help you."

Malvagio continued advancing. "But, the mayor spoke so very highly of you."

"Then again," Primo interjected, pointing to Malvagio, "he speaks very highly of him too so, that is no saying much, *eh?*" Primo chuckled to himself. Malvagio glared at him. Primo swallowed his laugh with a nervous gulp and bowed his head contritely.

Uncle Gio placed a stern hand on Fantina's shoulder, and angled her and Enzo toward the door. "You two should run along home. These gentlemen do not need you here."

Fantina resisted. "But, Uncle Gio—"

"Fantina!" Uncle Gio cut her off abruptly, "I do not need you here!"

Fantina paused, a stung look on her face. She took a step back. "Right. I guess I don't belong."

Uncle Gio regretted his tone, but remained resolute. He looked to Enzo. "Take her away," he urged, "I will join you later."

Enzo scanned the church, noting Malvagio's crew closing in. He nodded. He reached for Fantina's arm and took a step toward the door when suddenly, Malvagio raised his silver tipped walking stick to block the way. Primo cringed, anticipating the sword that he was sure would soon follow.

Fantina, still upset from being turned away, was nevertheless more than a bit perturbed by Malvagio's gall in forcing her to stay. She shot him a brassy look. Malvagio smiled unpleasantly. "I would like you all join me now instead," he said, tightening his grip on the silver handle of his hidden blade.

"COOOO!" Up above, Bianca fluttered a perfectly timed diversion. Malvagio and his crew looked up. Uncle Gio reached forward quickly, grabbed the rope attached to his pulley and counterweight mechanism and thrust it into Enzo and Fantina's hands.

"Hold tight," he ordered. He unhooked the rope from the side of the scaffold, setting the 'elevator' loose and the counterweight plummeting toward the ground. Primo lunged forward to make a grab but missed as Fantina and Enzo were yanked upward to safety. The counterweight smashed to the ground forcing Malvagio back, but as Uncle Gio turned to flee, Malvagio's crew emerged from the shadows, their rat faces now clearly visible.

Up above, Fantina and Enzo leapt off the rope onto the top level of the scaffold beneath the vaulted ceiling. Bianca cooed urgently near the open window.

"This way," Enzo called.

Fantina hesitated. "Wait, we have to help him!" She looked down over the edge. Scampering up the sides of the scaffold, four of Malvagio's rat-men were closing in. The other two held Uncle Gio fast in their paws. Uncle Gio looked up, locking eyes with Fantina. "Go, now!" he shouted.

"Oh rats," Fantina frowned.

Enzo stepped up beside her. "No. They are *Pantegane*. We call them ratters," Enzo said quickly. "I will explain later." Enzo grabbed Fantina's hand and pulled her toward the window. He nodded to Bianca, "Have Nicos and Dimitris meet us at *Campo Formosa*." With that, in a golden flash, Bianca transformed into her faerie form and fluttered away.

Fantina turned to Enzo, her mouth agape, "Did you...? Did she...?"

"Yes and yes, but later!" Enzo nodded as he shoved Fantina up and through the window.

Fantina emerged from the window onto the high roof of *San Lorenzo*. She paused a moment to find her balance then stepped up onto a low parapet that encircled the roof's edge. Enzo pulled himself through as well and scrambled up after her. "Keep going."

"Where?" Fantina asked. "There's nowhere to go!"

Suddenly, the four pursuing ratters burst out from the window, their teeth gnashing as they scampered onto the roof. Fantina spun about, considering quickly. "Never mind. This way's good," she said as she sprinted gingerly across the roofline.

When Fantina got to the edge she slid to a halt, turning back toward Enzo. "Now what?"

"Hang on," Enzo shouted as he ran past, grabbing Fantina's hand. Fantina screamed as Enzo jumped, pulling her straight off the roof's edge. They landed together on the peak of an adjacent rooftop, terra-cotta tiles smashing beneath their feet. Enzo steadied Fantina. "Are you all right?"

"You made me jump off the roof!" Fantina blurted out, her mouth agape.

Enzo looked back, considering the distance with a shrug. "Oh...it was just a little jump," he justified. Fantina stared at Enzo incredulously.

Just then, the ratters leapt down onto the roof as well. Fantina backed into Enzo as the ratters spread out then closed in on them. "Any more ideas?" Fantina asked.

Enzo scanned the roof looking for an escape route. They were surrounded. Then he paused as he spotted a tall, metal pole—a lightning rod—strapped to a chimney. He shot Fantina a quick look. "Yes...duck."

With that, Enzo grabbed the lightning rod and yanked it free. The ratters lunged. Enzo swung the rod in a wide arc overhead connecting with the closest ratter and sending it plummeting off the roof into a canal below. The remaining three ratters regrouped and charged forward again. "Behind you," Fantina warned.

Enzo spun about, twirling the rod like a fighting staff and beating back each new assault. As dangerous as this all seemed, Fantina was sure that she'd been in worse fixes before. Just then, another ratter got smashed across the face and tumbled from the roof into the canal below. Okay, she thought, maybe not worse, but definitely just as perilous.

Suddenly, Fantina's eyes locked on something, beyond the rooftop, out across the canal—a small balcony extending out over the water from a rugged, old house on the other side. The balcony was narrow, but would do for a landing. She crinkled her nose then narrowed her eyes, thinking deeply—her 'inventing look.' An idea sparked. Fantina turned to Enzo. "Ready?"

Enzo looked worried. "For what?"

Fantina grabbed hold of the lightning rod and smashed the end against the tiles beneath their feet. "Hang on." The tiles broke free and sent Fantina and Enzo sledding down the roof slope toward the canal below. At the last possible moment, before dropping off the edge, Fantina jammed the end of the rod hard onto the edge and pole-vaulted herself and Enzo up, over and onto the balcony across the canal. One ratter tried to follow but came up short and splashed down below.

On the balcony, Enzo caught his breath, eyeing the distance cleared over the water. He stared, wide-eyed, at Fantina. "You are crazy!"

"Oh...it was just a little crazy," Fantina justified.

Enzo considered a response but instead caught sight of the ratters, scampering down the walls across the canal to give chase. He dropped the lightning rod and grabbed a clothespin bucket hanging from a clothesline strung between the balcony and the ivy-covered wall of a quaint, Venetian cafè across a small *piazza* below. Fantina looked, then nodded...she understood. She grabbed onto Enzo's shoulders. "Go."

Enzo and Fantina leapt from the balcony, hanging onto the bucket, zip-lining over and across the *piazza*. Just before hitting the wall of ivy, they let go, bounced off a striped, canvas awning over the cafè seating area and flipped to the pavement below. Enzo landed first, just in time to reach out and catch Fantina in his arms.

Fantina paused for an awkward moment in Enzo's embrace, while *Carnevale*-costumed patrons at the cafè applauded the festive acrobatic display. Enzo smiled and took a slight bow.

Fantina cleared her throat. "You can put me down now."

Enzo hesitated. He had heard the words, but somehow it took a moment before it fully registered that Fantina was still in his arms. Fantina waited patiently, glancing toward the ground. "Right here would be fine."

"Oh...absolutely." Enzo set Fantina down promptly, but delicately...and perhaps a bit slowly, but Fantina didn't mind. She eyed Enzo curiously as he set her onto the pavement. Evidently, none of this seemed strange to him—talking to pigeon faeries, fighting ratters... Fantina thought she was definitely owed some explanation.

Enzo would have agreed and would have clarified everything for her right then, but in that moment, the four ratters climbed out of the canal across the *piazza*—dark, wet and ready to pounce back into the chase. Enzo grabbed Fantina's hand again. "Time to go."

Enzo pulled Fantina out of view into a dark alley along a narrow canal. "Wait," Fantina said as she freed her arm and squared up to him. "Who are you?"

Enzo paused—the chattering sounds of the pursuing ratters getting closer. He seized the curved bow iron from the front of a gondola docked in the canal, then, with a sharp twist, he unseated the iron and swung it in hand, wielding it like a deadly scimitar. "I am a gondolier," he answered.

Suddenly, the ratters scrambled into view and charged. With expert agility, Enzo dodged, parried and attacked, smashing one ratter through a window, clubbing another into the canal. Enzo shot a look back at Fantina. "Run that way. Nicos will find you." Fantina stared at Enzo wide eyed, glanced down the dark alleyway uncertainly, then ran.

The ancient, stone walls of Venice passed in a blur as Fantina fled. She thought for a moment about doubling back to see if she could help, but then, how could she? She had no idea what they were up against. She was pretty sure now that everything she had seen, since that golden pulse had washed over the city at sunset, was real, but she was still a bit stunned by it all. It was as if a page from the wondrous stories her father had told her had suddenly sprung to life before her eyes all at once, and it was more fantastic than anything she could have ever imagined. Fantastic, frightening, and a bit overwhelming she thought to herself as she ran. She didn't think she could take any more surprises tonight.

Fantina stopped. She had been running on instinct, without paying attention to where she was going, and now, she had no idea where she was...again. Voices and the sounds of *Carnevale* had faded in the night, and she found herself alone in the dark.

Just then, a faint noise arose from somewhere beyond. Fantina squinted into the darkness of the alleyway before her, and saw what she thought might be a person approaching fast. Then she heard the noise more clearly, galloping hoofbeats on the cobbled alleyway, getting closer. She stared as two shapes passed in and out of the dim moonlight—they were definitely horses, but the sound of their hooves was thunderously loud...and hollow.

Fantina gasped as the horses charged into view and pulled to a halt before her. They were towering, powerful, muscular...

and bronze. Moonlight glinted off their metallic skin as they looked down at Fantina with curious expressions.

"I am Nicos," the first horse said to her in a deep, resonating voice. "Are you all right, little one?"

"Of course she is not all right," the second horse, Dimitris, chimed in sounding a bit brassy. "You think Enzo would have called for us if everything had been all right?"

"Do not mind Dimitris," Nicos consoled Fantina. "He has been grumpy ever since Paris."

"You had to bring up Paris again…" Dimitris snorted. He turned to Fantina. "It was very stressful time for me."

"Do not bore us with the details," Nicos chimed in. "Look at her. You are making her ill."

Fantina's face went blank. She felt dizzy. Two giant, talking, bronze horses—it was 'one surprise too many.' Her eyes rolled back and she fainted straight away. Nicos glared at Dimitris. "Nice going."

"What? I did nothing."

Nicos scanned the alleyway then bent down low. "Get her up. We should go."

Dimitris gently nudged Fantina onto Nicos' back, then tossed a glance down the alleyway as well. "What about Enzo?" he wondered. "What you think is keeping him?" Just then, Enzo swung around a corner and landed before them. "Ahhhh!" Dimitris flinched. "Sorry."

Enzo rushed over to check Fantina, then looked to Dimitris for an explanation. "What happened?"

Dimitris tried to look innocent. "It was not me. I think Nicos scared her—that big, booming echo voice of yours." Nicos rolled his eyes with a snort.

"Come," Enzo leapt up onto Nicos' back behind Fantina. "We have to take her in."

Nicos shot Enzo a cautionary look over his shoulder. "Are you sure you want to do that? Someone is not going to like it."

"No choice," Enzo said. "Something is going on, some-thing...murky. We have to warn Leo and the guild."

Nicos and Dimitris nodded. Enzo held fast to Fantina as the bronze horses turned and galloped away, their echoing hoof-beats fading in the night as they disappeared back the way they had come.

CHAPTER TWELVE — SOMETHING MURKY

Fantina awoke, unsure of where she was. Light from a colored glass chandelier high above cast a glow through the space—a towering multi-floored chamber open down its center—a library of sorts with floors upon floors of ornate and sturdy wooden shelves that housed a massive collection of worn and ancient books. Each floor was connected to the others by a series of oddly angled staircases and bridges that climbed or spiraled upward to the topmost floors that lay hidden beyond the dim light.

Fantina sat up on a small cot that had been placed in the center of the room. She was alone...or was she? She turned slowly as if sensing a presence behind her. And there, at the edge of the shadows, was Leo, the great winged lion of *San Marco*, watching her. Fantina jumped and fell off the back of the cot.

"Be careful," Leo purred. "You have already had a bit of a bumpy night."

Fantina rose and backed away warily. "It's you, the lion that my father used to tell me about. The sentinel in the night. The fierce protector of Venice."

A deep, resonating voice behind Fantina stopped her in her tracks. "He is just a big kitty cat, really." Fantina spun. Towering over her, were the bronze horses, Nicos and Dimitris. Fantina held in a gasp and paused, then reached up and tapped Dimitris' bronze nose. "Hello," he nickered. Fantina stared speechlessly.

"Do not scare her again" Nicos interjected. "Can you not see she is still a little discombobulated?"

Dimitris shot Nicos an odd look. "Discombob—what? Ah, well, we certainly not mean to do that." Dimitris turned back to Fantina. "But Bianca said you met her earlier, so we assumed—"

"Bianca?" Fantina questioned.

"The one with white feathers," Dimitris explained. Right on cue, Bianca fluttered in from above and landed on a stair railing to straighten her dress. Fantina smiled uncertainly.

"Where are you from little one," Nicos asked.

Dimitris cut in. "We came here originally from Constantinople in 1204, after 4th Crusade. We spent some time in Paris when that horse thief, Napoleon, raided Venice in 1797—"

"Dimitris please, do not monopolize the conversation."

"I was just explaining our history."

"Boring," Nicos yawned.

Just then, Enzo appeared on an upper level overlooking the chamber, Contessa beside him. "Oh good, you are awake," Contessa noted, then looked to Leo. "How is she now?"

Leo considered. "A little confused, I would say."

Fantina looked about cautiously but held her ground. "Well, let's see," she summarized. "—jumped off a roof, chased by giant rats and rescued by bronze horse statues...what could be confusing?"

Dimitris cleared his throat, "Uh, actually, we are about 96 percent copper. Many people historically are confused about this. You see—"

"Boring!" Nicos repeated.

A door on the third floor suddenly swung open. Cosimo strode in and crossed urgently down a slightly skewed staircase toward Leo. Behind him, Jester Joe, Eva and some of the other *Carnevale* street acrobats filtered in and crowded forward at the rail, to see Fantina standing down below. Cosimo stared sternly at Enzo, not pleased at all. "You brought her here? This is not allowed."

Enzo leapt over the rail and slid down a column to go stand beside Fantina. "She was in trouble."

Cosimo grumbled. "You put us all in trouble...the entire guild. She does not belong here."

Fantina paused, a thought spinning. She looked at Enzo, Cosimo and the others as if suddenly placing them in a memory. "The Gondoliers," she whispered. "You watch over the city with help from..." she glanced at Leo, "the sentinels. You defend those in need and protect Venice from harm. You're the secret guild from my father's stories." The room fell silent. Cosimo glanced uncertainly at Fantina, then at Contessa and the others.

Leo stepped forward. "Not secret, but an unspoken tradition. The last line of defense between the Glim of this city and the reality of a new and more logical world."

"Glim?" Fantina asked.

Leo paced before her. "The spirit…energy…the magic that flows through Venice, sustains it, and holds back the ruin of time."

"And it continues to fade," Cosimo chimed in. "If the mayor does not want us, and the city does not need us—"

"Of course they need us," Contessa interrupted. "What would Venice be without its magic? Just an old city with some very bad plumbing problems."

"Or worse," Leo said as he wandered toward a dark corner of the room.

Fantina eyed Leo curiously, "Then why do you hide?"

Cosimo sighed. "The mayor does not care much for old traditions. He believes Venice must forget the past to embrace the new century of progress. He just needs one excuse to crack down on us, outlaw the guild and seal the fate of the sentinels."

"Seal the fate?" Fantina wondered as she looked to Leo standing still in the shadows. "That doesn't sound good."

Nicos clopped up beside Fantina. "Do not worry, little one. There will always be hope."

At that, Leo turned sharply. He didn't look so sure about that. Hope, he knew, could be beaten down by darker things in the night. Fantina edged closer, studying his face. "Without hope, the Glim fades?"

Leo turned to Fantina, a concerned look in his eyes. "...and the Murk rises," he said.

Fantina stared uncertainly.

"Fear. It is what grows and strengthens murkier things when the glimmer of hope becomes weak," he explained.

Cosimo scanned the room and the faces of the gathered Gondoliers. "The guild must remain unseen," he said. Murmurs of agreement filled the room.

Enzo shook his head and stepped forward decisively. "But her uncle has been carried off by Malvagio and his *Pantegane*. We have to step out and rescue him. It is what we are here for."

Gondoliers nodded.

Leo strode back into the light, resolute. "He does make a point, Cosimo. Ratters have been nothing but trouble since they first came to Venice."

Contessa agreed. "And Malvagio...bit of a rat himself. I always knew he was up to no good."

"They are searching for something," Enzo explained. "He spoke about a journey, and...something golden."

Fantina's eyes suddenly sparked, recalling words from distant memories. She closed her eyes, to see them clearly. "To find what is golden, the journey must start, with an open mind and a worthy heart."

Cosimo exchanged a puzzled look with Contessa then turned to Leo. Leo nodded solemnly. "Malvagio has the stolen journal."

Fantina took a step toward Leo, amazed. "The treasure of Marco Polo is real?" Murmurs rose in the room. Jester Joe, Eva and the others stared at Fantina curiously. "Fortune and glory," Fantina whispered to herself.

Cosimo turned to Leo. "How does she know of this?"

Fantina squared up to Cosimo and the others. It all made sense to her now. "Stories my father used to tell me, stories about old Venice, the sentinels, the Gondoliers—the stories my Uncle Gio saves from being forgotten." She nodded with certainty. "They took him to make him solve the clues, unravel the secret...find the treasure. I have to get him back."

Fantina spotted a shuttered doorway across the room. Before anyone could intervene, she made a dash for it. Cosimo tried to intercept her. "Wait, you cannot go out there."

Fantina threw open the door but froze, her eyes widening. The doorway was sealed by a thick pane of glass, like a floor to ceiling window, or perhaps more precisely, a giant porthole. Outside the window, a colorful assortment of fish swam by. Fantina stared out, dazed, into the depths of the Venetian lagoon, moonlight filtering down through the water from above.

"Oh, this is good…" Fantina said incredulously, "because things weren't strange enough I suppose."

Cosimo, Enzo and Contessa stepped up beside her. Contessa smiled. "Welcome to *Ca' Vecchia*, the council chamber and headquarters of the Guild of Gondoliers."

Fantina paused, face to face with a large, bug-eyed fish through the glass. "That's a fish. This whole place is under water—"

"Okay," Contessa interrupted defensively, "so we have had a bit of a sinking problem over the last century or so."

Fantina raised an eyebrow. "A bit?"

Cosimo turned decisively. He was still upset that rules and tradition had been ignored, but now that Fantina was here, he had to decide what was best for her...and for the guild. "It is not safe for her up there," he said. "Until we learn what is going on, she stays here."

"But Uncle Gio needs my help," Fantina argued.

Cosimo eyed Fantina crossly, then motioned to Bianca, perched and ready. "The pigeon patrol will cover the city by air," he said. Bianca saluted. Cosimo then motioned to Nicos and Dimitris. "Wake the frog squadron, scout every alley and walkway." He turned to Joe, Eva and the others. "And the Gondoliers will crisscross every canal. We will find him."

Leo nodded to Cosimo, then joined Nicos, Dimitris and Bianca as they headed out, up the stairs toward the top of the chamber.

Enzo took a step forward as the Gondoliers turned to go. He knew that Cosimo was not happy with him, but he was sure that this time— "I can help," he blurted out.

Cosimo paused. He turned, his expression grim, inflexible and clear that he was not in the mood for further discussion. "No." He shook his head. "We will take care of this. You stay here." Cosimo tossed a glance at Fantina. "Keep her out of trouble, and do as I say for once." With that, Cosimo and the others disappeared up the stairs.

Enzo watched them go, stung. It wasn't the first time he'd been told to stay behind. He wasn't a full-fledged Gondolier, but despite his years, he knew that, if given the chance, he could step up into the guild and prove his worth. But his uncle didn't seem to want to give him that chance.

Fantina noted Enzo's downcast look. She turned as Contessa joined them with a consoling shrug. "Do not take it personally. Cosimo has always been a bit of a hot head." Contessa chuckled, looking for a reaction. "Hot head, you understand? Him with the eating-fire all the time? It is a joke." Fantina and

Enzo remained unresponsive. Contessa sighed and rolled her eyes. "*Beh*, never mind."

Enzo crossed away, discouraged. Contessa placed a comforting hand on Fantina's shoulder. "Do not worry. The Gondoliers have protected Venice for many years. It will take more than a few murky rats to change that."

Fantina narrowed her eyes, considering. She didn't feel so certain. Could the fabled guild that, until today for her, had only lived in the stories her father had told, really protect the entire city of Venice? She wondered if the more practical world outside had simply passed them by. If the Glim was fading, as Cosimo had said, how long could Venice depend on the Gondoliers to protect it from harm? It seemed that Malvagio had fooled the city into believing in him rather than the eternal hope of Venice. Maybe a few rats wouldn't tip the scales, but what if there were a few more? Fantina watched with growing uncertainty as Enzo disappeared down a dim corridor.

CHAPTER THIRTEEN — A FEW MORE

Uncle Gio, held captive between two ratters, marched along a walkway beside an old, rundown boathouse near the shore of Malvagio's *Lido* watchtower and work site. The boathouse looked abandoned. Its wooden plank walls were rough and splintered, rotted in sections where the water lapped at its foundation. Only an occasional puff of steam drifting out through cracks and gaps in the walls betrayed that something was still happening inside.

At the lagoon inlet, the roughneck crew paused, turning together to stare at the new arrival. Uncle Gio slowed. Even through the darkness he could see that something about them wasn't quite right. Their round, black eyes shone like glass; their hunched forms and pointed noses twitched in the evening air. "More ratters," Uncle Gio murmured to himself.

The fact that Malvagio's crew was made up of ratters didn't seem to surprise Uncle Gio all that much. He knew much more about Venice and its secrets than he had wanted to admit even to Fantina. The stories that he had preserved and restored over the years were filled with fantastic oddities that most would have simply written off as myth, but Uncle Gio had always known of the power of Glim and Murk. He knew the places where ordinary history became intertwined with the extraordinary.

You see, ratters, despite their transforming shape and size, were descendant from the commonplace rodents of centuries past that had roamed far and wide, often hiding away amongst the cargo in merchant ships arriving in port from strange, new lands. Those rodents had pestered sailors and travelers as they scampered across continents and scurried through cities, lurking and listening in the shadows of streets and taverns...and Genoese prison cells.

In 1348, a plague of flea-infested rats had arrived in Europe. Disease and devastation had followed, and somehow, as despair took hold and hope faded, the rats began to change. A second wave of the plague made its way to Venice in 1630, and, at the tipping point between hope and fear, the *Pantegane* began to emerge in the night. Just as the Glim had bolstered the strength of cities and given rise to the sentinels, its opposite, which in hushed whispers became known as Murk, allowed the metamorphosis of viler things that crept in the dark.

Now, the *Pantegane* had taken their place as Malvagio's shadowy crew of ratters, searching for the shiny reward at the heart of the rumors spread by their own kind so many centuries ago.

Uncle Gio cast one last, guarded glance at the ratter crew staring at him from the lagoon inlet. While he had always known that they were out there, lurking in the night, they were more in number than he had realized. Malvagio had somehow managed to gather them all into his service, and Uncle Gio knew that whatever they were working on did not bode well for Venice. The ratter escort prodded Uncle Gio onward and into the *Lido* boathouse.

Inside, steam hissed menacingly from an array of exhaust pipes that lined the hull of an imposing, iron-sided vessel, the Scylla. Named for the fearsome water beast of ancient Greek mythology, it rose from the surface like a mechanical monster—a metal nautilus assembled from enormous, curved panels riveted at the seams, with sleek paddle wheels on either side to propel it through the tide. Uncle Gio slowed as he approached it, both awed and intimidated at once.

At the bow stood Malvagio's captain, his white rat, now mutated into a menacingly large ratter. Clothed in a trim uniform and a long marauder's jacket, she had the look of a vile mercenary about her. She stared down at Uncle Gio with piercing, red eyes, an unsettling glance that made him wonder if there was more behind her gaze than simply blind devotion to Malvagio. She looked dangerous and evil.

Primo met Uncle Gio at the gangway and motioned him on board. "Come along. I have been waiting for this for eight years," Primo griped. "You had better have some answers, *eh?*"

Uncle Gio hesitated. He knew what Malvagio was after, but he also knew that he would never betray Venice to such a man, no matter the consequence to him. He was old and unbreakable, tough like leather, and there was nothing Malvagio could do to force him to talk. He followed Primo up onto the deck.

Their footsteps echoed on the metal as they stepped past
the sinister ratter captain and an equally intimidating crew of
twelve more uniformed ratters who edged closer, gnashing
their teeth as if making ready to pounce. Uncle Gio braced
himself, but the ratters, kept in check by their captain, stayed
back.

Iron hinges squealed as Primo pulled open a large, metal
hatch. It swung heavily then slammed against the deck, rever-
berating through the hull. Primo signaled. "This way."

Uncle Gio hesitated a moment, uncertain about stepping
into the strange, metal monster. It looked a little…constricting,
he thought. The ratter captain grinned and chattered menacingly to her crew. Uncle Gio eyed them warily. He reconsidered.
Staying on deck with the crew might prove even more uncomfortable, so he crossed quickly and followed Primo below deck.

Behind a polished, metal desk at the far end of the boat cabin,
Malvagio sat—papers, maps and charts spread out before him.
The iron walls of the room were lined with steam pipes, gauges
and mechanical levers, unadorned with anything that might
have suggested warmth or comfort. It was a cold space for a
frigid encounter. Uncle Gio and Primo paused just inside.

From a drawer, Malvagio pulled out the journal of Marco Polo. He opened it decisively, turning to a particular yellowed page. He read. "Bring siren's gift and search awhile; Where tolls the bell on a cursed isle."

Primo shot Uncle Gio an expectant glance then prodded him forward toward the desk. "Go on, now. Sirens and bells... Tell him. What does it mean?"

Malvagio turned the open journal toward Uncle Gio and slid it across the desk to him. Uncle Gio narrowed his eyes, taking a moment to consider Malvagio, then Primo pressuring him from behind. He gave the journal a passing glance, then off-handedly pushed it back across the desk to Malvagio. "It is a fairy tale. There is nothing to find."

Primo frowned and plopped himself gloomily into a chair against the cold wall. "I knew it. That is what I have been sus-pecting too for a while." Malvagio glared at Primo. Primo backtracked. "I mean...if I had an opinion which, of course, I no have, *eh?*"

Malvagio shifted his stare to Uncle Gio. He knew that if anyone could decipher the words of the journal and uncover their true meaning, it was this man. The unabridged history of Venice, painted on its many walls and passed down through generations was archived with him. He was the best. The mayor had been quite certain. Even that little girl had confirmed it. Malvagio just needed to figure out how to force him to cooperate. How to threaten—

Malvagio stopped short. He smiled. "Then again, maybe we are asking the wrong person about this." Malvagio turned to Primo. "The girl...she seemed to know something."

Primo thought back. "She did?" Malvagio shot him a cold glance. Primo nodded quickly. "Oh yes, she did. You were saying that first part from the book...about how the journey must start with a worthy heart, *eh?* And it was like she was saying, 'hey, I remember this.' It was very interesting, no?"

Uncle Gio shifted uncomfortably. Malvagio reached forward to retrieve the journal with a grin. "So, maybe we will just go find the girl, and have a little chat with her instead."

Uncle Gio quickly leaned forward and placed his hand on the journal, eyeing Malvagio sternly. The threat had worked. He might be old and unbreakable, but Fantina...

Uncle Gio slowly spun the journal back toward himself and considered the page before him. "There is a story," he began, "about a young fisherman centuries ago. His name was Nicola, and he was engaged to be married to a lovely young woman, Maria."

"Oh, this is going to be good," Primo grinned as he scooted forward, scraping his chair across the metallic floor.

Malvagio cringed at the sound. "Primo!"

Primo stopped scooting abruptly. Malvagio shot him a cold warning glance then turned back to Uncle Gio impatiently. Uncle Gio continued.

"Days before the wedding, while Nicola was out at sea, a beautiful *sirenetta*, a mystical sea creature known as a siren—"

"A mermaid?" Primo blustered excitedly. "He means a mermaid, part fish and part wo—" he stopped himself, his cupped hands hovering over his chest. He noted Malvagio's stern stare. "Never mind," Primo hushed.

"In any event," Uncle Gio went on, "she tried to tempt Nicola with her song, but he refused her. The siren was so moved by his faithfulness to Maria, that she ran her hand through the water and crafted, from the sea foam, a veil of delicate lace which she gave to the fisherman for Maria to wear at their wedding. The lace was so beautiful that afterwards Maria dedicated herself to the art of lace-making, trying to recreate the gift for others."

Primo nodded enthusiastically. "The siren's gift. But where is it?"

Uncle Gio hesitated, weighing the peril of his cooperation against the risk that Malvagio might track down Fantina if he refused. But Malvagio was already grinning.

"The island of lace. The island of *Burano*," Malvagio stated, quite pleased with himself.

Primo applauded innocently. "I love that place," he cheered. "All the pretty doilies and handkerchiefs and little doll clothings... Can we go, boss?"

Malvagio eyed Uncle Gio, satisfied, then nodded. "Set course, full steam." Primo leapt up and hurried back onto the deck outside.

Uncle Gio watched Primo go, then turned to contemplate Malvagio. Rabidly poring over maps and charts of the northern lagoon at his desk, Malvagio had an intense look in his eye. Obsession had taken hold, and obsession...can lead to terrible things. Uncle Gio shook his head knowingly.

Malvagio looked up, and caught Uncle Gio's glance, and for a moment, he hesitated. It was a familiar look that Malvagio recognized well, like that of a disapproving father. "What is it?" Malvagio bristled.

"What you want, you will never find," Uncle Gio stated plainly.

Malvagio paused, a twinge of self-doubt chipping at his confidence and bravado. He shook it off and scowled at Uncle Gio. "Of course I will. With you and the journal, nothing will stop me."

Uncle Gio raised an eyebrow to consider, then shrugged. He turned back to the ancient journal and turned a page, carefully, respectfully.

Malvagio returned to his charts, but was too distracted now to concentrate. He glared at Uncle Gio. "What do you mean?" he asked angrily. Uncle Gio looked up slowly, in no hurry to answer. Malvagio stared impatiently.

"The treasure of Marco Polo," Uncle Gio finally began, "has been hidden for centuries. Even if I tell you where to look, it will never be yours. It is protected. There are secrets that are not meant for us to know, wondrous places that will never be found. That is what I meant." Uncle Gio closed the journal on the table as if he had simply stated a fact that was not subject to change.

Malvagio hesitated, his expression growing dark. He knew he would do anything to succeed, but Uncle Gio sounded so sure that he would fail. It was a certainty that reminded Malvagio of his father. Well...a kinder and gentler version of his father, without the mocking tone and complete disregard for a young boy's fragile sense of self-worth. But the disapproving tone...that was a near perfect match.

Malvagio suddenly sprang from behind his desk, enraged by the thought. He seized his walking stick, ready to draw his sword and strike— He paused, staring at Uncle Gio. He still needed him...for now. Malvagio turned abruptly and stormed out.

CHAPTER FOURTEEN — WONDROUS PLACES

Fantina stepped out from a dark corridor into a round, marble-paved *piazza* at the center of a cluster of old Venetian buildings. Filtered moonlight shimmered down from above. Overhead, an arching glass-panelled dome glistened, water and sediment from the lagoon bottom swirling just outside. Fantina stared in awe. The *piazza*, the buildings, just like the towering Gondolier council chamber, they were all part of a small section of ancient Venice that had sunk and settled beneath the waters of the lagoon.

Fantina crossed slowly through the *piazza*, on a walkway flanked by rows of stone statues—mythical creatures of fabled times long ago that now adorned the stately banners and flags of various Italian cities. The noble and nurturing She-Wolf of Rome was first, standing above the infant figures of Romulus and Remus, the legendary founders of Rome. The Rampant Bull of Turin was next followed by the Double-Headed Eagle of Trieste. Fantina studied the finely chiseled details of each statue. They were beautiful and powerful.

She stopped at the end of the row before the last statue. She had seen this heraldic creature before, in the over-painted mural at *San Lorenzo*, battling Leo in the skies above the lagoon. A sharp, chiseled beak…wings tucked beside its broad lion shoulders, it was fierce and majestic.

"That is Gen, the Griffin of Genoa," Enzo interrupted the moment. He was sitting alone on a stone bench at the edge of the sculpture garden. "She fought with the Genoese against Venice years ago," he explained.

Fantina looked from Enzo to the statue uncertainly. "You mean she was—"

"Alive," Enzo nodded. "Like Leo and the other sentinels." He rose to join Fantina looking up at the statues. "Long ago, every city had a defender, a champion to channel the Glim, back when hope was strong."

Fantina gazed up at the stone griffin, its eyes mighty but altogether lifeless. "So what happened?" she asked.

Enzo considered, staring at Fantina. "Come see," he said.

He took her hand and led her along the walkway, past the statues, toward an arched entrance into an old, stone-faced building at the far end of the *piazza*. On the arch's keystone above the door was the face of a sculpted lion staring down at Fantina as she passed beneath. Fantina looked up at the face. It was Leo, but then again, not Leo. She realized that there were probably hundreds of statues, and many of the lion of *San Marco*, throughout the city. She wondered if years ago, when the Glim was still strong, if they all came alive, if they all were part of some wondrous story of Venice—a story that was slowly fading away.

Fantina stepped with Enzo in through the arched doorway, wondering what new surprises she might learn inside. She tossed a last glance up at the keystone lion as she passed beneath and nearly stumbled over the threshold. She could've sworn that the lion had smiled at her.

Enzo and Fantina stepped into a large circular space—an elegant atrium decorated, from floor to vaulted ceiling, with millions of small and colorful, mosaic tiles. Fantina spun about in awe. The edges of the room seemed to blur and disappear in the puzzle of pieces that flowed over every surface depicting people and places and times long past.

Fantina stopped before an enormous, curved wall beneath a lofty, marble arch. On the surface, a finely detailed mosaic showed a lone gondolier on a misty night standing on the back of his gondola while lighting a gas street lamp with a long flame-tipped staff. A gilded scroll border inlaid near the bottom of the mosaic image dated the scene at 1162. Enzo stopped before it and pointed.

"Over eight centuries ago, that was part of the job—illuminating the dark streets and alleyways of Venice. It was given to the small band of boatmen who ferried Venetians about the city."

Fantina studied the image curiously. The delicate tiles that made up the picture had a glassy quality about them that made them shimmer in the dim light as she stepped closer.

Suddenly, she stopped short. The mosaic mist that hung over the water seemed to swirl before her eyes. She blinked uncertainly then tossed a curious look toward Enzo. Did he see it too?

Enzo returned Fantina's look carefully, as if weighing whether or not he should continue or save further explanation for another day. Maybe this was all too much. Then again, Fantina had already seen plenty of strange things since arriving in Venice, so the Gondolier Guild's mystically moving, mosaic wall archive of Venetian history should seem relatively normal by comparison.

Fantina eyed Enzo expectantly, like she had heard him debating whether or not she could handle more of the truth. She crinkled her nose, nettled by the thought.

Enzo noticed and understood. No stopping. He crossed over to Fantina as the mosaic tiles above, below and throughout the atrium continued to swirl and change, depicting the unfolding story.

"You see," he explained, "by the early 12th century, Venice at night had become a dark and dangerous place. Bandits roamed the streets preying on people who had wandered too far from the crowds, or those who had gotten lost in the night. The ruling *Doge*, he promised to make Venice safe. So first, he installed the gas street lamps throughout Venice, and he told the gondoliers to crisscross the city every evening and light up the night. But secretly, he also asked them to patrol the waterways, to defend his city against all those who would do it harm."

Fantina took a step back in astonishment as, just then, the street lamp pictured in the mosaic brightened. The mist seemed to clear and two figures that had been concealed in the darkness of the image till then were revealed—a masked bandit and a victim held at knifepoint. Enzo noted Fantina's stunned expression, and continued. "And so, the guild of Gondoliers was born."

Fantina gazed intently at the scene which now, without question, was definitely swirling before her. The bandit pushed his victim aside and squared off against the gondolier. Then, the gondolier, in a blur, leapt from his boat toward the bandit, spinning his flame-tipped staff which suddenly flared sending a giant fireball straight at—

Fantina jumped back, blinking. The image had returned to how it was before. She stared at Enzo, as if wanting to make sure that she hadn't just imagined the whole thing. Enzo nodded with a shrug...she wasn't crazy.

Enzo then ran his finger over the mosaic scroll border at the bottom. The date zipped forward to 1311. The image above reconfigured to depict a Venetian skyline at sunset—orange, red and pink tiles creating a stunning visual effect. Before the mosaic sky, the silhouette of a gondolier was looking out over the city.

Fantina stepped close, and again, the image began to change. As the sun sank behind the rooftops, a fine, flickering mist rose from somewhere within the glassy tiles, up toward the gondolier who extended his arms, palms down, and directed the glowing pulse out over the city. Fantina smiled in wonder.

Then, from the background, bathed in the flickering light, the tiled image of Leo stepped forward to stand beside the gondolier. "People found hope," Enzo explained, "and the cities everywhere glimmered at night."

Enzo waved his hand, drawing Fantina's gaze across the vaulted atrium ceiling to other areas where the mosaic images were swirling as well. Beneath one arch, the noble She-Wolf of Rome watched over her city from the rim of the Colosseum. Nearby, the streets of Turin were guarded by their brawny Bull. Across the atrium, the Double-Headed Eagle soared above Trieste, and Gen, the Griffin, stood sentry over Genoa.

"The sentinels of each city woke and promised to stay as long as they were needed," Enzo explained. "As long as the power to wake them remained." Enzo paused before a small balcony overlooking the sculpture garden outside. Fantina joined him and looked out at the rows of lifeless, stone statues.

"But hope faded," she guessed.

Enzo nodded. "The sentinels withdrew to Venice where the Glim was still strong, but eventually they all went to sleep. There are few that still wake—Leo, Nicos and Dimitris..." Enzo held out his hand, palm down, as if trying to sense an invisible wave of energy. He sighed. "The Glim barely rises these days. My *Zio* Cosimo says that one day it will end here too."

Fantina looked to Enzo, concerned. "You mean...Leo..." Fantina followed Enzo's glance to a large, stone, pedestal at the far end of the sculpture garden—no statue on top...yet.

Enzo nodded. "Then, we will be on our own." Enzo moved away. Fantina glanced again at the empty pedestal, then followed.

Enzo led Fantina past a trio of green, marble frogs spouting water into a fountain at the center of an inner courtyard. Smooth and polished with time, Fantina slowed briefly, half expecting them to hop away when they spotted her. She was beginning to expect the unexpected everywhere she looked, as if everything she thought she knew for sure was suddenly a possible surprise waiting to happen. But the marble frogs didn't move a wink, so she continued on.

At the far end of the courtyard was a large iron door, a sort of modern vault set in the stone wall. "Times are changing," Enzo explained as he stepped close. "My uncle thinks we can hold everything in place the same way it has been done for centuries, but I think we need to try some things that are new. Luckily, I hear that Venice is the source of all things...fanticulous," he smiled.

Fantina watched curiously as Enzo reached up to a panel beside the vault door and pulled a small lever. With a hiss of steam, the panel whirred open and an odd, bi-ocular contraption telescoped out toward him. Enzo pressed his face to the eyepieces and the device scanned him with a hum. He then entered an access code on a row of mechanical, spring-loaded buttons. Electricity hummed, gears whirred, and the iron vault door slid open on a metal track. "This way," Enzo motioned to Fantina.

Fantina looked at Enzo, intrigued, ready for the unexpected surprise she was now sure was waiting to happen. She followed him inside.

Through the vault door, Fantina paused, awestruck, wondering what turn her reality had just taken. In place of old stone, the walls were sleek like polished steel, shiny and bright, in a cavernous industrial space ribbed with iron girders and divided into multiple bays for different research projects. A hazy cloud of steam and the steady hum of hissing turbines and clicking gears hung in the air. It seemed like a space where anything might be possible, and Fantina braced herself as she began to sense several shapes moving toward them.

Fantina let out a short gasp as she spotted a team of frogmen, similar to the ones who had caught her earlier. Unlike those, however, these were geared out in lab coats and safety goggles, carrying clipboards and jotting notes as they ambled along through the laboratory. They acknowledged Enzo with various nods and croaks as they passed.

"So, what do you think?" Enzo asked. He indicated toward the first bay where, standing at attention inside the space, was a gangly frogman decked out in traditional gondolier garb—striped shirt and straw hat—with a gondola bow iron scimitar sheathed on his belt. He stared at Fantina and croaked quite seriously.

Fantina chuckled to herself. The frogman eyed her, not amused, so Fantina swallowed her laugh.

"It is my prototype G-1000 GondoSuit," Enzo explained. "Traditional styling with a new century twist."

Enzo nodded to a second frogman technician who flipped a control switch. Suddenly, a static electrical charge washed over the Gondo-Suited frogman. He flickered for a moment...then disappeared. Enzo grinned proudly. "Optic-refracted camouflage. Perfect for patrolling the canals of Venice unseen."

Just then, the invisible frogman tried to unsheathe his unwieldy sword. It got caught on a wire and shorted a circuit. The suit fizzled and reappeared. The frogman technician shook his head wearily.

"Uh...a work in progress." Enzo shrugged self-consciously and motioned to the frogmen, "Put it in the 'tweaks' pile." The frogmen croaked and headed over to a long aisle of shelves filled with inventions that still needed an adjustment or two...or three.

"Here." Enzo turned back to Fantina regaining his confidence. "This one works." He grabbed a small device from a nearby workbench—a small, rounded metallic bud with a spiral antenna jutting out from the top. "It is a communicator based on Marconi's new radio wave transmitter. I gizmoed it up a bit, made a few modifications... I put one inside my ear," he demonstrated, "then when I turn the receiver on—" Enzo flipped a tiny switch. A blue spark swirled around the antenna and zapped him. "Yeow!"

Enzo yanked the bud from his ear and tossed it back on the workbench. He stared at it for a moment then turned to Fantina awkwardly. "It really does work, you know…"

"—a work in progress," Fantina said. She smiled and moved on.

Enzo paused, as if recalibrating his invention in his head. His little 'gizmology tour' was not unfolding as impressively as he had hoped. One more mishap and his chance to dazzle Fantina, he thought, would most definitely fizzle out.

Fantina stole a quick glance at Enzo over her shoulder. Despite the misfires, she couldn't help feeling a bit charmed by the effort. She knew inventing wasn't always an exact science. Sometimes…kitchens blew up, right? But she found herself secretly hoping for a bit of luck with whatever Enzo decided to demonstrate next.

From a workbench in the next research bay, Enzo grabbed a pair of metallic mesh gloves with tubular tips extending from each finger. He slid them on and connected them to a pair of thin tubes that ran along his arm and into a compressed fuel tank on a belt pack. The contraption looked complicated, Fantina thought...and dangerous. "I thought this one up for my uncle," Enzo explained as he finished strapping in. "You know...Flame boy?"

A twinge of dread passed through Fantina's face, but she managed a quick smile to hide her concern.

Enzo pointed his fingertips at a target. A lab-coated frog-man in the bay, standing beside the bull's-eye, gulped nervously and ducked behind it. Enzo flicked a trigger switch on his palm. A flint ignitor clicked twice and then...nothing. Enzo frowned. "Still a little glitchy, I guess. Back to the pile."

Fantina sighed. Enzo looked so disheartened. She crinkled her nose and narrowed her eyes...thinking. "What if...?" Fantina opened her mini toolkit belt pouch and grabbed a pair of needle-nose pliers. "Maybe if you adjust the fuel primer—" Fantina tweaked a screw on Enzo's fuel belt and—WHOOSH! a burst of flame shot out from each fingertip and incinerated the target. The ash fell away revealing the wide-eyed and slightly singed frogman behind.

Enzo stared, speechless.

Fantina shrugged. "That was great," she said with a grin. She then moved on.

Enzo watched her. He nodded. There was definitely something about her, he thought.

Fantina and Enzo continued on to a bay near the back of the lab where a large pipe resembling a jumbo-sized, pneumatic message delivery tube, tunnelled away through the wall. A steam-powered piston hissed, cranking water into a large hydraulic pressure tank. "This is my RTT, Rapid Transit Tube," Enzo announced. He turned a dial on a control panel, scrolling through the various Venetian districts—*Cannaregio*, *Castello*, *Dorsoduro*, *San Marco*, *San Polo* and *Santa Croce*. "Anywhere in Venice, five minutes or less."

Fantina nodded, impressed. "Very Verne."

Enzo stopped suddenly, staring at Fantina strangely.

Fantina noted and began to explain. "I mean it's very inventive. See, there's this writer—"

"Jules Verne," Enzo completed Fantina's thought.

"You've heard of him?"

"He is my favorite," Enzo smiled. "His stories...his ideas,"

"—are amazing," Fantina finished.

Fantina and Enzo paused, lost for a moment in each other's mutual admiration. Nearby, a lab-coated frogman observed the awkward silence. "Ribbit."

Enzo snapped out of his trance and turned away abruptly trying to look busy. Fantina smiled. Enzo was definitely distracting, she thought, but even so...she didn't mind so much.

Fantina reached curiously for the hatch door into the transit tube and pulled...

"No wait—" Enzo warned.

The hatch door swung open as a gush of water burped through the tube and a black, torpedo-shaped capsule came to a splashing halt at the hatch opening. Enzo stood drenched, head to toe. "I am...still working out the kinks," he sputtered.

Just then, the top of the transit capsule slid open revealing a lanky frogman decked out in bluish green, lagoon-camouflage fatigues—a frog commando. He hopped out, croaking intel. Enzo listened intently, then croaked back before turning to Fantina.

Fantina gasped. "Wait, you just spoke Frog?"

Enzo considered. "Well...yes. He does not understand Pigeon."

Fantina crinkled her nose curiously. The frogman shrugged.

"He spotted a steamboat heading out into the north lagoon," Enzo said. "Malvagio. And your uncle is with him."

"I have to go after them," Fantina said.

Enzo hesitated. "I am supposed to keep you out of trouble."

Fantina squared up to Enzo, resolutely. He could see that her decision had already been made.

"So...I guess I had better go with you," Enzo said. Fantina smiled.

The frogman shook his head and croaked, apprehensively Fantina thought, and Enzo shot him a quick look. "Well then my uncle does not need to know, right?"

The Frogman responded with an uncertain nod then saluted as Enzo motioned Fantina toward the open capsule.

"This way," Enzo said. He climbed in and offered Fantina a hand.

Fantina hesitated. While the red, cushioned seat inside looked comfortable enough and the blinking control panel lights were impressive, she nevertheless had her doubts. "I thought you were still working out the kinks on this."

Enzo stammered a bit but did his best to sound confident. "Not to worry, it is completely safe." Fantina looked to the frogman who shrugged casually.

Great, she thought. Not at all reassuring. She crossed her fingers for luck as Enzo slid the canopy shut.

Fantina settled back into her reclined seat behind Enzo as the sound of pressurized water filling the tube outside swelled around the capsule. Enzo flipped a series of switches on the small control console then settled into a jumper seat that folded up from the floor panel before Fantina. "I know what you are wondering," he said. "Is this the invention that blew up half the lab? Right? That is what is bothering you?"

Fantina stared at Enzo blankly. "Well it is now!"

Enzo considered. "Oh. Never mind then. Ready?"

Fantina rolled her eyes and gripped the sides of her seat tightly. Too late for doubts, she thought. "Sure," she answered as convincingly as she could.

Suddenly, a sound like a powerful whirlpool roared outside, and Fantina felt the capsule rocket forward in the tube. In seconds, they were speeding along, spinning and banking hard like a runaway cart in a carnival ride. Enzo shot a concerned look toward Fantina. "Are you all right back there?"

Fantina grinned. "Your uncle has to try this," she laughed excitedly.

CHAPTER FIFTEEN — THICKENING FOG

Moonlight shimmered on the still waters just off the northern side of Venice proper. The quiet promenade along the shore was mostly deserted as people wandered inward toward the sounds of ongoing *Carnevale* festivities humming faintly in the distance.

Then, the surface of the water began to bubble and churn as a shape rose from below. The R.T.T. capsule broke the surface, skimming along the water like a skipping stone. As it slowed to a halt, the canopy slid open and stowed itself beneath the back side of the vessel. Fantina sat up, noticing now that the capsule was actually Enzo's battered, black gondola.

Enzo pushed a button and the front bow iron rose into place like an antenna to complete the transformation. Fantina shot Enzo a quick look. Maybe it wasn't as shiny or as elegant as other gondolas she had seen since arriving, but it was definitely more impressive. Enzo sighed, more than a bit relieved by the glitch-free demonstration.

Fantina turned and scanned the horizon urgently, looking for any sign of Uncle Gio or Malvagio's boat. "I don't see anything. It's too dark."

Enzo leaned forward and opened a small storage compartment in the front of the hull. He grabbed two, plain, Venetian harlequin masks and handed one to Fantina. "Here, try this."

Enzo slid his mask on. The eyeholes suddenly lit up and glowed green. Fantina watched curiously, then put her mask on as well. Through the mask, the dark lagoon brightened with a hazy tint, and details previously hidden in the night became visible.

Fantina looked toward a low bank of fog. Off in the distance, she saw the faint imprint of a steam-powered boat, chugging away in the darkness. Fantina pointed. "There."

Enzo spotted it too, then lowered his mask. "Where could they be taking him?"

"The mermaid story," Fantina whispered to herself. She set her mask aside, remembering…"The siren's gift."

"What?" Enzo asked.

Fantina explained. "It's a story my father told me...the second part. Come on, they're getting away." Fantina grabbed the gondola oar and jumped up onto the back end of the boat. She gave it a quick sweep, almost losing her balance, then turned to Enzo desperately. "Can this thing go faster?"

Enzo tossed Fantina a confident glance. "I did mention that I have done some work on it, right?" Enzo flipped a switch on the control console. With a hiss of steam, a hinged side panel on either side of the hull opened and two hydrofoil water skis descended onto the water's surface.

Fantina looked impressed. "Very, very Verne."

Enzo smiled then pressed a throttle lever forward. A steam piston rumbled to life, and the gondola quickly gained speed, rising up on its water skis as it started forward.

Fantina slid back down into her seat, marveling at Enzo's ingenuity. She wondered, though, about the mysteries still out there in the dark night ahead. Nothing so far had been what she imagined it would be when she had first arrived. Instead of finding in Venice a place where she could belong and make her mark, all she had found was trouble. Along with her 'big splash' she had made a 'big wave,' just as Uncle Gio had warned.

She sat quietly, feeling uneasy...and guilty. Venice was full of secrets, some enchanting, others dangerous, and the only family she had left was now caught between the two. She knew that somewhere deep in her memory were the clues to the mystery she had to remember...to make things right.

Fantina braced herself against the wind and spray as the gondola sped away into the darkness and the thickening fog.

CHAPTER SIXTEEN — THE SIREN'S GIFT

The island of *Burano* appeared, as if from a dream, through a bank of mist on the water. Colorfully painted houses and shops crowded along the narrow walkways joined by quaint, arching bridges over winding canals. The mist swirled past the bow iron of Enzo's gondola as he and Fantina approached, creating a delicate pattern in the wind that looked like a breath of fine, handmade lace, the kind for which the island artisans were famous.

That was part of the legend of *Burano*, the island of lace, the story that Fantina had once heard, now stirred by the fragment of a poem that she had recalled from deep within her memory.

"We are here," Enzo said quietly. "What now?"

"I don't know," Fantina said. "The lace from the story...if it's not just a story...he'll have to take them to it. Where would it be?"

Enzo thought for a moment. "The school," he suggested.

Fantina turned curiously, "School? What school?"

The *Scuola Merletti*, Lace School of *Burano*, was located in the palace of *Podestà* of *Torcello* at the edge of *Piazza Galuppi*. It was an impressive, brick, noble residence that had been restored and converted into a school under the patronage of Queen Margherita back in 1872. She and King Umberto had taken a 'special interest' in Venice and the surrounding lagoon since it had become part of the Italian kingdom six years earlier. And among the many places their interest was felt, *Burano* and its dying art of lace-making was one. Lace-making had a rich tradition on the island, and the King and Queen, for some reason, had seemed intensely determined to preserve that history.

Old-time artisans who had learned the craft generations ago from even older artisans were sought throughout the *Veneto* region and brought to the school to re-teach it. They studied and reproduced the intricate patterns of vintage lace that had been created at the height of *Burano's* prominence—an archive of lace that was then kept at the school—a type of museum of the past.

Like cobwebs lining an ancient and secret passage, panels of delicate lace dating back through the centuries hung on display along the walls of the palace corridors and quivered in the evening breeze wafting in from a window that had just recently been forced open. Shadows moved across the smooth, marble floor, through dappled moonlight, toward the inner chambers of the school as Malvagio, Primo and a handful of ratters passed through. Between them, Uncle Gio, the journal of Marco Polo in hand, led the way.

"Where are you taking us?" Malvagio demanded.

"To the siren's gift," Uncle Gio said. "The oldest piece of lace on display here at the school—the one that they say was made from sea foam and given to the bride, Maria."

Primo slowed, staring spellbound at the fluttering lace on the walls. "It is all so pretty," he sighed. "Maybe we can stop to see the exhibit of dolls while we are here," he asked hopefully, pointing to a darkened chamber across the hallway. "I heard they are all dressed up in the little, lace dresses and bonnets, and—" Primo stopped short. Malvagio didn't look interested... at all. "Never mind," Primo finished abruptly, "maybe another time would be better."

Uncle Gio glanced curiously toward the doll room, as if he had seen something move in the shadows. He wasn't sure, but it looked a little bit like—

"Well?" Malvagio glared, "What is it?"

Uncle Gio turned back and pointed toward a wide archway leading away to a different wing. "This way," he said as he continued on. Malvagio and his ratters followed.

Primo paused a moment, tossing a suspicious look from Uncle Gio back toward the doorway to the doll room. But all was dark and still, so Primo turned away and hurried to catch up to the group.

Just inside the shadowed, doll room doorway, Fantina and Enzo breathed a sigh of relief. "That was close," Enzo whispered. "But I think no one saw us." Just then, Enzo bumped something behind him in the dark. He spun. Two large, piercing blue eyes stared back at him. "Ahh!" He gasped and jumped back, falling to the floor.

Fantina stepped forward. The eyes belonged to a cherubic, porcelain face attached to a lovely, antique doll pulling a tiny, toy wagon on a display shelf beside an assortment of other angelic dolls. In fact, the whole room was wall-to-wall dolls, all dressed in dainty, lace finery.

Enzo picked himself up quickly, trying to downplay his miscue. "Uh...creepy, little doll...just surprised me."

Fantina hid a grin. "Absolutely. Could be dangerous, you never know."

Enzo paused as Fantina stepped past him. He shot a suspicious look at the delicate doll with baby blue eyes from the display shelf, then raised an eyebrow with a shrug. "You never know," he agreed.

At the doorway, Fantina looked out to where Malvagio had disappeared. Enzo joined her. Distant footsteps and the unsettling sound of ratters chattering echoed faintly through the hall. "We have to get him away from them," Fantina said.

Enzo nodded. "But we will need some sort of diversion. Do you have any ideas?"

Fantina crinkled her nose and narrowed her eyes, thinking deeply. Then, she smiled.

In the central chamber of the *Scuola Merletti*, exquisite samples of the most intricate lace patterns ever created were framed and preserved behind glass. It was the 'rare works' archive that Queen Margherita herself had set up, a collection that was quite impressive...and complete.

Tucked away in a corner of the room, in an unassuming, rustic wooden frame, was the most remarkable piece of all. It was a lace veil with a swirling pattern of such fine thread work that it looked almost like spun glass and reflected even the dimmest of light in the room so that the veil itself shimmered. "The siren's gift," Uncle Gio said as he stopped before the frame.

Primo crowded close to see. "So, this is why King and Queen were so interested in lace."

"Yes," Malvagio said as he pushed past Primo. "A little too interested."

The phrase struck Uncle Gio as odd, and he suddenly wondered if there was more to the king's assassination two years ago than what everyone had been told.

You see, in July of 1900, an anarchist named Gaetano Bresci had emerged from a crowd to shoot King Umberto for reasons that were dubious at best. He was captured and convicted for his crime, but many believed, despite the official account, that he had not acted on his own. And when, less than a year later, Bresci was found dead in his prison cell under extremely suspicious circumstances, the notion that someone had taken measures to silence the rumors surrounding the assassination seemed quite probable.

But with both the king and his assassin dead, the story died as well. Queen Margherita's 'interest' in Venice and the lace of *Burano* faded shortly thereafter, and whatever mystery might have been at the heart of it was abandoned…until now.

Uncle Gio stared at the lace veil framed and preserved on the wall before him. It was definitely a clue, but only the first part. He had helped Malvagio find it, but if he could get away, Malvagio would be no closer really than he was before. After all, according to the journal, only a 'worthy heart' could find the treasure.

Suddenly, the glass in the frame shattered with a blow from Malvagio's walking stick. Uncle Gio ducked aside, and Primo flinched as the pieces fell away exposing the delicate lace beneath. Malvagio sneered. "Protected, is it? So, now what?"

Uncle Gio eyed Malvagio warily then scanned the journal. "It says we should search awhile…where tolls the bell." He paused and looked around. "I see no bell tower. Oh well." Uncle Gio took a step away, but Malvagio stopped him with his walking stick and backed him up against the wall.

"Give me that," Malvagio said as he reached forward to snatch the journal from Uncle Gio. He read. "Bring siren's gift and search awhile, Where tolls the bell on a cursed isle."

Primo groaned. "Cursed? I no think I like that so much. Why does it always have to be so scary? Just once, it would be nice if we could look for something cheerful and sweet like—" Primo suddenly paused. A faint, familiar melody of plucked notes—the 'Carnival of Venice'—drifted in from the dark hallway. Malvagio, Primo, Uncle Gio and the ratters all turned to see...

At the main entrance to the room, rimmed by the dim moonlight, was a doll—blonde hair, blue eyes and a frilly, lace dress. She sat on her tiny, toy wagon rigged with the windup motor from Enzo's gondola music box. As the tune slowly wound down, gears turned and the wagon crept forward along the smooth floor till it ground to a halt, mid note, just inside the room.

Primo beamed. "Oh...pretty." Malvagio eyed the doll suspiciously, then motioned to his ratters. They quickly spread out and began creeping toward it. Malvagio and Primo edged closer as well.

Uncle Gio, on the other hand, quickly scanned the room, now certain of what he had seen earlier in the shadows. And back near a side exit into another hallway, he saw it again—an escape route and two friendly faces.

Fantina and Enzo peered cautiously around the edge of the exit, motioning for Uncle Gio to follow them to safety while the ratters closed in on their 'dolly diversion.' Uncle Gio nodded and took a cautious step toward them, then paused. He shot a quick look at Malvagio with the journal, then the lace on the wall. If he left now, the siren's gift would certainly be stolen and lost forever, but if he took it...

At the front doorway, the ratters converged on the doll, ready to pounce. Primo stepped close, crouching down to pick it up. He stared at it curiously, then glanced into the empty hall behind it. He shrugged, turning back toward Malvagio. "There is nobody here."

Just then, a low hum rumbled across the floor. The doll in Primo's hands shuddered...and spun its head toward him, its blue eyes glowing fiercely. Primo jumped back and dropped the doll with a shriek. Ratters recoiled.

At the side exit, Enzo turned to Fantina, impressed. "The windup wagon was very clever. And the doll—" Suddenly he paused, considering, "Wait a minute, how did you make the doll turn its—"

"I didn't," Fantina cut him off.

"Then why is it moving?"

Just then, Uncle Gio dashed up beside them, the ancient lace of the siren rolled up under his arm. "Maybe I was not supposed to take this, *eh?*" Uncle Gio said.

Across the chamber, the doll sprang to its feet, eyes cold and piercing, assessing the intruders—the ratters, Primo, Malvagio, and...

Malvagio followed the doll's glance to the side exit where Uncle Gio stood with Fantina and Enzo...and the lace. Malvagio's face darkened. "Stop them!" he shouted.

In that same moment, the doll opened its jointed jaw, emitting an ear-splitting cry that echoed through the chamber like an alarm. "Waaaaaaahhhhh!" Primo backed away uncertainly as a loud hum arose from the hallway beyond in response. Primo froze as the source of the hum became clear.

"The baby dolls!" Primo shouted in terror.

Charging forward from the hallway outside, a wave of dolls, rushed into the chamber, ferocious eyes glowing, lace bonnets and dresses flying.

Uncle Gio turned to Fantina urgently. "So, what is the escape plan?"

Fantina and Enzo considered briefly then turned to each other. "Run!" They shouted.

Primo ducked for cover while the ratters scampered to chase after Fantina, Enzo and Uncle Gio. Malvagio retreated as well, fending off the assault with his walking stick as the dolls swarmed, biting and scratching, like a litter of rabid kittens.

Fantina glanced over her shoulder as she, Enzo and Uncle Gio made a mad dash down a dark corridor toward the back exit of the school. Ratters, closing in, were quickly overrun by the dolls and disappeared in a roiling sea of thrashing lace. Enzo quickened his pace anxiously, tossing Fantina a self-righteous glance. "I knew it...creepy, little dolls—"

Fantina nodded quickly. "Yeah, I guess you really never know."

Fantina shot a look at Uncle Gio as she ran, wondering. Did *he* know? He didn't seem surprised by anything that had happened tonight. It was as if, for Uncle Gio, this was all normal. It made her wonder further, about her father and all the stories he had told her. Were there other secrets that he'd meant to share before—?

Fantina jumped as an adorable, little, curly-haired, ballerina doll in a lavender, lace tutu leapt for her heels, teeth gnashing. Fantina kicked it back and sped up. As soon as they weren't being chased by giant rats…or possessed baby dolls, she would ask Uncle Gio to fill her in on anything and everything that he knew about Venice and the world of the Gondoliers. All things considered, it was time she got the whole story. Fantina threw open the back door and rushed out into the night, Enzo and Uncle Gio close behind.

Enzo bounded onto his gondola and powered up the engine while Fantina helped Uncle Gio in. The hydrofoil water skis lowered into place with a hiss of steam. Uncle Gio nodded, impressed. "They definitely do not make these like they used to."

Enzo grinned proudly. "My own design, based on the Parsons steam turbine of 1884—"

"Go now! Chat later!" Fantina yelled as she tossed an uneasy glance back toward the school.

"Not to worry," Enzo assured her. "I locked the door behind us."

Just then, the windows on either side of the school door shattered outward as the wave of frenzied dolls burst through the glass from inside. Uncle Gio turned casually to Enzo. "Maybe we should go now." Enzo's expression paled. He nodded.

The mob of daintily intimidating dolls raced toward the water, shrieking ferociously and waving their tiny fists as the gondola began to accelerate away. In another instant they would leap aboard and swamp it and—

Enzo slammed the throttle forward. The engine roared and sent a spray of water out the back that fell like a wet baby blanket and doused every doll along the shore. The mob fell silent, staring blankly at each other and pouting like scolded children, their lace finery now dripping with lagoon water. "WAHHHHHHHH!" they cried as the gondola rose up on its skis and sped away into the misty night.

CHAPTER SEVENTEEN — A NEW MORNING

Cosimo maneuvered his gondola through a narrow canal in the *Cannaregio* district as the first hint of the new morning began creeping from the eastern horizon. In the daytime, he reasoned, it would be more difficult to continue the search for Fantina's uncle. Bianca and her patrol could still canvas the city in their pigeon form, but Leo would need to return to his ledge on the clock tower in *San Marco* overlooking the *piazza,* where he would turn to stone once again.

Cosimo couldn't remember a time, certainly not in his life, when the Glim was strong enough to last longer than one night before fading at dawn. And every evening, when the magic returned, it somehow felt...thinner, like the energy that recharged the spirit of Venice had diminished ever so slightly and was not quite as hopeful as the night before. He had led the Gondoliers into the new century convinced that tradition and the old ways could survive, and that Venice would always be protected, but more and more, he was having doubts about what might last into the future.

Cosimo furrowed his eyebrows and cast an uneasy look at the brightening sky. If he seemed grim, inflexible and humorless to Enzo and his fellow Gondoliers, it was only because he sensed that Venice was at the tipping point. Like no time before in its history, the city stood at the edge of hopeful light and utter darkness. He was sure that someday soon the balance would be tested, and the battle would be fought. He swept his oar and glided onward through the canal.

The night was quickly retreating as streaks of sunlight stretched over the rooftops of Venice and Enzo's gondola slowed near the landing at the *Riva Degli Schiavoni*. Along the promenade, signs of the previous evening's festivities were still visible. Flowered garlands and ribbons waved gently from lampposts, while a scattering of costumed revelers (who had perhaps been celebrating a bit too much) slept off their exuberance on the park benches beneath.

Fantina left Enzo at the gondola controls and edged back toward where Uncle Gio sat studying the lace veil in his lap. The threads swirled in delicate, translucent patterns, but whatever secret they were meant to reveal remained hidden. "What do you see?" Fantina asked.

"Nothing," Uncle Gio said as he gently rolled up the veil again. "It is only a part of the clue. To use it, one would have to —"

"—take it to where a bell tolls on a cursed island," Fantina finished eagerly.

Uncle Gio looked at Fantina curiously. "You remember the poem?"

"Why didn't he tell me it was real?" Fantina asked.

Uncle Gio considered. "I am sure he would have, when he thought you were ready."

Fantina stared at Uncle Gio incredulously. "Ready? Look at me. I have exactly one outfit, and the last decent meal I had was when I stowed away on a bread truck out of Paris. I've been ready for a little fortune and glory for quite a while now."

"Fortune and…? No," Uncle Gio explained. "I meant… ready to understand."

Fantina hesitated. She'd admit she'd been caught a little off guard by Venice and the whole world of Glim that she had stumbled upon, but maybe if someone had explained it to her earlier, things wouldn't seem so strange to her now.

Just then, Fantina noticed a small girl in a shining mask and a silvery costume of overlapping petals sitting on the pier beneath a glowing street lamp, her feet dangling over the water. She looked awfully young, Fantina thought, to be out alone at night, and yet somehow she had a look of wisdom about her, as if her youthful appearance was just part of her *Carnevale* costume.

Then the faint, glowing mist that Fantina had seen rising through Venice the evening before, reappeared, flickering downward this time, as if chased away by the morning light. And the girl, sitting at the water's edge, transformed.

First, the petals of her costume rippled like scales along her body as her legs joined together into a mermaid tail. She shared a moment—a gentle look with Fantina—as if she knew that the lace veil from *Burano*, the siren's gift, was now in Fantina's care. Then, as the Glim retreated further into the city beneath her, her arms became fins, and her face narrowed into that of a silvery fish. She flopped onto her side then leapt from the pier into the Venetian lagoon and disappeared beneath the water's surface.

Fantina froze for a moment. She shook her head. Okay, she admitted to herself, even if someone had explained everything to her in advance, it would all still be very strange. She turned back to Uncle Gio. "So, it only happens at night?"

Uncle Gio rose, and looked out across the quay to the empty *Piazzetta San Marco*, as the darkness dissolved in the early morning glow. "People are dreaming," he explained. "And when you dream, everything is possible. So hope is strongest at night."

"But so is fear" Enzo said as he leapt up onto the landing, holding the gondola's docking tether. "Murk and Glim rise and fall together these days. Malvagio's rats will have to hide until it is dark again too."

Fantina considered, then nodded decisively. "So we'll have a head start." Fantina reached for the lace, but Uncle Gio held it back.

"What do you mean?" Uncle Gio asked. "We need to warn the mayor about Malvagio. And this," he said, holding the veil protectively, "needs to be kept safe…and hidden."

"Wait, what?" Fantina asked. "We're not going to go find the treasure?"

Uncle Gio paused, pondering Fantina's expression. He could see that spark of adventure in her eyes. She was definitely her father's daughter, so maybe she would know… He shook his head. "If there is a treasure, hidden by Marco Polo years ago, then it is part of the past, the mystery of Venice. It must be preserved that way." Uncle Gio stepped up onto the landing then turned back to Fantina and Enzo. "Go someplace safe, and wait. Once the *carabinieri* have Malvagio in custody, I will meet you at home, and we will talk more about this." Uncle Gio paused a moment, noting Fantina's disappointment. "Then I will tell you about everything."

Uncle Gio crossed away as the sun washed over the *piazzetta*. Fantina stood in Enzo's gondola, shaking her head in wide-eyed disbelief. "Well, that wasn't quite the way I saw this going."

"Maybe he is right," Enzo said with a shrug. "We need to stop Malvagio and his *Pantegane* first…before it is too late."

Fantina wondered. 'Too late?' She felt like she had spent so much time waiting for things. From as early as she could remember…the next port beyond the horizon, the place where her father and mother would settle down, the end of a story…

there was always something just out of reach. And then it was 'too late.'

Fantina's father had tried to explain to her before he had passed away, that she needed to 'look closer.' Tomorrow would come with new surprises no matter how much she tried to plan. 'Don't wait for tomorrow to enjoy today,' he had said.

Fantina had crinkled her nose, not quite understanding what he meant in that moment, as they sailed onward, under the stars, toward a distant morning. She had always looked beyond, past the horizon, and wondered about what was coming so she could be prepared. She would watch her father at the helm, hands sturdy on the wheel, and believe that he knew every turn and destination. She wanted to chart each day of every journey toward what she thought would be solid ground. But that to-morrow hadn't come, and then…she was alone.

The orphanage was not what she had planned either, but she'd been in worse fixes, she had told herself. She had to make it on her own, be confident, strong (or fake it), just as her father had taught her. Despite her resolve, however, she had still felt tossed in the tide.

So when Fantina received the letter from Uncle Gio, she had set out eagerly for Venice, deciding to try something different. Venice, after all, was anything but solid ground, and maybe taking a chance and allowing herself to be part of something that she couldn't entirely plan on her own was what her father had been urging her to do. Or, as he had put it more simply: 'Do not stay in the boat. Dive in and hope for the best.'

The *Rialto Pescheria* Market sprang up every morning on the *San Polo* side of the *Rialto* Bridge. A fishy aroma washed through the open air *portico* and *campo* as fishermen, returning from a night on the water, brought their evening catches to old fishmongers setting up shop along the south bank of the Grand Canal. In addition to providing locals with a daily supply of fresh fish, the fish market was also the hub for all the latest news—rumored, real or otherwise—that had been netted throughout Venice and the surrounding lagoon the night before.

As Cosimo turned into the Grand Canal, he spotted Joe and Eva docked at the market, speaking with an old fishmonger, knee-deep in clams and mussels. And though it didn't strike him as peculiar immediately, Cosimo did note the wary glance that the fishmonger cast his way before turning back to his work. It wasn't the usual greeting of high regard that Cosimo and the Gondoliers generally received, but Cosimo wrote it off to a long, hard night or perhaps the earliness of the morning.

"What news?" Cosimo asked as he drifted up beside Joe and Eva.

"Trouble up in *Burano*," Eva said. "A break in at the *Scuola Merletti*."

Cosimo narrowed his eyes with a grim look. "Malvagio?"

"Ah, well, uh, no no," Joe explained nervously. "Actually...word on the canal is that *we* did it."

"What?" Cosimo looked confused.

"Someone is, well, spreading a tale that, ah, the Gondoliers have taken up burglary," Joe said.

Cosimo turned and watched as guarded glances from the vendors slowly became suspicious looks. He could feel the change, like an unsettling chill in the air, and he knew the cause. "Malvagio is stirring up fear."

"You think he is trying to strengthen Murk and weaken Glim?" Eva asked.

Joe shook his head doubtfully. "No no. Lies will not work. Well, not entirely. He may turn a few people against us, but..."

Cosimo wondered as he watched the old fishermen leaving the market behind and heading back out through the canals of Venice. The rumors would spread fast. "Not just a few people," he explained, "he needs to turn everyone...make all of Venice think we are dangerous...fear us." He shared a troubled look with Joe and Eva. "And there is only one way to reach all of Venice."

CHAPTER EIGHTEEN — UNSPOKEN TRADITION

The inner *loggia* of the Ducal Palace was an open colonnade that surrounded and overlooked the palace's central courtyard like a grand, rectangular balcony. It was connected to the courtyard below down a massive set of steps known as the Giants' Staircase, named so on account of the enormous statues of the Roman gods Mars and Neptune that loomed on either side at the top.

Now, the story was that in 1355, the *Doge* Marino Faliero, had been beheaded for treason at the top of the stairs, and the giant statues were then placed there at the main palace entrance to dwarf any future ruler and diminish any delusions of grandeur and self importance that he might entertain.

Of course the current mayor, Filippo Grimani, needed no reminder of his diminutive stature or status. Every day of his mayoral term had been one of hesitation and self-doubt. So standing, as he was now, between the figures of Mars and Neptune made him feel no more diminished than usual.

The disturbance last night at the *Scuola Merletti* did have him more agitated though, and consequently, the tips of his handlebar mustache were both drooping quite low from having been tugged all morning since he was awoken by the news. Chaos during the annual *Carnevale* festivities would reflect badly on Venice…and on him. He would have to act quickly to tidy up the mess.

He was consulting with a trio of city officials when Uncle Gio arrived at the main entrance into the palace courtyard, the *Porta della Carta*. It was called the 'Paper Gate' because it was the place where Venetians could submit written complaints or report any suspicious activities to the authorities, and that was exactly what Uncle Gio wanted to do. He gripped the rolled up lace veil from *Burano* tightly in his hands as he stepped in through the entrance.

Uncle Gio paused uncertainly for a moment, noting the commotion on the stairs and the company of *carabinieri* assembled in the courtyard. Could the news about Malvagio have already gotten to Mayor Grimani? Did he know about Malvagio and the *Pantegane* and their devious plot?

"They have been deceiving us all this time…" the mayor called out as he spotted Uncle Gio and waved him forward. "…hiding their true intentions. But not anymore."

Uncle Gio nodded, relieved. "Ah, so you have heard. You know what is going on." He began unrolling the lace veil to explain—

"Yes, of course. Those Gondoliers have gone too far this time," the mayor grumbled.

Uncle Gio stopped unrolling abruptly. "Gondoliers?"

Mayor Grimani waved off the other city officials and descended the stairs toward Uncle Gio. "They have become a nuisance in the city," the mayor continued. "Roaming in the night, answering to no one… They ruined the *Burano* doll exhibit and stole from the lace archive."

Uncle Gio hesitated. He glanced again at the *carabinieri* then discreetly tucked the veil away behind his back. Evidently, the truth about what had happened last night had already been distorted by someone, and trying to set the story straight while holding the very lace that had been stolen did not seem like the best plan.

Mayor Grimani tugged his right mustache nervously as he continued. "I promised to lead Venice into the new century, and no 'unspoken tradition' is going to hold us back. When we catch the ones who did this, I will see them locked up for a good, long time." The mayor turned on the stairs to survey his *carabinieri*. They stood at attention, awaiting orders.

Uncle Gio retreated a step nervously. Other than the stolen veil now tucked into the small of his back, he had no proof of anything that had happened. He couldn't accuse the mayor's 'Protector of Venice' of anything illicit with only a crazy story about Malvagio and his shadowy crew of giant rats...an army of vicious, animated dolls...and a mythical, as-of-yet, only rumored treasure. He would end up behind bars himself.

Uncle Gio attempted a casual smile, but it came off a bit forced and peculiar. "Ah, well, I see you are busy," Uncle Gio said suddenly. "I will go...get back to work, *eh?*" Uncle Gio turned and crossed quickly back the way he had come.

The mayor paused a moment to watch Uncle Gio curiously before proceeding back up the stairs. A bit of an odd, disheveled man, he thought. Though Uncle Gio was absolutely the best restoration historian and had come highly recommended, Mayor Grimani had always been somewhat uncomfortable around people who reminded him of the past. The guest list of his upcoming *Carnevale* Ball would be exclusively for modern Venetian high society—elegant people who would help him remake the city for the new century—

Mayor Grimani stopped short at the top of the Giants' Staircase and spun about. There was nothing elegant about Uncle Gio and yet... Mayor Grimani squinted suspiciously, eyeing Uncle Gio closely as he passed through the Paper Gate into the *piazza* beyond. There, tucked in his belt behind his back...a roll of delicate lace.

Chapter Nineteen — work in progress

The 'tweaks' pile in Enzo's lab contained an assortment of gizmos, gadgets and contraptions that Enzo had designed and built in his effort to keep the Gondoliers in step with the changing times. But even with his eye on the future, Enzo often invented with a nod to the past.

His fire-finger gauntlets were an homage to the flame-tipped staffs the first gondoliers had used to light the gas street lamps of Venice in the 12th century. From the sketches of Leonardo Da Vinci, Enzo had adapted a mini, back-mounted, over-the-shoulder catapult; and, in tribute to the Venetian lagoon itself, he had made a portable, steam-powered, water canon that would shoot pulses of seawater with enough force to disable a foe. At least…that's what they were supposed to do.

Enzo sat in the middle of his lab reworking the mechanisms and moving parts that weren't yet working in quite the way he had imagined them. Although he was constantly being reminded that he was not a full-fledged Gondolier in his uncle's eyes, he had a sense that sometime soon Cosimo might need some serious help. He wanted to be ready, just in case.

Fantina stepped toward Enzo, a gondola bow iron scimitar in hand. It was a bit unwieldy to carry around she thought. Her nose crinkled; her eyes narrowed.

"Is something wrong?" Enzo asked as he spotted her.

"Hmm? Oh," Fantina said, "I was just thinking."

"Ah," Enzo nodded. "You have an 'inventing look.'"

Fantina paused, somewhat surprised but quietly pleased that Enzo had not only noticed but understood. It had been quite some time since anyone, besides her father, had truly caught on to all her peculiarities. She handed Enzo the bow iron and a page where she had made some design notes. "If you made all these parts spring-loaded," she explained, "you could fold it up, and carry it hidden."

Enzo looked at Fantina's notes and smiled. "A secret weapon. I will try that."

Enzo watched as Fantina returned to the tweaks pile. He found himself hoping that after all the mess with Malvagio was sorted out, that she would stay—

"I think I need to leave," Fantina said suddenly. She had been tinkering with one of Enzo's unfinished contraptions, but set it down anxiously. "My uncle doesn't need me here. Maybe I should just move on."

Enzo set aside his work. "You cannot go," he said almost without thinking. Fantina shot Enzo a curious look. "I mean, you should...I could show you around a bit and...I really need some help here and you could..."

"What?" Fantina asked.

"Stay," Enzo said quietly in what sounded more like a request than a suggestion.

Fantina hesitated, and just like before, she found herself both surprised and quietly pleased. She narrowed her eyes, thinking.

"Is that your 'inventing look' again?" Enzo asked.

Fantina shook her head. "No, this is my 'Do-you-have-anything-to-eat-I'm-really-hungry' look."

Enzo smiled.

Tucked away along a narrow passage in the *Dorsoduro* district, the *Cucina Segreta,* or Secret Kitchen, was a quaint but over-looked, little *trattoria* restaurant with an abundance of charm (if not paying customers). The district, bordering the *Giudecca* Canal on one side and the Grand Canal on the other, was far enough from the more well-traveled walkways of *San Marco* and *San Polo* that it seemed a place apart, where you might only find a particular locale if you knew both which way to step and which direction to look at the same time. Enzo, of course, knew both.

In a back booth—a rustic table for two built inside half of a giant, empty, oak wine barrel—sat Fantina and Enzo. A heap-ing helping of seafood *linguini ai frutti di mare* rested on the table between them, but seemed to be disappearing mostly in Fantina's direction. Enzo watched, nibbling on a bread stick and thoroughly impressed by Fantina's uninhibited appetite.

Just then, *Signora* Sofia, the matronly owner of the *tratto-ria* emerged from the back kitchen area. She was a rotund but sprightly woman wearing a long gingham apron and carrying a big, steaming, copper pot with a ladle at the ready. "You need some more, *eh?*" She spooned out another helping of the seafood pasta onto Fantina's plate. "Eat. It is good for you."

Sofia tossed a curl of calamari to her only other lunchtime customer, a stray cat waiting patiently by the door, before turning back to Enzo and Fantina. "Enzo, it is about time you come in here with someone. Not to misunderstand, when you come here alone, I am happy to feed you, but…a crowd of new people, the kitchen humming, food flowing out into happy faces…" Sofia trailed off pensively and sighed. "Well, a girl can dream."

Fantina chuckled. Enzo nodded and swirled a forkful of *linguini*.

"Of course, then I would need some help in the kitchen." Sofia turned abruptly to Fantina. "You know how to cook?"

"Oh, uh, not really," Fantina confessed between mouthfuls. "I'm more of an explorer…and inventor."

"Ah, another gizmologist." Sofia shook her head disappointedly as she crossed back into the kitchen. "You kids these days. So modern. You have to learn to appreciate things that do not change over the years. Like my secret recipes."

Enzo called after her. "Not to worry. All of Venice appreciates your secret recipes."

Sofia poked her head out of a window from the kitchen area. "Really?" She scanned the empty restaurant. "Then someone forgot to tell Venice." She disappeared back into the kitchen.

Fantina considered as she finished a mouthful. Maybe the *Cucina Segreta* was a little too secret, she thought. Venice had so many secrets, and the more she uncovered, the more there seemed to be. Uncle Gio wanted to keep them safe and hidden, but maybe it was time to try something different.

"If this place weren't so secret," Fantina called out to Sofia, "you could make a fortune." Enzo looked at Fantina. He could see that she was thinking about more than just *Signora* Sofia's restaurant. She had 'fortune and glory' on her mind.

Just then, Sofia appeared at the kitchen window again. She raised an eyebrow at Fantina and Enzo as if somehow she understood as well. "Maybe yes. But then...maybe no. Not all fortune is measured in riches," Sofia explained. "Some is measured in smiles and spaghetti sauce." With that, she disappeared back into the kitchen.

Fantina watched her go, not quite sure if she understood that one. She turned to Enzo.

Enzo shrugged then finished up his *linguini* with a final slurp. As he did, a splatter of sauce flew across the table splashing Fantina across the face. Enzo dropped his fork, flustered. "Oh, sorry. I did not mean—"

Fantina laughed, cutting off Enzo's apology. She stuck out her tongue as far as she could to lick her cheek then grabbed her napkin to wipe the rest.

Enzo tried not to stare, but he couldn't help himself. He was enchanted.

Fantina tossed a glance toward the kitchen where *Signora* Sofia was now singing an old Venetian tune to herself. It was something Fantina had never heard before, and yet...there was something familiar about the sweet, romantic melody. It was as if somehow everything in the moment seemed like it...belonged exactly where it was.

"So," Fantina asked tentatively, "she said you usually come here alone?"

Enzo hesitated. "Yes, I…have no one really that…" Enzo stopped himself. He was staring again, but this time at a small drop of spaghetti sauce still clinging to Fantina's forehead.

Fantina eyed him curiously. "What…"

"You still have some…" Enzo pointed. Fantina understood and grabbed her napkin. She wiped but missed it. Enzo leaned forward and gently took Fantina's napkin in his hand. He dabbed her forehead slowly and wiped it clean, catching her eyes in a look that seemed to stretch the moment.

Fantina stared back at Enzo. She felt unsure, like she wanted to stand her ground, or maybe dive in and hope for the best. Enzo was odd…in a good way, and though she was used to being on her own, Fantina was beginning to feel like maybe she didn't need to be.

Fantina suddenly realized she was still staring, and sat back in her seat to hide a blush. She grabbed her napkin from Enzo and gave her face one final wipe. "There, how's that?"

Enzo smiled. Fantina's forehead was clean, but now she had a saucy smudge on her cheek. "Much better," he fibbed.

A distant bell was chiming three o'clock by the time Enzo and Fantina left the *Cucina Segreta*. They wandered along the *Zattere* promenade, the quay of the ship builders, and stopped to watch craftsmen fashioning gondolas in an old *squero,* a boatyard on the bank of the *Rio San Trovaso* canal.

On the *Ponte dell'Accademia,* the bridge between *Dorsoduro* and the *San Marco* district, Fantina stopped to admire the handrails covered in padlocks which Enzo explained was a tradition started by couples who would attach a lock to declare their…love. Fantina and Enzo both froze for an awkward moment, then hurried across the bridge to the other side.

Finally, high above the rooftops of Venice, Fantina and Enzo looked out from the towering *campanile* in *piazza San Marco* as the afternoon sun began to sink toward the western horizon. Venice was stunning, Fantina thought. Her first day had been…extraordinary, and more than ever before, she wanted to stay and just be surprised by what might happen tomorrow.

She tossed a quick glance toward Enzo and smiled. Of all the surprises that day, he had been the most— She stopped herself. Well, other than the magic animals, talking statues, the hunt for the lost treasure of Marco Polo… okay, so he wasn't the most surprising thing she'd seen since arriving in Venice, but he was somewhere on the list. She wondered. Maybe Uncle Gio, once he got to know Enzo, would like him too.

Long shadows were already stretching across the cobbled walkway as Uncle Gio stepped quickly, checking over his shoulder as he went. He had been taken by an uneasy feeling after he had left the Ducal Palace, and was convinced that his decision to warn the mayor had unintentionally made him a target of the citywide search now being conducted.

He had ducked into St. Mark's *Basilica* to evade one group of *carabinieri* and had spent the rest of the afternoon hiding in doorways and down twisting alleyways unsure of where to go. Now, the light was beginning to fade, and echoes of pursuing footsteps, seemed to be closing in.

Uncle Gio paused a moment at the top of a bridge. More shadows, these small and twitching, scurried past across walls lit by the rapidly approaching sunset. Uncle Gio hurried onward.

When Uncle Gio entered his house, he immediately pulled the lace veil out from where he had tucked it. He crossed to his cluttered shelves, searching for a place to hide it, but knew that no place here would be safe enough. Darkness would soon chase out the last rays of the sun, and outside he could hear the swell of chattering voices getting closer. He turned quickly and crossed up the spiral stairs toward the attic above.

The sky was a deep orange outside the open shutters of the balcony window in Fantina's attic room. Uncle Gio closed the door behind him as if hoping to buy some time before he'd be forced to face the inevitable night and everything the Murk would bring with it. He paused, with a sudden thought, then opened Fantina's suitcase and sifted through her gizmos. If he could get back to Fantina—

The sound of someone entering downstairs startled Uncle Gio to his feet. He crossed to the balcony and half considered climbing out onto the roof, but the distance to the hard walk-way below made him reconsider. Then suddenly he glanced up to the rafters, looking for movement. She was his best chance now, but there wasn't a feather in sight.

Uncle Gio sighed and looked at the delicate lace veil in his hands. If the mayor and the *carabinieri* didn't stand up to Malvagio, then Malvagio would never stop. He would steal what he wanted and demolish whatever obstacle stood in his way to find the hidden fortune at the end of the journal's story. Maybe the mystery and magic of Venice was in grave danger, and the only way to preserve it now would be to find it. Maybe Fantina was right.

Just then, a faint cooing sound caught Uncle Gio's ear. He turned to find a white pigeon perched on the balcony railing. Uncle Gio smiled and nodded, almost a bow—a gallant gesture to greet a true lady.

On the balcony above the entrance to St. Mark's Basilica, Fantina and Enzo stood watching the setting sun as people in the *piazza* below gathered to begin another evening of *Carnevale*. Fantina looked to the clock tower nearby where the bronze Moor statues stood frozen, still minutes away from sounding the six o'clock hour. On the ledge below them was Leo, waiting as well.

Now that Fantina knew what it was, she was anxious to see the Glim rising up as it had yesterday, eager for that moment when everything ordinary became extraordinary. She glanced again at the people below, wondering. "Do they see it too?" she asked Enzo. "The glow, the magic…Leo…"

Enzo hopped up onto the balcony parapet, looking out over the piazza. "Some still do. Others can just feel it. For most though, the Glim and everything about it faded from sight years ago. It is the two thirds of the world they do not see anymore."

Fantina pondered the idea. It made her sad somehow to think that most people would never appreciate the wonders she had seen since arriving in Venice. They would go about their business, their lives, never knowing how amazing Venice was…how fortunate they were to be a part of it.

As the sun made its final dip toward the orange horizon, a white pigeon came fluttering with great effort toward the balcony. Held in her tiny talons, was the rolled lace veil from *Burano*. "Bianca!" Fantina called as she spotted her and rushed forward to guide her in.

Then, in that moment, the sun sank away and the faint golden pulse that Fantina remembered from the night before rose up from the streets and swept across the city. It was, however, much fainter tonight. In fact, where once it had seemed like flickering stardust, now, Fantina thought it was more like a dim haze barely brightening the darkness.

Bianca's feathers slowly curved inward and became her dress as the Glim washed over her and revealed her faerie form. She landed heavily on the parapet beside Enzo, cooing breathlessly. Enzo listened intently.

"What happened?" Fantina asked.

"Your uncle has been taken away by the *carabinieri*," Enzo explained. "Arrested. The mayor suspects him of being in league with outlaws."

"Outlaws?"

"The Gondoliers." Enzo considered. "Malvagio got to the mayor. Now he will use the *carabinieri* to track us by day and his ratters to hunt us by night, until he gets his hands on what he wants."

Bianca nodded then cooed urgently, pushing the veil toward Fantina. Enzo listened, and translated, "Unless…"

Fantina looked at the veil. She understood. "Unless we get it first."

Enzo nodded. "So your uncle sent the clue to you."

Fantina took the veil from Bianca, unrolled it partway with an uncertain look. "But, I can't... I don't know where..." She closed her eyes recalling the words of the journal from memory. "Bring siren's gift and search awhile, Where tolls the bell on a cursed isle." Fantina opened her eyes, bewildered. "But I don't know anything about a cursed island."

"Maybe it is talking about *Poveglia.*" Fantina and Enzo turned. Dimitris stood above them. "Hello," he nickered.

Fantina stepped close. "*Poveglia?*"

"It is south in lagoon, a little far, which is why, back in days of old it was used for sick people."

"Sick?" Enzo asked.

"Yes," Dimitris continued, "Bubonic plague was very bad in 1347 and again in 1630. People who began to show signs were taken by force out to island and abandoned there to die."

Fantina and Enzo exchanged a look, a bit wary.

Dimitris' face suddenly brightened. "It will be very interesting to go."

"Uh, wait a minute," Enzo objected. "Are you sure that...I mean, it does not really sound like a...healthy sort of place to visit."

"Oh, that was long time ago," Dimitris reassured. "There is no more plague to worry about."

Enzo sighed with relief.

"It is the mysterious voices and mist that appears from nowhere and traps those who have mistakenly set foot on that island of the damned that worries most people," Dimitris finished.

Enzo froze. "Wonderful." He turned to Fantina. "Maybe we should just stay here. It sounds like the curse has everything pretty well protected."

Just then, in a gust of evening air, Leo landed on the balcony beside Fantina and Enzo. "It may not be enough," he said.

Fantina stared at Leo as he straightened up before them. Unlike yesterday when he had leapt down from above, with a powerful sweep of his wings, graceful and majestic, he somehow seemed diminished tonight. His golden mane seemed stiffer in the breeze and his coat had taken on an ashen color in the early dusk. "Things have changed," Leo explained. "Malvagio is on the move, and every day he is stepping closer to his goal."

Dimitris looked out over the *piazza,* as if sensing the shift. "Murk is getting stronger."

Leo nodded and stepped close to Fantina. "It is not just about the treasure, you understand? He wants more than that."

Fantina considered. She wanted Leo to clarify, but she took a step back, somewhat self-consciously as if she suspected that she already understood, and worse yet, that she herself was guilty of wanting the same thing: fortune and glory.

Enzo pushed his concern aside with a decisive nod. "So how do we stop him?"

"Go with Fantina and help her," Leo said. "Find what needs to be found."

"With you?" Fantina stepped forward pleadingly. "You'll come with us, right?" She reached forward to take hold of Leo, but then, she stopped herself. She could see now that his ashen color was not just from the dim light of dusk. He was dusty, like he was covered in a stony powder that made him look old and...brittle.

"*Poveglia* is too far for me to go." Leo paused, looking deeply into Fantina's eyes. He saw her concern, her uncertainty, but also the spark of something more. "It is up to you now."

"But what about Uncle Gio, the others and...what about you?"

"Do not worry. We will take care here as best we can. Your destiny is down a different canal." Leo turned to Enzo. "They will be looking for your gondola. It may be safer to figure out something else."

Dimitris clopped forward assuredly. "It will be dangerous. Glim is weak tonight, but Nicos and I will take them as far as we are able. Right, Nicos?" Dimitris turned to the pedestals next to his where Nicos and the other two *Quadriga* horses stood overlooking the *piazza*. He paused, suddenly realizing that Nicos, as yet, had not interrupted him even once. Fantina and Enzo edged closer to see. The early evening light glinted off Nicos' cold, bronze flank. He was still. He had not woken, and Dimitris sighed knowing that he would never again.

CHAPTER TWENTY — THE CURSED ISLE

Poveglia stood like an abandoned moment in time, at some distance from Venice proper, within view of the lagoon inlet at *Malamocco*. The neglected, stone ruins of a 14th century octagonal fortification and crumbling buildings overrun by wild brambles presented a rather foreboding welcome by themselves, but, when coupled with the tales of past horrors on the island, and the ghost stories that had arisen since, the approach was altogether intimidating.

The evening sky was almost completely dark with only a sliver of the waning moon reflecting on the still and undisturbed waters surrounding the island when the tips of Dimitris' bronze ears appeared in the tide at the water's edge. His eyes, wide and alert, appeared next, then his neck as he rose up in the shallows. On his back were Fantina and Enzo, each outfitted with a peculiar brass cannister and copper-tubed breathing apparatus. Fantina pulled the gizmo from her mouth, both impressed and relieved. "Hmm...these things actually work."

Enzo removed his as well, needled by Fantina's doubt. "Why do you sound so surprised?"

Fantina backpedaled. "Oh. Well...I'm surprised in a good way. Like, 'Hurray! we're not dead.'"

Enzo paused uncertainly to consider the 'compliment,' "Uh...thank you?"

Fantina smiled then quickly slid down from Dimitris' back and stepped toward a path through the brambles.

Fantina, Enzo and Dimitris moved cautiously along an overgrown path toward the island interior. There was a slight breeze that whistled through the thicket and gave the vague impression of voices wailing in the wind. Enzo shook his head, as if acknowledging the obvious. "They know we are here," he said anxiously.

"Who?" Fantina asked.

"The ghosts."

Dimitris nickered. "You mean thousands of doomed spirits of dead that have been stranded here on this completely isolated and forsaken island over centuries?"

Enzo stared at Dimitris, dumbstruck. "Yes, Dimitris, those ones. Thank you."

"No problem, but, if you ask me, those stories are a bit far-fetched. I do not really believe in ghosts and all that supernatural business."

Fantina raised an eyebrow. "...says the giant, talking, bronze horse." Fantina continued on through the thicket as Enzo followed with a sigh. Dimitris paused to consider.

"Ah, I see what you mean. You may have point."

The massive, stone walls of a long, rectangular building appeared like a dim shadow against the dark sky as Fantina, Enzo and Dimitris stepped out from the bramble thicket. Two centuries old, the *Tezon* was the largest of the buildings left standing on *Poveglia*, and the most chilling. Two rows of gaping holes in the side wall marked where windows had once been, windows behind which thousands of quarantined Venetians had been confined and eventually had lost all hope.

Fantina peeked in through the main entrance where a rotting, wooden door had fallen off its hinges years ago. Enzo looked in over her, and Dimitris over him. The room was cavernous—a wide chamber open from the rubble-strewn floor below to the collapsed rafters above. Fantina stepped inside leaving her footprints in the thick dust as she crossed to the center of the space. Enzo followed. "Wait, where are we going?" Dimitris asked?

Fantina stopped and turned to Enzo. "The bell tower... Where's the church?"

Enzo paused, unsure. "I am not so sure there is one. No church or bell tower on this island."

"But there has to be," Fantina said.

"Unless," Dimitris reasoned, "we have been lured here under false pretenses as part of elaborate scheme to protect treasure and catch us in trap."

Fantina looked to Enzo...another touch of concern. Enzo shot Dimitris another incredulous, dumfounded look. "Thank you, again."

"No problem."

Fantina turned to continue on through the room when suddenly she paused. A fine mist, like a thin layer of fog was rolling in from each of the holes in the wall where windows used to be. It swirled as it flowed down over the rubble and seemed to converge on Fantina and Enzo at the center of the room. Enzo retreated inward standing back-to-back with Fatina.

"Do not worry, I am coming!" Dimitris called as he stepped forward into the doorway. His bronze body, however, too wide to pass, got wedged in the opening. "Ah, maybe not."

Then, suddenly, the mist stopped. The swirls spun together and coalesced into forms and shapes—ghosts of people who had been sent to die on *Poveglia* centuries ago. Their bodies floated weightlessly over the remains of the room, their hair and clothing drifting slowly about them. Some were old, others young, but all bore the dark symptoms of the plague on their faces and in their sunken eyes. They settled in a circle around Fantina and Enzo, motionless, terrifying, and staring...

"Hey Angela, look! We have visitors." The initially fearsome and ghostly face of a young fisherman with a bushy mustache melted into a friendly grin, as his equally jovial, ghostly wife floated forward and stopped before Fantina.

"Yes, I can see that, Luigi. They look frightened, white as a ghost. No pun intended, *eh?* But I do not blame you. Luigi is a little spooky with his scraggly face and dark circles under his eyes."

"Hey, why do you have to be so judgmental? I was very sick when I died."

Fantina and Enzo exchanged a look. "Hello," Fantina said.

"How about that," Angela grinned. "It has been so long since we got a nice greeting. Most people...just a lot of screaming, then they go running away."

"Well, you don't seem cursed," Fantina said.

"I would not go that far," Luigi noted. "I am, after all, stuck here with her." Angela shot her husband a frown. Luigi rephrased. "I mean, we are all stuck out here with nothing to do all day."

"And the night life on *Poveglia* is just dead," Angela explained. "No pun intended. What I would not give for one more night of excitement."

Luigi sighed, "Yes truly, then I could die a happy man."

Angela groaned then smacked Luigi on the back of the head. Luigi's left eyeball popped out. Enzo caught it on reflex. "Ah!" he yelped, then tossed it like a hot potato.

Angela snatched it mid-air and slammed it back into Luigi's eye socket. "*Stupido*, you already died a happy man."

Luigi rolled his re-seated eye. "Of course I did." He turned to Enzo ruefully, "Do I not look happy?"

Enzo considered, but before he could answer—

Luigi clarified. "What I meant is that everyone is destined for a touch of greatness before they leave this world. If we could find some little bit of useful purpose, get some closure, then we could move on from here."

"Ah, well," Dimitris chimed in, "if you could help me get unstuck from door, that would be very usefully purposeful of you."

Fantina, Enzo and every ghostly face turned to look at Dimitris, then Luigi raised an eyebrow and looked to his wife with an odd expression. "Angela, there is a talking horse statue stuck in our doorway."

"Yes, I see that. I wonder what he wants."

Enzo stepped forward. "We are looking for something hidden here on the island."

"Hidden where 'tolls the bell,'" Fantina explained. "A church bell tower, maybe?"

"Ah, you are thinking of the church of *San Vitale*?" Luigi suggested.

"Yes, perfect," Fantina nodded excitedly. "Where is it?"

"Well, it is gone of course."

"Gone?"

"It was torn down in 1805 by that French hooligan who plundered Venice."

"Napoleon," Dimitris tensed up and snorted indignantly.

"Ah, you know him?"

Dimitris sniffled sadly. "It was very stressful time for me."

Fantina had a sinking feeling. "So there is no bell tower?" she asked.

Angela floated forward to console Fantina. "No, not anymore, dear."

Fantina sighed. She exchanged a disheartened look with Enzo.

Angela continued. "They saw no point in having a bell tower after they destroyed the church, so they turned it into a lighthouse."

Fantina paused, her face brightening.

The *Poveglia* lighthouse rose up through the bramble thicket as if it were trying to climb the tangled vegetation covering the island and escape. The brick façade was old and worn but still looked sturdy—a fortress strong enough to stand through time and guard a secret.

The door creaked ominously as Fantina pushed it open and looked into the empty space. It was a plain, square room, with a crumbling, stone staircase at the far wall that wound its way up toward the uppermost floor of the tower high above. As

Fantina stepped inside, a breeze stirred the thick layer of dust on the floor, whisking it into the air and somehow thickening the darkness.

Luigi and Angela peered in at the doorway. "There is nothing in this place anymore," Luigi said. "Only the view from the top, where the bell used to be."

Fantina looked up the precarious staircase with certainty in her eyes. "Then that's where we have to go."

Luigi and Angela floated upward as Fantina and Enzo climbed the tower stairs. Fantina smiled to herself as they went, feeling that spark of adventure within her, and with that, the sense that her father was there guiding her along the way. The stories he had told her long ago were somehow clearer in her memory, as if now that she needed them, they had risen from deep within.

Up and up they continued until near the top, a stone step beneath Fantina's foot broke loose and crumbled away. Enzo quickly reached out and pulled Fantina to safety, holding her close as the step tumbled to pieces down at the bottom of the tower. He sighed with relief...still holding Fantina for what he began to realize was an awkwardly long moment. Fantina waited patiently, in no real hurry to be released from the embrace. Angela nudged Luigi who nodded knowingly.

"Oh!" Enzo cleared his throat and took a quick step back. "Bad step."

Fantina smiled. "Good catch though. Thanks." Fantina turned and continued up while Enzo paused. He looked to Angela and Luigi who assured him with a smile and a 'thumbs up' before floating up after Fantina.

Fantina paused and looked in through the doorway at the top of the tower stairs. With weathered brick walls and a dirty, mosaic floor neglected through time, the space was dimly lit by the waning moon, and open on all four sides, overlooking the ruins and bramble thicket below. Outside, the ghosts lingered around the base of the tower where Dimitris waited as well, curiously looking up along the exterior wall. "Are you there yet? What do you see?" he asked.

At the center of the room was an old mirror and lens set over a rusty, iron brazier—the lighthouse element added by the French a century ago. Enzo scanned the otherwise empty space, a bit confused. "There is nothing here," he said. "What are we supposed to do?"

Fantina pulled the rolled lace veil from her jacket, remembering again the poem her father taught her years ago. "Bring siren's gift and search awhile, where tolls the bell on a cursed isle." She shook the veil open and continued. "Beneath the pattern you will see, the key to solve this mystery."

Angela smiled. "Oh, how exciting. What could that mean?"

Fantina looked about as if hoping the answer would reveal itself somehow. "A pattern…" Fantina repeated.

Enzo reasoned, "like the one on the veil?"

Fantina held up the lace. The swirling thread work was quite detailed, but seemed rather nonspecific.

Angela stared at the veil as she floated about. "It is beautiful," she said. "So delicate, so...familiar, like…" She turned to Luigi, but he wasn't there.

"Like the pattern on the floor I think." Luigi, hovering high above near the rafters, was looking down on the room. The mosaic of small, marble tiles on the floor beneath the brazier, though dusty with time, seemed a close match for the swirling pattern on the lace. Enzo and Fantina smiled.

The sound of the iron brazier being dragged to the side of the tower room echoed in the night. It was a low and rasping noise, almost guttural, as if a long dormant monster on *Poveglia* were waking from a nap. The ghosts circling the tower looked about frightfully then dissolved back into a mist and dissipated into the brambles while Dimitris looked up the tower wall uncertainly. "Enzo! I am beginning to have bad feeling."

Through the thicket, at the shoreline, a rat picking over some washed up bones looked up curiously. He twitched at the sound with a glance that might have seemed fearful if you knew nothing of ratters and Murk. But when a second rat came scampering from the brambles, black eyes gleaming wickedly, it was clear that these rats weren't bothered by fear at all. They seemed strengthened by it. They scrambled into the tide and swam away.

With the brazier moved aside, and a quick sweep to remove centuries of dust and debris, the mosaic at the center of the room was revealed. It was an intricate pattern of small, colored tiles that gave the appearance of random waves and crests of sea foam flowing across the floor.

Fantina and Enzo stepped forward with the veil, noting the identical swirls in the lace and matching its design to the mosaic. The veil fluttered over the floor, shimmering in the dim moonlight, making it seem as if the patterned swirls were spinning like water in a current.

Fantina followed the movement to a spot near the edge of the veil where the swirling pattern ended. Beneath the veil at that spot, was a single, dull, grey tile. Fantina folded back the veil to look. Amid the other tiles in the design, it was the least impressive, the least colorful and most easily overlooked part of the mosaic.

"Beneath the pattern," Fantina said. She flipped open her tool pouch and pulled out a small pry bar to work the tile loose. Enzo stepped closer. Suddenly, the tile popped up, revealing a small hollow carved down into the stone sub-floor.

Fantina hesitated and shared an expectant look with Enzo, then reached into the hollow. As she felt around inside, her finger brushed against something cold and metallic. She looked to Enzo wide-eyed and pulled an iron skeleton key from beneath the floor. It was old but still intact, blackened by an ancient process to protect it against rust over centuries of time. Fantina held it up for Enzo to see. "The key to solve the mystery."

"Oooh a mystery," Angela bubbled with excitement. "Finally a little something to liven up the night life."

"We may get more than a little something," Luigi said, looking out the north side of the tower.

Enzo shot a wary glance at Fantina then crossed to see. Out in the lagoon, a cloud of smoke trailing behind it, Malvagio's Scylla was steaming briskly toward *Poveglia*.

"He found us," Enzo said anxiously. "We have to get out of here."

"Do not worry," Luigi nodded with assurance. "We will help you." He floated higher and struck a heroic pose. "Finally, after centuries of just wafting around aimlessly, we will fulfill our destiny and—" Luigi stopped short as he looked down to the base of the tower where Dimitris waited...alone. "*Ei*, where did everybody go?" Luigi groaned. "Does nobody around here want closure besides me?" He slapped his forehead in frustration.

Angela swooped in, caught Luigi's eyeball as it popped out and slammed it back into its socket. She glanced out where the other ghosts had disappeared. "*Beh*, maybe another day. Good luck," she said as she and Luigi dissolved back into mist and disappeared.

A trace of the dim moonlight filtered down into the water surrounding *Poveglia* as a faint cloud of sediment rose in the shallows. Through the cloud, a vague shape appeared—Dimitris with Fantina and Enzo astride. Their underwater breathing gizmos left a small trail of bubbles as Enzo pointed the way through the tide and Dimitris veered off into deeper waters.

Fantina looked up cautiously, hoping that they would miss Malvagio by a comfortable distance, but as they continued forward, a growing shadow appeared on the surface above. Dimitris paused briefly as the Scylla's iron hull, faintly rimmed in the moonlight, skimmed over them. Fantina and Enzo held their breath as the shadow passed, then managed a sigh of relief.

The relief, however, was short lived. A swirl of bubbles and silt was approaching them now through the murky water, and by the time Fantina and Enzo saw the drift net, it was too late to escape. Dimitris turned and angled away but the net swept over them catching Fantina in its twisted mesh. Enzo grabbed Fantina's hand, but before he could pull her clear, he was snared in the net as well. Dimitris turned back to help, but Enzo waved him off, pointing him back toward Venice.

Dimitris understood. He would go for help. He exchanged a final glance with Fantina and Enzo, then trudged away along the muddy lagoon bottom.

Steam hissed as Fantina and Enzo were hoisted up like netted fish and deposited onto the deck of the Scylla. They looked up and froze, surrounded by a dozen or so ratters, black eyes shining, pointed teeth gleaming.

"Welcome aboard," Malvagio said as he emerged through the hatch from below. "Did you think you had gotten away?"

Fantina stood her ground at first, but shuffled back along the deck in terror when Malvagio's white, ratter captain appeared and quickly scampered over to her. Unsettled by the ratter's piercing, red stare, Fantina looked to Enzo for help, but he was still tangled in the net and surrounded by the rest of the ratter crew. Fantina gasped as the captain circled her menacingly, as if looking for a moment to strike.

"Leave her alone," Enzo shouted as he rose to Fantina's defense. The ratters chattered with laughter as they pulled the net tight about Enzo's feet, dragging him back down onto the deck.

The ratter captain then rushed at Fantina, her paws grasping, searching... Fantina struggled desperately, but couldn't escape.

Then suddenly, the ratter captain's eyes flared. She pulled the old skeleton key from Fantina's pocket. Fantina reached to grab it back, but a sharp snap of the captain's razor teeth forced Fantina to pull her hand back quickly.

Malvagio grinned as his ratter captain scurried back to his side with the key. He snatched it greedily. "At last."

"It's just a key," Fantina said. "We don't know what it opens."

"Ah, but I think perhaps you do," Malvagio grinned. He motioned below deck and Primo stepped up, the weathered journal of Marco Polo in hand. Primo opened it, scanned the text and read.

"Then banished fires, and dragon's bone; Will point the way to traitor's home." He looked up, pondering the rhyme for a moment, then shook his head. "I got nothing. What about you?"

Fantina paused, exchanged a quiet look with Enzo. Malvagio glared at her impatiently, then motioned to his captain. In a flash, she scampered over to Enzo and gripped him, a sharp claw at his throat.

"Okay," Fantina said quickly, "Maybe I remember something."

"Fantina, no," Enzo interrupted. "Do not tell him anything." The ratter captain tightened her grip, leaning Enzo backward out over one of the Scylla's churning paddle wheels. Enzo gulped. "Uh, on second thought, yes, tell him something."

Fantina looked at Enzo, concerned, then closed her eyes, thinking back. "My father once told me a story…" she began, "about a fire in Venice a long time ago. A young glass-blower's furnace burned through his neighbor's wall. And since many of the houses back then were built of wood, by the time the fire was put out, an entire neighborhood was gone. The *Doge* threw the glass-blower into the palace prison and ordered all the glass furnaces in Venice to be moved out of the city, north for safety."

Malvagio grinned. "To *Murano*—the island of the glass-blowers." Ratters chattered excitedly, as the ratter captain dropped Enzo back onto the deck, and scurried off to the helm. Malvagio nodded to her. "Full speed," he ordered.

"Ah, I understand," Primo nodded excitedly. "Banished fires, *eh?*" He checked the journal's text again. "Uh…but what about this other part," he gulped. "…a dragon?"

Fantina paused, crinkling her nose. In a flash, images flooded her mind: an exploding canon; the bamboo-framed ink drawing of the dragon in Uncle Gio's house; the fiery dragon swirling toward the Genoese ship in the battle of Chioggia, its gaping mouth ready to devour— "No," Fantina said quickly, "I can't think of anything."

Malvagio studied Fantina's face. She was lying, of course. But how could this young girl know so much about the secrets he was after? Since he had stolen the journal from the Venetian

Grand Exposition eight years ago, he had studied each page intently, looking for the clues that would reveal the treasure's final resting place. He had followed Marco Polo's route from China, excavated the Nicobar Islands, razed villages near Ceylon and Calicut. Through India and Persia he had dug, and he had lain to waste the Greek island of Tenedos. But…nothing.

All the while, he had kept moving, staying one step ahead of the authorities on his trail. Of course, after he had arranged the timely assassination of King Umberto I, the trail had cooled. The Murk that gave rise to his ratter crew had darkened Malvagio's heart, and had turned his quest to prove his father wrong into his obsession to succeed at any cost. And that had brought him back to Venice where he had set in motion his final plan to uncover the treasure.

Malvagio looked at the key in his hand. He was closer now than he had ever been, and this girl before him had gotten him there. He slipped the key into his breast pocket as he eyed Fantina suspiciously.

"I realize I have been somewhat warm and friendly till now, so you may have gotten the wrong impression of me," Malvagio said as he edged closer with a menacing glare. "Let me be clear. The treasure of Marco Polo will be mine, and you had better start remembering, anything and everything, if you ever want to see your uncle alive again." Malvagio stopped, face to face with Fantina, then turned abruptly and disappeared below deck.

Fantina caught her breath, unable to breathe for a moment. Uncle Gio was in grave danger, and she and Enzo were in serious trouble. What a pain in the neck she had turned out to be. She stood shivering while the Scylla steamed off into the night.

Chapter Twenty-One — Fire and Glass

The fires of *Murano's* glass factory furnaces cast a hazy, orange glow into the night sky, silhouetting Malvagio's steam-hissing vessel as it churned its way through the island's main canal.

There had always been an aura of mystery about *Murano*. Detached and almost a kilometer north of Venice proper, it had been ideal for the decreed relocation of glass-blowing artisans by *Doge* Pietro Gradenigo in 1291. But beyond the geography, it was the whispered rumors that made *Murano* truly isolated.

Though most never spoke of it, the ever-burning glow on the horizon had spurred the belief that the island was still the home of a dragon that had arrived in Venice in 1295 with a 'certain explorer' returning from the Far East. Other stories claimed that the dragon was a beast that had roamed in *Arezzo* or terrorized the Greek island of Cephalonia centuries earlier and had been slain when Saint Donatus spit on it. No, really, the tales were strange and fanciful, but while they, like so many others, had faded into folklore, the sense that *Murano* yet concealed some unknown and dangerous mystery remained, and most Venetian locals seemed content to leave that notion undisturbed.

Fantina marched alongside Enzo and between the dozen ratters from aboard the Scylla, as she led Malvagio and Primo from the shoreline of *Murano*. Light from a glowing furnace inside a glassworks factory, bounced through shelves of multi-colored, blown-glass wares—from vases and bowls to mini statuettes of butterflies and unicorns—washing the group in a kaleidoscope of color as they passed.

Then, at the far edge of the fire's glow, Fantina stopped. Malvagio and the others stopped short behind her. "What is it?" Malvagio asked.

"Well, if the story is true," Fantina explained, "then the dragon's bones are in there." Fantina pointed across a small *piazzetta* to an elegant curved colonnade wrapping the back of a large, brick building—the church of *Santa Maria* and *San Donato*.

Now, the church of *Santa Maria* (as it was initially consecrated) was first built in the seventh century, but it had been rebuilt at least twice since then. The exotic, Byzantine style and architecture came with the redesign in 1125, when *Doge* Domenico Michele, added both the name and relics of Saint Donatus to the rededicated church.

So now, centuries later, commingled with the rich mosaics and sweeping arches of the nave, were four, long, curved bones, hung on the back wall behind the altar. Most people didn't even see them there, and of those who did, most had no idea what they were.

"Are you sure it was a dragon?" Primo asked as he rechecked the journal then stared up at the bones skeptically. "I mean, maybe a whale or a sea cow, or—"

"Primo!" Malvagio bristled.

"Nevermind."

Malvagio grabbed the journal from Primo's hands and shoved it into Fantina's. He then gripped his walking stick fiercely, threatening to unsheathe the menacing blade within. He drummed his fingers on its silver handle expectantly.

Fantina exchanged a nervous glance with Enzo, then ran her hand over the ancient pages of the journal, and read. "Then banished fires and dragon's bone, will point the way to traitor's home."

As if on cue, everyone looked up at the bones, then looked off in the direction they pointed...or rather, the many different directions the four curved bones pointed. Primo scratched his head. "This makes no sense at all. What traitor's home? How does anything here point to a traitor's home, *eh?*"

"Maybe not anymore," Enzo said. "This church was restored years ago. Redesigned, rebuilt...maybe the clue is gone."

Fantina reread the text nervously. She knew it was up to her. If she couldn't make sense of the verse, Malvagio would have no use for them anymore. She wondered if Uncle Gio had failed or refused to reveal the meaning behind the previous clue, or if he had been forced to point Malvagio toward *Poveglia*. She shuddered, suddenly afraid that her quest for fortune and glory had taken a dark and deadly turn. "I...don't know," she stammered.

Malvagio stared coldly, his grip tightening on his sword's handle as he drew it out. "Then that is extremely bad news for you." The ratters began chattering to each other and closing in. The ratter captain grinned, her red eyes glowing—

Just then, the windows of the church exploded inward as a team of frogman commandos, wielding bow iron scimitars, stormed in ready for action. While ratters ducked the shards of glass and turned to meet the assault, Fantina slammed the journal shut and pulled Enzo away, retreating toward the back of the church. "This way!"

Malvagio slashed and parried as frogmen leapt about, keeping him and his ratters occupied. He paused though, as he spotted Fantina and Enzo escaping through the melee. He pointed with his sword. "She has the journal. Stop them!" he yelled. The ratter captain snarled and gave chase.

Fantina and Enzo slid to a halt before a large double door beneath an archway at the back of the church. Enzo pushed, but the door wouldn't budge. Fantina spotted a side door and rushed toward it. "This way," she called.

But before she could reach the door, the ratter captain appeared before her, blocking her way. A sinister grin, sharp claws glinting in the dim light, the ratter captain stepped toward Fantina, her red eyes fixed on the journal. Fantina stood her ground but hesitated. No way to fight, nowhere to run, she didn't think she could fake her way out of this fix. She braced herself, clutching the journal tightly, when suddenly—

Eva, outfitted for her *Carnevale* wind dancer aerial ballet, sprang downward from the balcony above on her silken scarves. She grabbed onto Fantina, hugging her from behind. "Come with me. This way."

The surprised ratter captain slashed forward, but Eva and Fantina were already springing back upwards to the balcony.

Then, the double door behind Enzo came smashing inward, battered open by the giant, bronze, hindquarters of— "Dimitris!" Enzo cheered. Dimitris spun about as Cosimo and Jester Joe charged in beside him.

Cosimo stepped between Enzo and the ratter captain spinning a flame-tipped gondolier staff in hand. "I will take care of this. You and Eva get them out of here," he ordered. Joe nodded and quickly extracted Enzo, pulling him out of the church.

"Wait," Enzo pleaded. "I can help."

"You have helped enough today," Cosimo said angrily. Enzo withdrew a step, stung. But his uncle was right. All he had done was expose Fantina to danger and the Gondoliers to disrepute.

Cosimo shot Enzo a final stern look. "Go." He then spun back to face the ratter captain as Joe pulled Enzo away.

A thin trail of smoke rose into the night sky from the stacks of two inconspicuous fishing boats idling in the canal. Contessa turned at the helm of the first one as Fantina and Eva leapt aboard. "There you are. We were worried about you." Contessa leaned close to Fantina. "Although I have to say, I had a sense that you would be just fine. There is something about you, *eh?*"

Just then, Joe and Enzo leapt aboard. "Go! Cosimo will join us later," Joe explained. Contessa nodded knowingly then winked at Fantina. "Flame Boy is busy." She gunned the engine as Fantina turned to look.

Back before the church, an arc of fire shot across the *piazzetta,* forcing the ratters back. It was Cosimo, just as Fantina had seen him that first evening at *Carnevale,* breathing flames and lighting up the night. Silhouetted against the orange glow, the ratter captain and her crew clashed with Cosimo and the frogmen. They charged forward, claws to blade, then retreated as Cosimo spun about, connecting with his staff and blasting another burst of flame.

Fantina cringed as she saw what seemed like the ratter captain connecting with a slash, forcing Cosimo back. She clutched the Marco Polo journal tightly as Contessa throttled forward and chugged away from the shore in a hiss of steam.

The ratter captain paused, suddenly locking eyes on Fantina. She shrieked an order, and her ratters turned and scurried away from the clash into the darkness. Cosimo tried to intercept them, but stumbled, leaning heavily on his staff. He was hurt. The ratter captain grinned, then turned and disappeared with her crew.

Ratters scrambled on board the Scylla, its engine hissing angrily as if it were anxious to give chase. But instead of casting off, the ratters all rushed below deck. A violent blast of steam spewed from the hull as twelve panels on the side of the vessel opened, each releasing a small, one-passenger water-cycle, a hissing engine mounted between two water skis and a seat. The ratters leapt on, gunned their engines and sped away after the fleeing boat.

Fantina glanced back as the water-cycles sped closer. "They're catching up," she yelled.

Enzo dashed up to the helm beside Contessa. "Not to worry, I made a few tweaks to this boat too." Enzo pulled a small, inconspicuous lever. A panel with knobs and buttons swung out near the helm controls.

Contessa shot Enzo a look with a proud smile. "My little gizmologist."

With that, Enzo flipped a switch. A streamlined daggerboard folded out from the front of the keel while two water turbines emerged from the sides. A button on the panel switched from red to blue. Enzo nodded to Contessa. Contessa grinned. "This is going to be fun."

Contessa punched the blue button and braced herself as the turbines squealed. Steam coursed through them, churning the water on either side of the boat. Fantina, Enzo, Joe and Eva held on tightly as the boat accelerated, its bow rising up on the front daggerboard. It then launched itself, soaring, like a water rocket, across the water's surface.

Twelve ratters on their water-cycles blasted through the spray kicked up by Contessa's boat as it sped away. They zigzagged back and forth in the canal trying to avoid the massive wake, but two slammed into it and rode it like a ramp, soaring up and out of the canal where they crashed through a glassworks factory. They smashed into the factory furnace, which exploded in a shower of steam, fire and colored glass.

A small crowd of late night *Carnevale* revelers, walking along the northern promenade of Venice proper, looked up curiously as an arc of fire lit the sky over *Murano*. They "Oohed," "Ah-hed," and applauded at what they assumed was a festive, *Carnevale* fireworks display.

Contessa's boat soared out from the fireball over *Murano's* main canal and sped onward into the open lagoon. Fantina glanced back. Through the smoke and haze, ten ratters emerged, still in pursuit. Fantina turned nervously toward Joe and Eva. "We're going to need some help!"

Joe nodded confidently. "Ah, well...help is on the way," he said. "Look!" Fantina followed Joe's glance…

Galloping along the south shore of *Murano* was Dimitris. He whinnied triumphantly as the second 'fishing boat' came soaring around the side of the island, Cosimo at the helm. Like Contessa's boat, it was tweaked up and cruising, steam and spray blasting out the back as it closed in behind the pursuing ratters.

Fantina looked concerned. "We're still outnumbered, unless—" Fantina paused…and looked closer.

Fanning out behind Cosimo's boat at the end of four tow lines, were four waterskiing frogmen decked out in pairs of Enzo's Da Vinci water shoes. Atop their shoulders were six more leaning into the spray. "That'll work," Fantina nodded.

With a signal from Joe, Cosimo swerved right. Contessa zigged left. Then, with synchronized precision, they both zagged back putting Cosimo on an intercept course with the ratters. As the two paths crossed, the top frogmen leapt from their pyramid, snatching ratters right off their water-cycles and slamming them into the lagoon. Six went down, the remaining four continued the pursuit.

Joe and Eva vaulted from the back of Contessa's boat onto two of the vacated water-cycles as they zipped past, then spun about to rejoin the fray.

On the northern promenade of Venice, the crowd pointed excitedly as Contessa's boat sped closer. She was being pursued by the four remaining ratters on their water-cycles, who, in turn, were being chased down by Cosimo's boat towing four waterskiing frogmen. The crowd applauded. It was quite a show.

Contessa suddenly cut right, leaving the north lagoon and ducking into *Sacca Della Misericordia*, a wide basin leading in toward the *Rio Noale* canal. Joe and Eva veered off to either side while the ratters followed her in.

As Cosimo turned to pursue, the frogmen skiing behind him swung in a wide arc, straight toward the banks of the *Rio Noale's* left fork. Two let go and sank beneath the water; the other two, their frog eyes wide with panic, soared up onto the bank and skimmed along the cobblestone walkway, sending pedestrians at the water's edge scrambling and diving aside.

Enzo cringed. "Well," he said to Fantina, "at least it is not too crowded tonight." He spoke too soon…

In the Grand Canal, elegantly decorated *bissone* longboats with crews of colorfully uniformed oarsmen rowed gently along in the *Carnevale* Regata parade. Like other boat parades held during the year and down through the centuries, it celebrated the city's bond to the water and was quite the spectacle. Led by a gilded, ceremonial barge, known as the *Bucintoro*, and followed by fancy six-oared *caroline* and sleek twin-oared *pupparini* and *mascarete* boats, the colorful procession flowed along the festive route past *piazzas* and palaces, while hundreds upon hundreds of spectators watched from windows and gathered at the banks of the Grand Canal, lit by street lamps and twinkling amber boat lanterns.

Near the end of the procession, Mayor Grimani, dressed in silken costume finery, waved from the back stoop of his long, gilded parade boat as it approached the tall arch of the *Rialto* Bridge. Behind him, two *carabiniere* patrol steamboats brought up the rear.

Suddenly, Contessa's boat shot out into the Grand Canal turning right into the middle of the parade. The ratters soared out after her, narrowly missing parade boats as they pursued. Cosimo and the remaining two frogmen zipped out last. Their towlines clipped the bow of a *pupparino* and sent it spinning into a *mascareta*. The frogmen exchanged a doomed glance and let go, disappearing beneath the water as the boats collided and swamped each other.

Contessa swerved back and forth against the flow of the parade. "Have we lost them?" she asked. Fantina and Enzo scanned the crowded canal. Through the growing confusion and chaos, they spotted two of the ratters weaving through and closing in.

"No," Fantina said, "they're still behind us."

"We will take care," Jester Joe chimed in as he and Eva reappeared from a side canal and sped past on their water-cycles heading straight for the two ratters to intercept. They closed the distance and, at the last second, split wide revealing one of Eva's silk chords held between them. The ratters' beady eyes went wide but too late. The chord swept them off their seats and slingshot them backwards across the canal.

Their water-cycles, however, careened out of control heading straight for a long, 16-oared *bissone*. Terrified oarsmen dove overboard as the water-cycles lopped off the bow and stern of their boat in an explosion of wood, metal and steam. Spectators gasped.

At the rear of the procession, the Mayor rose, alarmed, and motioned his *carabiniere* escort forward toward the commotion. Fantina spotted them approaching. "More trouble," she noted to Contessa.

Just then, Cosimo sped up alongside Contessa's boat. "Take the canals through *Dorsoduro*," he said as he pulled close. "Get out of sight. The mayor will not sit still for this."

Fantina stepped to the side of the boat, clutching the journal tightly. "It's okay. We got the journal back."

"And all the ratters..." Enzo added, "They are all gon—"

Before Enzo could finish the thought, a ratter raced past between the two boats, snatching Fantina and the journal onto his water-cycle and continuing on. Enzo's jaw dropped. Cosimo grumbled. "I will get her. You go, now!" Contessa nodded, throttled forward before Enzo could object, and disappeared down a narrow side canal.

Fantina struggled against the grip of her ratter captor while the water-cycle sped away, darting back and forth between boats. Spectators along the shore recoiled at the sight, some stunned, others fleeing in fear.

Some distance back, Cosimo maneuvered through the parade, trying to keep Fantina in sight. The *carabiniere* patrol boats steamed closer, boxing Cosimo in near the base of the *Rialto* Bridge. Cosimo was trapped.

Cosimo suddenly leapt up and vaulted away, springing across the parade boats with his Gondolier staff in hand, chasing after Fantina on foot.

The ratter gripping Fantina grinned as he caught sight of Cosimo trying to catch up. In seconds he would be gone down a side canal. There was no way the Gondolier would catch—

Suddenly, a deafening roar reverberated through the canal. Spectators froze, scanning the sky. The ratter looked up as well. A flowing mane and gaping jaw was the last thing he saw.

Soaring down from above, Leo swooped out of the night sky and snatched the ratter out of his seat and off of Fantina. With his wings spread wide and his claws locked on the squirming ratter, Leo rose high overhead, while below, spectators backed away from the growing chaos.

Fantina leapt forward to seize the water-cycle controls as it spun about. The parade had become a tangle of boats, crisscrossing the canal, bumping, tipping. People cowered, staring up at the ferocious lion in the sky with fear in their eyes.

And then, Leo felt it. He looked at the tip of his right wing where a feather flickered like a dying candle and suddenly turned to stone. It cracked off and fell to the water below. Then, he felt a twinge in his paw. He looked down as one of his claws went grey. Its pointed tips chipped and broke away, sending the ratter plummeting downward. The crowd screamed as the ratter fell onto their heads then scrambled away. Leo hesitated, his limbs slowly stiffening.

Fantina looked up at Leo, eyes narrowed with concern, but turned back just in time to see the rapidly approaching bow of the Mayor's boat, and nowhere to turn. Fantina leapt up and somersaulted onto the deck of the *bissone* as her water-cycle exploded through the bow. She landed at the mayor's feet, the journal of Marco Polo in hand. *Carabinieri*, swords drawn, boarded the boat and surrounded Fantina.

"Seize her," the mayor fumed as he surveyed the ruined parade and panicking crowd. The *Carabinieri* moved in to detain Fantina when suddenly—

Leo landed on the roof of the Rialto Bridge with a roar that shook the surface of the Grand Canal. The *Carabinieri* turned their swords on him as the crowd fled in terror.

"No," Fantina pleaded, "don't be afraid. He's here to help us."

On the shore, standing amid the people rushing away, Cosimo looked to Leo with a knowing expression, a sense of foreboding. Leo's golden mane looked faded, his expression hard...as stone. A glow, like the last rays of a sunset, began to drain from his limbs, slowly changing them...transforming him.

Leo looked to Fantina sadly. Fantina stared back, wide-eyed, and somehow, she understood. Leo leapt, spreading his wings and soaring upward, even as bits of stone began to flake off and rain down on those below.

Cosimo looked to Fantina, now firmly in custody, then turned to get one last glance of Leo before he disappeared in the night.

The darkness was passing quickly and the horizon was already hazy with the first glow of morning. Rays of light, like grasping fingers, crept over the Venetian rooftops reclaiming the city below from whatever magic might have been there hours before.

A mechanical hum broke the silence. The Bronze Moors atop the clock tower swung their hammers to chime the early hours of the new day. And nearby, on the ledge just below them, Leo struggled back into his spot overlooking the *piazza*. His golden mane, now pale and brittle, stiffened as he did. Sunlight washed over him, and the Glim, receding from the tips of his wings and stone limbs, left him...motionless.

Chapter Twenty-Two — Over the Bridge

Fantina stood still, flanked by a contingent of *carabinieri,* in the center of the Great Council Hall of the *Palazzo Ducale*. An exhibit of traditional *Carnevale* costumes lined the walls beneath gilded ceilings and huge painted frescoes of Venetian history. The room was impressive, but Fantina was more interested in what was going on at the far end of the hall. Two city officials were examining the Marco Polo journal, while the mayor perused a long list of formal charges.

"Vandalism, desecration, demolition... You, young lady, are a menace."

"I can explain," Fantina interrupted.

"You ruined my parade and my boat. And you stole the journal of Marco Polo!"

"Now wait a minute," Fantina corrected. "A menace? Maybe. A pain in the neck? Definitely. But a thief? Not a chance. I just took it back from the person who already stole it, before."

The mayor stared at Fantina. "Really? And who might that be?" he asked skeptically.

Before Fantina could answer, the gilded doors behind the mayor swung open. Malvagio strode into the hall like a man in charge. "You," Fantina gasped.

"Ah, *Signore* Malvagio," the Mayor greeted him. "It is so good of you to come to help us."

"Yes it is," Malvagio agreed. "And thank you for moving me here into the palace. My old residence was so…damp." Malvagio grinned. The Mayor nodded compliantly.

Fantina took a defiant step forward. "But you're—"

"—the Lord High Magistrate of Venice," Malvagio completed the thought. "Appointed to protect this city from criminals like you." The *carabinieri* saluted as Malvagio stepped up beside the mayor. Fantina retreated a step, alarmed. Malvagio had seized control.

The mayor rose to the tips of his toes, straining to reach as he pinned a shiny, new, silver service medallion beside the bronze one on Malvagio's breast pocket. "Venice is a city of progress, now," the mayor explained. "We must have order. You and your vigilante friends have roamed the shadows of Venice long enough."

"Uh, no, no," Fantina interrupted. "I just got here yesterday."

"And look at the mess you have made." The mayor motioned to the *carabinieri*. "Take her across the bridge."

"Bridge? What bridge?" Fantina asked. Two *carabinieri* seized Fantina and began marching her away toward a doorway at the opposite end of the room.

Malvagio watched her go, quite pleased with himself. "Do not worry. Your gondolier gang will be joining you shortly," he sneered.

Fantina struggled, pleading with the mayor. "Don't trust him. He's lying to you. You need the Gondoliers."

Malvagio moved past the mayor and strode to the city officials to reclaim the journal. "What this city needs," he said, "is a dose of reality, not old stories and fantasy."

Fantina stopped, managing to free an arm. "It's not just a story," she called out urgently. "Glim is real."

The Mayor looked at Fantina uncertainly. He had heard stories and had…seen things. Or maybe he hadn't really, he tried to tell himself. Things got confusing in the chaos of *Carnevale*. He wanted things to make sense. It was a new century, after all, and rumors and illusions in the dark of night did not make sense. And yet, there was something about Fantina. Maybe there still was something…magical out there, and maybe… Venice needed it.

Malvagio stepped close, intimidatingly close. The Mayor hesitated, then relented. "Maybe…not anymore."

Fantina's eyes dimmed. It was just as Leo had said. Hope had faded; fear had grown. "Then we're on our own," Fantina sighed. The *carabinieri* seized her again and hurried her out through the doorway.

The corridor was dark and narrow, and the stone walls felt cold and thick. Fantina marched between the two *carabinieri* uncertain of where she was going, her footsteps echoing on the hard floor. They arrived at a short flight of steps and crossed up into a narrow passage. As Fantina walked onward she suddenly realized where she was. The dim morning light filtered in through two small windows blocked with stone screens. It would be the last sunlight she would see. She was crossing the Bridge of Sighs.

Outside, the morning was grey and cold and drained of color. An ominous groan rose from the water, like the city itself had lost hope and its ancient foundations had slumped their shoulders and settled further into the mud.

Bianca, perched atop the bridge, cooed mournfully as Fantina passed through inside. She then turned and fluttered away down the canal. But as she disappeared, three rats rose from the water. They chattered to each other, then scampered off after her.

CHAPTER TWENTY-THREE — A SHOW OF FORCE

Everything looked unusually still. The water of the Grand Canal was like glass, as if that morning's ocean breeze had simply refused to stir it. The grey sky above was cloudless but overcast all the same, dimming the sunlight through a haze of uncertainty. And that's when they came.

Marching in columns of two and armed with fully modern *carcano* rifles, the 'improved' *carabinieri* of Venice emerged from the inner courtyard of the Ducal Palace. Each now wore a plain, white and chillingly expressionless, full-face, Venetian *Bauta* mask and tricorn hat as part of their new, martial uniform, as they moved in lockstep across *Piazza San Marco…* with new orders.

From the palace balcony, Malvagio smiled, enjoying the sight and sound of his new Venetian Police Force, his V-Troopers. Boots echoed on the pavement as the procession fanned out, spreading into the city.

At the Grand Canal, an old gondolier sat on the stern of his boat sipping his morning *cappuccino*. He looked up as a squad of V-Troopers marched into view. Two broke off from the group and ordered the gondolier from his boat. He stood uncertainly, his cup in hand.

The lead trooper, the eyes of his mask hollow and dark, stepped forward, smashed the cup away with the butt of his rifle and pulled the gondolier roughly onto the stone walkway.

Locals watched, confused, fearful, some hurrying away, others closing themselves in behind wooden shutters, as the V-Troopers marched onward with the gondolier and a handful of other detainees in custody.

The marionette show at the royal gardens was abruptly halted by a squad of V-Troopers. Puppeteers were rounded up on charges of rabble rousing and sedition, their marionettes confiscated as symbols of malcontent. Stories of old Venice were deemed no longer appropriate, and the V-Troopers had strict guidelines to follow. 'Cancelled by the order of Magistrate Malvagio,' read the banner draped over the puppet stage.

The show of force continued, in every *piazza* and down every alleyway. V-Troopers kicked through doors, pushing their way in to search for any sign of association with the outlaw gang of Gondoliers. Even the homes of those who professed to know nothing of the guild were ransacked in the search.

When the V-Troopers burst through the door of Uncle Gio's home, they found no one there. Regardless, they trampled in, emotionless in their blank-faced masks, and merciless, toppling his shelves of books and smashing works of art. In the attic, they kicked aside Fantina's travel-worn suitcase, spilling her gadgets and gizmos across the floor. One V-Trooper spotted her book. He grabbed it, suspiciously tearing through pages then tossing it aside. The V-Troopers then marched back out the way they came, trampling Jules Verne underfoot as they left.

In *Campo San Polo*, a small *piazza* in a quieter *sestiere* of Venice, shopkeepers and street vendors were already beginning their preparations for the continuing *Carnevale* festivities when a column of V-Troopers marched in. Locals looked up warily as the V-Troopers halted with measured precision at the *piazza's* edge to assess which of them posed the most threat to Malvagio's new authority.

Seated behind her fotune-telling table, Contessa motioned subtly to Jester Joe and Eva. "It has happened. Warn Cosimo. Tell him to be careful. Go."

"No no...what about you?" Joe asked nervously.

Eva scanned the *piazza*, plotting an escape route. "We will get you out of here."

"Not to worry. You go. I will slow them down for you." Contessa smiled slyly. "Go." Eva and Joe nodded uncertainly, then backed away and ducked down a narrow alleyway.

Contessa shuffled her tarot deck as the V-Troopers advanced toward a hapless fruit vendor. "*Ei!*" She called out. "Over here. I have some information for you."

The masked V-Troopers paused, then diverted and marched in an intimidating row to Contessa.

Contessa nodded submissively. "Come. I can see that you are looking for something, answers to burning questions. I can help you...tell you your future." The V-Troopers hesitated, exchanging blank looks. Contessa flipped a few cards and leaned over them, studying them as if to discover their hidden meaning. The V-Troopers shrugged and leaned in as well. Suddenly, Contessa looked up. She grabbed a card and held it high...an artfully drawn image of a man on the back stoop of his boat, a Gondolier. "Ah, here it is, your future." She considered the card a second time then shrugged. "*Beh*, what can I say? I see what I see. It does not look too good for you."

The V-Troopers straightened up, bristling. They overturned Contessa's table, scattering her deck of cards across the pavement, and seized her. Contessa rose without resisting. "Okay, okay. Not the fortune you were hoping for. I understand. How about...no charge, *eh?*" The V-Troopers pulled Contessa into a group with several other 'suspicious' locals, then marched the group away.

Contessa glanced down as they left the *piazza*. The pavement was damp—a slick, thin layer of water covering the stone and swirling beneath her scattered tarot cards. Contessa watched as the Gondolier card spun about then sank. She looked to the grey sky, concern in her eyes.

Chapter Twenty-Four — A sinking feeling

Joe, Eva and a handful of Gondoliers gathered together in the council chamber of the Gondolier headquarters. Enzo sat on the skewed staircase nearby. It was dark…and desperate.

"The magic of Venice has gone to sleep," Cosimo stated with certainty. "The Gondoliers are no longer welcome. Many have been arrested, and Malvagio controls the *carabinieri*. The Mayor has given him the city."

"Then we should take it back," Enzo said urgently. Joe and Eva exchanged an uncertain look.

"There are too few of us left," Cosimo continued. "And if we cannot raise the Glim, Venice will fall." Just then, the walls of the chamber groaned, as if in agreement. Enzo touched the stone wall beside him. It was forebodingly damp.

Cosimo and the others looked up as Bianca appeared, fluttering down from the upper levels of the chamber. She landed on Enzo's outstretched hand, cooing wearily. Enzo listened then nodded. "They have taken Fantina over the bridge, into the palace prisons."

Cosimo shook his head. "Then escape is impossible."

"This is my fault," Enzo sighed. "I got her mixed up in this. We have to rescue her."

"And who will fight with us?" Cosimo asked. "The city's hope is lost. The time of the sentinels is over. Leo and the others cannot help us anymore. We face this threat alone."

Gondoliers nodded. Joe and Eva paused, glancing upward, suddenly guarded. "Actually," Joe said, "we may not be alone after all."

Cosimo and Enzo followed Joe's glance. Peering down from the uppermost floor, two black eyes pierced the dim light —a rat perched on the railing. Then, behind the rat, two dozen masked V-Troopers appeared, their blank, white faces staring down through the chamber.

Bianca cooed in alarm.

Cosimo shot an unsettled look at Bianca, then motioned to the Gondoliers. "They followed her. To the stairs!"

The Gondoliers rushed up the staircase to defend. Enzo took a step to follow, but Cosimo stopped him. "Find a way to help Fantina," he commanded. "We will hold them here."

Enzo sighed, exasperated. "Why send me away again?" he asked. "When are you going to believe in me? I can fight."

Cosimo softened his gaze for a moment and put a hand on Enzo's shoulder. "I know you can. I have always known. But the old story ends here. Today, you need to do as I say. You are the future, and you must go on."

Cosimo and Enzo locked eyes. Enzo understood now. Cosimo had always known that this day would come, that the old ways would fade and that Enzo would have to step up to make sure that even if they did, they would not be forgotten. It was up to him now, to carry on the traditions of the past in a new and modern century. Cosimo pat Enzo on the cheek, then turned to join the fray. Enzo nodded and hurried away through a tunnel corridor.

Chapter Twenty-Four

Enzo ran out through the sculpture garden in the covered *piazza*. Outside the glass dome, lights flickered—curious streaks that sliced down through the lagoon water.

Up above, searchlights tracked across the surface. A dozen patrol steamboats, with an intimidating army of V-Troopers on board, converged near the tip of *Giudecca* Island, just across the canal from the Ducal Palace and *San Marco*. They closed in around a small, unassuming building, seemingly little more than a single story hovel, but actually, just the top of the sunken *Ca' Vecchia* council chamber tower.

Malvagio watched from the bow of the Scylla as Primo stepped up beside him. "Boss, we found them, but…why? We no need them anymore."

Malvagio stared out coldly over the water. "We do not. But when we crush the Gondoliers, we will crush the magic. And then…no one will stand between me and my city."

Malvagio signalled to his V-Troopers. They nodded. A sturdy barge with a massive bronze battering ram on its prow steamed forward toward the Gondolier tower. Primo watched uncertainly. How would crushing the Gondoliers get them closer to the treasure? Malvagio and this whole undertaking were making less and less sense to Primo with each passing day.

Inside, Cosimo stepped up to join the other Gondoliers as they readied themselves for the V-Trooper assault. "Remember, we have the advantage here. This is our home, and there is nothing they can send our way that we cannot defeat." The Gondoliers cheered, their voices rising up through the tower.

Up above, the V-Troopers hesitated, then unexpectedly stepped back from the railing and retreated the way they had come. Joe and Eva exchanged a puzzled look. Cosimo wondered. "Well, that seemed a little too easy."

Suddenly, an explosion rocked the chamber. Stone and timber fell in a shower of debris down the center of the tower. The Gondoliers ducked for cover as a rushing sound swelled above them. Cosimo looked up with a grave expression. "Oh no."

The battering ram barge backed away from the tower, as the dust of debris cleared. Malvagio smiled. A gaping hole had been bashed through the side wall, and now, a torrent of lagoon water was rushing in.

Gondoliers leapt over railings and retreated down stairs as a gushing waterfall poured down on top of them. Cosimo raced toward a tunnel corridor, calling for the others to follow. "Fall back!" Joe, Eva and the remaining Gondoliers hurried after him as the flood of water chased them down.

Enzo opened the hatch door of his Rapid Transit Tube and threw a small pack of items into the back of the gondola capsule.

Outside, the roar of rushing water swelled. Enzo hesitated. 'Find a way to help Fantina.' That was what Cosimo had told him to do. He gave his laboratory one last look then leapt into the gondola capsule. Somehow, he felt that whatever was happening outside, he would not be coming back here for a while…if ever again. He had always believed that change was coming, and that change was a good thing, but right now, all he would have hoped for was for things to remain as they had always been. Enzo reached out and closed the hatch door, and moments later, the pressurized roar of water through the tube whisked him away to safety.

Cosimo led the Gondoliers out past the statues of the old sentinels, a wave of lagoon water, already knee-deep, rushing in around them. Suddenly he paused, noting a cluster of bundles drifting down from the lagoon surface outside the glass dome. Cosimo's eyes widened. With a sense that time had finally run out, Cosimo raised his arms, motioning desperately to the remaining Gondoliers. "Hurry!"

Just then, the bundles touched down on the top of the dome…and exploded. Glass shattered. Water, or rather, what seemed like the entire Venetian lagoon, came pouring down in a violent rush. Gondoliers got trapped in the sudden deluge and were swept away through arches and doorways.

Cosimo dove for the entrance to the Archives building and pulled desperately on the door. He strained against the weight of the water crushing against it and against him. Above the entrance, the sculpted keystone lion stared out over the *piazza* with what seemed a sad expression, the sentinels and ancient buildings…the world of the Gondoliers, would soon disappear, swallowed by time and the waters of the Venetian lagoon.

CHAPTER TWENTY-FIVE — OUTLAWS

A gondola drifted in a narrow canal, empty and abandoned, as a distant bell tolled. It was a new day, a dim and desolate day. A shuttered window swayed in the morning breeze, its hinges creaking ominously as if lamenting its age. The paved walkways and *piazzas* shimmered in the rising sun, but not with anything remotely magical. They were simply wet. A thin layer of lagoon water flowed over them now, everywhere throughout Venice, the tide seemed to have risen...or perhaps turned. A low, rumbling noise echoed across the water, rippling the surface as the heavy, stone walls of ancient buildings seemed to shift, settling ever so slightly.

In the *palazzo* prison, the stone walls dripped with moisture, droplets that traced their way down the thin cracks in the mortar to deposit themselves in puddles on the cold floor. The faint strains of a harmonica drifted in the air past the heavy, iron bars of prison cells filled with 'outlaws,' newly arrested in Malvagio's push for complete and unchallenged control.

In one of the cells, Fantina paced anxiously, while Contessa completed her doleful dirge on her harmonica with a flourish. Contessa looked up, listening for some applause, but got only a few coughs and a sneeze. She frowned. "Tough crowd."

Fantina pressed herself against the bars of her cell to look down the corridor. At one end, a stone stairway led up to sunlight, down the other way were more cells and deepening shadow. Fantina could see faces in the cells beyond, confused, disheartened, unsure. She paused as she spotted a prisoner slumped in the shadows in the furthest cell. He looked weary, and familiar… "Uncle Gio?" Fantina called.

The prisoner moved into a sliver of light reflecting off the damp stone floor. Uncle Gio rubbed his stubbled face. "Fantina? Are you all right?"

"Sure. I've been in worse fixes," she reassured him. Fantina couldn't quite think of any at the moment, but she thought it best to fake it for now.

"I am sorry, Fantina."

"No, no. Me and 'trouble' are good friends, remember?"

"But if I had told you sooner, you would have been ready."

"Told me?" Fantina asked. "Ready for what?"

Uncle Gio leaned close to the bars of his cell and locked Fantina in a glance. "I tried to hide this world from you...deny it. I was glad when your father decided to leave it behind."

Fantina hesitated, suddenly understanding. "He was a Gondolier."

Uncle Gio nodded. "Many years ago."

Fantina thought back to everything that had happened and all the stories her father had told her. Of course he was. Contessa considered as well, an uncertain look on her face. Even if she didn't remember Fantina's father, she had always sensed that there was...something about Fantina herself.

Fantina scanned her cell, thinking. "Don't worry, Uncle Gio. We're going to get out of here."

"Oh, I think not." The voice was followed by an unnerving chattering noise that Fantina recognized immediately. Malvagio stepped into view from the stone stairway, his white rat perched on his shoulder.

"Look who came to visit," Contessa said as they paused before her cell, "a dirty, good-for-nothing rat…" Malvagio's rat bared her teeth. "Oh," Contessa noted, "and a little, white mouse too." Contessa laughed. "It is a joke. You see…there is the rat…" she said, pointing to Malvagio, "…and the mouse," she continued, pointing to Malvagio's pet. "*Eh?*"

Malvagio eyed Contessa coldly, not amused.

Contessa sighed, "*Beh*, never mind."

"Joke if you want," Malvagio sneered, "but tonight, I will be the only one laughing." Malvagio glanced down the dark corridor of cells with a grin. "So much for the Gondoliers."

Fantina faced Malvagio defiantly. "They'll come for us."

Malvagio laughed. "No. I am afraid they are a bit swamped at the moment, and after the Mayor's ball this evening, things are going to be very different around here."

Contessa wiped her hand across the damp walls of the cell. "Yes…wetter," she quipped. "Venice is sinking. No Glim to hold back the ruin of time. You will be treading water by midnight." The rat leapt from Malvagio's shoulder and scampered away. Contessa chuckled. "Even your little friend can recognize a sinking ship."

Suddenly, Malvagio reached through the bars of the cell and grabbed Contessa roughly by the neck. "The Venice problem will be taken care of," he seethed. "Believe me."

Fantina rushed forward, pushing herself between Malvagio and Contessa. "Stop, let her go," she pleaded. She glanced down the corridor at the others in their cells, and caught Uncle Gio in a glance. "Let them all go, and I'll help you find the treasure."

Malvagio released Contessa and stared at Fantina, wickedly amused. "The treasure? Oh, no need to worry about that," he grinned. "I will uncover the treasure in my own way."

Malvagio locked eyes with Fantina coldly, his stare darker and more cruel than it had ever seemed before. But he paused. There was something...in Fantina's eyes that he couldn't understand. Even here in a dank cell from which she would never leave, there was...an unwillingness to accept what seemed painfully obvious. There was hope.

"They cannot help you," Malvagio said plainly. "No one can help you. The time of the Gondoliers is over, and Venice will cower before me. It is my time now." Fantina hesitated and shrunk back from the evil of Malvagio's stare. He turned and strode away up the stairwell.

Fantina grasped the bars of her cell resolutely. "We have to save Venice, no matter the cost."

Uncle Gio nodded, but Contessa looked concerned. "What is it?" Fantina asked.

Contessa hesitated, her eyes deep in thought. "He said he'll uncover the treasure 'his own way.' I am just wondering…at what cost *that* will be."

Seabirds roosting on sandbars between the Venetian lagoon and the sea looked up, suddenly attentive, as a steam-powered rumble disturbed the tranquility of early evening. Nearby, at the *Lido* inlet, a massive iron sea wall rose from beneath the water. Gears ground noisily as the wall locked into position, closing the inlet between the lagoon and the Adriatic, and shutting out the tide.

A little further to the south, at the *Malamocco* inlet, a similar wall rose to block out the sea as well. A third wall locked into place at the *Chioggia* inlet. Venice was now cut off, the three waterways into the Venetian lagoon, sealed.

But Malvagio's Gatekeeper Project was not quite finished. Beneath the surface, near each of the sturdy, iron walls that held out the sea, a great cloud of sediment stirred. Lagoon water swirled, drawn with incredible force into an enormous drainage pipe that snaked across the lagoon bottom, into a massive, steam-powered piston. The piston pumped the churning water on through to a second pipe out beyond the sea wall where it emerged, bubbling and sputtering into the Adriatic Sea. The lagoon was being drained.

CHAPTER TWENTY-SIX — PARADISE

Bathed in a dim sunset, a parade of elegant, water-taxis steamed along the *Riva Degli Schiavoni,* arriving at the quay before the Ducal Palace. On board, Venetian high society, city officials and dignitaries in elaborate costumes and masks, crowded forward, eager to attend the Mayor's annual *Carnevale* Ball.

Attendants in formal finery stepped in to help the invited guests from their boats which, for some reason, seemed to be docking a bit lower than usual along the stone landing of the *molo*. The tide was low, so low in fact, that the mooring posts to which the boats were tied seemed…exposed, barnacle encrusted and fragile.

The guests proceeded from the quay to the palace entrance where a crowd of locals gathered to watch the arrivals. A tall, bearded photographer, hefting his unwieldy, plate camera, jockeyed for position to get some candid shots of the attending luminaries. Some waved, others hurried past, but all noted the column of intimidating V-Troopers that lined the walkway to the palace to keep the uninvited from mingling with the privileged.

The *piazzetta* beside the Ducal Palace was filled with locals, blocked from the ball but intent, nevertheless, on celebrating the last day of *Carnevale*. V-Troopers, however, patrolled the entire area—on the lookout for anything they deemed suspicious. A man in a lion mask was immediately seized and dragged away, as stunned revelers were pushed aside.

Up above, the last glow of daylight faded over the rooftops as a lone, white pigeon, Bianca, fluttered to the clock tower ledge. She landed beside Leo, still as stone, and wondered if she could dare to hope for his return when the sun dipped away beyond the horizon.

Then, as the sky faded to night, a dim glow pulsed weakly and began to flow over the city. But unlike before, it quickly dissipated into a barely perceptible flickering mist. Bianca shook her feathers, struggling, but was unable to transform. She looked up sadly. Leo remained motionless, without a glimmer of life.

The procession of the Mayor's guests lined up before the Paper Gate of the Ducal Palace to present their exclusive tickets and enter the palace grounds. Standing close against one of the slender, marble columns before the palace, a masked guest in a flowing black cape watched and waited patiently. It was Enzo, looking for an opportunity.

V-Troopers, positioned at the gate, waved the photographer in but stopped a costumed count who couldn't seem to find his ticket for the ball. Despite his protest that he had been pick-pocketed, the V-Troopers marched him away to some dark holding cell to join the other suspicious detainees of the evening.

Enzo shrugged, half apologetically, as he pulled the missing ticket from his own pocket and merged into the procession of invited guests.

The palace courtyard was decorated grandly with banners and golden lights washing the Italian Gothic architecture in a festive glow. Guests milled about freely but under the watchful surveillance of V-Troopers positioned in each archway of the second floor *loggia* open to the courtyard below.

Then, Mayor Grimani, masked and costumed in garish renaissance garb, emerged from the palace through the Golden Staircase which was flanked by the two imposing statues of Hercules and Atlas. The mayor paused a moment to eye their impressive physiques, then tug the tips of his mustache self-consciously. Why did there have to be so many statues of big, strapping gods and heroes throughout the palace? Every staircase, every alcove...it was so stressful trying to measure up. The mayor straightened his silk topcoat and shirt ruffles before proceeding quickly to the railing of the *loggia* to look out over his guests.

"Welcome," he proclaimed as the courtyard below fell silent. "Welcome to you all on this festive evening of *Carnevale*. I am happy that despite all the recent unpleasantness in and about the city, you have all come to celebrate...the new Venice." The mayor raised his arms triumphantly, as the photographer below snapped a picture. Guests applauded tentatively, surrounded as they were by the expressionless, masked V-Trooper faces.

In the *palazzo* prison, Fantina, Contessa and Uncle Gio strained to hear the faint applause that drifted in through the stairwell at the end of the corridor where a stationed V-Trooper stood watch. Suddenly, a noise, like a pebble on the stone floor, drew the V-Trooper's attention. Fantina scanned the darkness uncertainly, then raised an eyebrow in surprise. Behind the V-Trooper, approaching from the prison stairwell, was a short boat paddle, floating in mid-air. Contessa turned to Fantina curiously, but Fantina nodded with a grin. "Watch this."

The V-Trooper, as if sensing the impending impact, turned just as the paddle swung downward and cracked him across the mask. He collapsed to the ground, out cold.

A static charge suddenly flashed and faded to reveal Enzo wearing the G-1000 Gondosuit. "Fanticulous!" Fantina smiled.

Enzo quickly grabbed the key from the fallen V-Trooper and rushed over to unlock all the cells. "Go up the stairs to the right," he explained as the people flowed out into the prison corridor. "Grab something from the *Carnevale* costume exhibit, and sneak out through the crowd."

Uncle Gio looked up approvingly as Enzo unlocked his cell. He shared a quick look with Fantina as she entered to help him to his feet. "All right," he admitted, "he is a good boy. You can be 'sidetracked' a little for that one."

Fantina smiled. "Let's go."

Enzo, in his Gondosuit, peeked around the gilded door jamb at the entrance to the Great Council Hall. All was quiet. He motioned for the others to follow as he crept stealthily into the chamber.

Uncle Gio stepped in next, outfitted in a traditional *Arlecchino* costume—colorful, jacquard doublet and a floppy, feathered hat. Contessa, followed in a blue and white *Colombina* dress with a flirty, flounced skirt and a snugly fitted bodice. She gave her outfit a twirl as she entered, quite pleased. "I like it," she smiled.

Uncle Gio caught himself staring and looked away awkwardly clearing his throat. "Uh...yes. Very nice."

Enzo motioned from the door across the chamber. "This way. The Mayor is still making his speech. We can get out—" Enzo paused. "Where is Fantina?" he asked.

"Do not worry," Contessa said. "She is coming. I think she is maybe having a little trouble with her costume."

"Trouble?" Enzo wondered.

"The style," Contessa explained. "It is a bit of a change for her."

Then, from a dark stairwell just outside the Council Hall, Fantina emerged. An exquisite, satin ball gown flowed from her shoulders to the floor. The bodice was beaded in pearls, the skirt draped with a sweep of sheer silk that swayed as she walked creating an illusion of waves swirling about her. Her hair sparkled with glitter and a jeweled tiara which connected to a delicate, silver mask over her eyes.

Contessa smiled knowingly as Enzo stepped toward Fantina. He hesitated, searching for the right words. "You look—"

"Don't say it," Fantina interrupted.

"—like magic," Enzo blurted out. Fantina paused. She wasn't quite sure how to respond to an observation like that. In all her travels she had never once looked like anything that anyone would have compared to…'magic.' With her dusty jacket and her cap pulled low over her eyes, she was more used to looking like…'trouble.' And yet… A subtle smile crept across Fantina's face, when suddenly—

"What is this?" Uncle Gio stood in a puddle of water beside Malvagio's miniature model of the Venetian lagoon. Contessa, Enzo and Fantina crossed over to take a look. Water was dripping from a hole punched through the bottom, and the lagoon was dry. "So that is his plan. He is going to drain Venice."

"To find the treasure…in his own way," Fantina concluded.

Uncle Gio looked to Fantina. "Unless we find it first."

Fantina crinkled her nose, reaching back into her memory, piecing together the clues from the journal. "...will point the way to traitor's home..."

Uncle Gio nodded. "You went to church in *Murano*, of *Santa Maria* and *San Donato*—"

"The one with the bones..." Enzo said. "Yes, but we found nothing."

"No," Fantina said, "it points the way." She looked to Uncle Gio hopefully.

"The church was restored by the architect Filippo Calendario," Uncle Gio explained, "who was arrested in 1355 for plotting with the *Doge*, Marino Faliero."

"Plotting what?" Enzo asked.

"Treason," Uncle Gio said. "He planned to throw out the city's authorities and take over all of Venice."

Contessa scoffed. "Does that sound like anyone we know?"

Fantina nodded. "So what happened?"

"He was arrested, tried and sentenced," Uncle Gio explained.

Contessa made a face and mimed a beheading with a finger slash to her throat. "He lost his head out there on the Giants' Staircase."

Fantina turned to Enzo. "The *Doge* was the traitor."

Enzo looked confused. "So, the traitor's home—"

"We are standing in it," Contessa completed the thought.

Uncle Gio turned to Fantina. "The poem. Do you remember the next part?"

Fantina closed her eyes, recalling her father's story. "Where Paradise, before you lies; Hidden beneath the starry skies."

"Paradise?" Enzo scratched his head, still not following.

Uncle Gio crossed toward a painted fresco at the far end of the room, a dark scene of a nighttime battle on the lagoon that covered the entire wall. "'Paradise' is the name of a painting done by an artist named Guariento in 1355 to decorate the Great Council Hall of the Ducal Palace..."

Enzo eyed the painting skeptically. "That is his idea of paradise?"

Uncle Gio shook his head. "No, it was painted over years ago. Guariento's 'Paradise' is beneath." Fantina smiled. Enzo watched curiously as Uncle Gio pulled Fantina's x-ray gizmo from his pocket and handed it to her. "Okay Fantina, do not blow it up."

Fantina took her ray-o-scope in hand and cranked it. An electric hum swelled as a faint cone of light beamed against the wall. Uncle Gio took a step back, lowering his hands again to protect his…vital organs. Enzo noticed and nervously followed suit.

Fantina angled the magnifying glass to cast a wider beam. The cone of light grew. Suddenly, the painted images faded, revealing a different painting underneath.

It was a scene of ancient Venice, but bright and fantastic. Leo and a flock of *fate* patrolled the sky; frogmen stood at attention along the shore; Gondoliers navigated near the quay while bright-bannered sailing vessels crisscrossed through the lagoon. "It's beautiful," Fantina nodded.

Then, in the background of the painting, off in the distance beyond the island of *San Giorgio Maggiore*, a stone monastery atop a small island became visible. The rising sun in the painting gleamed over the glistening stone walls and created a sunburst effect that vaguely resembled—

"X marks the spot," Primo crowed as he stepped into the Great Council Hall. V-Troopers followed, appearing in every doorway to block any escape.

Then Malvagio entered, eying Fantina and the secret scene revealed by her x-ray gadget. "Good of you to join the party."

Fantina quickly lowered her device. The image faded and returned to the painted battle scene. Malvagio stepped close, however, grabbed Fantina's hand and aimed the device back up at the wall. The monastery marked by the bright 'X' reappeared. Malvagio smiled. "At last. I have found it."

Primo, however, scratched his head with a little less confidence, looking from the painting to the drained model before him. "Are you sure? I no see that island here anywhere, boss."

The cone of light and the electric hum faded as Malvagio released his grip on Fantina. Uncle Gio pulled Fantina back, stepping defensively between her and Malvagio. "The lagoon has changed over the years," Uncle Gio explained. "Land has shifted. Islands disappear in the tide."

Malvagio tossed a glance at his model, then back at Fantina and Uncle Gio. His eyes flared, his obsession had fully taken hold and was about to pay off. "Yes. But soon, they will appear again." Malvagio laughed wickedly as Uncle Gio held Fantina close.

CHAPTER TWENTY-SEVEN — LOW TIDE

Under a black sky dotted with stars and lit only by the thinnest sliver of a new moon, water lapped at the sides of boats docked at the quay before the Ducal Palace. The water level, however, was well below the dock itself. Posts, covered in green algae and barnacles, now exposed to the air, creaked ominously as the boat tethers tightened around their necks, pulling them toward the muddy, lagoon bottom. All along the shoreline, the exposed foundations of Venice were leaking mud and sediment, slowly crumbling into the rapidly disappearing lagoon.

The ground beneath the feet of the guests at the ball suddenly shuddered. A web of cracks in the stone pavement shot out across the palace courtyard. Guests looked up at the Mayor with concern.

Just then, Malvagio and Primo emerged from the palace onto the *loggia* behind the Mayor. Fantina, Enzo, Uncle Gio and Contessa marched out as well between two columns of V-Troopers. The Mayor steadied himself on the railing uncertainly. "*Signore* Malvagio, something is happening. What is going on?"

Malvagio strode forward to the railing to address the guests below. "Do not worry. Everything is going according to plan."

"What plan?" the Mayor fumbled.

Malvagio turned pointedly to the Mayor. "There are going to be a few changes around here, starting with you." The Mayor stared at Malvagio, confused. Two V-Troopers stepped up on either side of the Mayor and seized him as murmurs of shock and confusion rose from below. Malvagio raised his hands to silence the crowd. "Venice needs a new vision for a new century," he proclaimed.

The Mayor struggled, but remained captive. "What new vision?" he demanded.

Malvagio closed his eyes, breathing in deeply as if he could smell the rising fear throughout the courtyard below and the city beyond. "My vision. One...with less water."

With that, he signalled to Primo who reached up and pulled a lever at the edge of the railing releasing a large banner that unfurled along the far end of the courtyard wall. It was a grand rendering of Venice and the surrounding lagoon area, but in place of the lagoon...was dry land. The space had been filled, parcelled off and built up with new homes, estates, merchant market centers and exclusive tourist resorts. Malvagio raised his arms to take it all in. "Under my rule, as your new *Doge*, Venice will become great once again, with a bright, new future."

The Mayor, still held fast, protested. "You cannot do this. Venice is protected—"

"By what?" Malvagio cut him off. "The Gondoliers? With thanks to you, that world is all but gone."

The guests below reeled in shock. Then, the photographer stepped out from behind his camera. He pulled off his beard to reveal a devilish goatee beneath. It was Cosimo. "But not gone yet," he announced.

V-Troopers started forward toward Cosimo when suddenly, another guest stepped forward, then another. They removed their masks—Eva and Jester Joe. Joe looked up to the loggia with an appreciative nod, Enzo's copper-tubed breathing gizmo in hand. Enzo smiled.

Malvagio seemed amused. "So, it seems that some of you managed to cheat death. But, do you think there are enough of you to challenge me?"

Cosimo considered. Guests exchanged glances, then began to step forward as well, removing their masks. Some were Gondoliers who had survived the attack on their headquarters; others were old-timers, perhaps Gondoliers of an earlier age; still others were simply guests at the ball, willing to take a stand.

Enzo tapped his ear, activating his Marconi earbud transmitter and sharing a look with Cosimo. "Maybe tonight, we are all a little bit Gondoliers." Cosimo nodded.

Malvagio frowned and motioned to his V-Troopers. "Seize them."

V-Troopers advanced, leveling their rifles at the crowd, when suddenly, Cosimo threw off his cloak, revealing his hands, now outfitted with Enzo's flame-throwing gauntlets. With a flick of his wrist, Cosimo shot an arc of fire out at the V-Troopers who stopped in their tracks.

Up in the *loggia*, Fantina nodded to Enzo. "That is soooo 'him.'"

Enzo grinned, "Just wait…"

Just then, down below, all the 'Gondoliers' threw back their capes and costumes as well. They were all armed with an array of strange and fanciful weaponry from Enzo's arsenal of inventions: gondola bow iron scimitars; portable, steam-powered water canons; gear and pulley slingshot contraptions…

Uncle Gio nodded, impressed. "Very Verne."

"Absolutely," Fantina agreed.

Enzo smiled proudly. "I finished my tweaks," he explained as he flicked his wrists forward. Two electrodes, shaped like tuning forks, slid out from his sleeves and locked into position on the back of his hands. An electric hum zipped from a power belt around his waist down his arms and sparked a mini lightning bolt at his fingertips. Fantina smiled.

The V-Troopers hesitated—surrounded, outnumbered and out-weaponized. They dropped their rifles in dismay.

"Idiots!" Malvagio fumed. "You think you can trot out your desperate little gang with their pathetic, little gadgets and win the battle? I will show you an army."

Malvagio looked up at the perimeter wall of the palace, raising his arms wide as if summoning all that was dark and evil. Hundreds upon hundreds of rats appeared, silhouetted against the starry night sky, eyes glinting, scampering into position to surround the courtyard.

Fantina joined Enzo as he stepped up to shield Contessa and Uncle Gio.

Cosimo and the Gondoliers below squared up to face the impending attack, while the ball guests retreated a step in alarm. Malvagio looked down on them with contempt and a superior grin that could only be described as...aristocratic. "Your Glim has faded beyond all hope. It is time for fear to take over. And fear is much more powerful."

With that, the dark shapes along the wall began to change. Bathed in the murky night, the rats swelled, transforming into an army of ratters, bigger and meaner than before. Malvagio's white rat scurried down to stand beside him as her form altered and she became his sinewy ratter captain. She shrieked, red eyes glaring.

The ratter army swarmed downward, claws digging into the stone walls as they charged. Gondoliers rushed forward to fight.

A handful of ratters leapt into the second floor *loggia*. Enzo spun, loosing a discharge of electrical jolts that zapped them back over the railing. Down below, Cosimo ducked and fired, scorching a throng of advancing ratters with a wall of flame. Ratter squeals filled the courtyard.

Gondolier acrobats flipped and tumbled, bow iron scimitars flashing. Jester Joe swung his water canon toward a column of ratters and blasted them soundly through an archway into a stone wall. Eva swung her silk cords like bullwhips snapping ratters down in their tracks.

Uncle Gio stumbled backward as a ratter lunged for him. He was trapped with nowhere to retreat. The ratter closed in, claws raised and ready to slash, when suddenly…

"Hey you," Fantina called. The ratter turned just in time to see a boat oar smash him across the face. Fantina completed her swing, looking quite pleased. "Pretty handy with an oar, I'd say."

Uncle Gio nodded, but suddenly spotted a ratter charging at Fantina. "Behind you!" he warned. Fantina spun on the instant, swinging her oar and connecting with the second ratter as it lunged. Fantina looked dumbfounded at the oar in her hands, then up at Uncle Gio. "It must be a family thing," Uncle Gio suggested.

Just then, another low rumble shook the ground. A large crack opened down the center of the courtyard as people dove to one side or the other.

Malvagio rushed down the front staircase protected by his ratter soldiers as an enormous, armored vehicle tore into the palace courtyard. Fantina looked closer. It was Malvagio's Scylla, but modified with large tractor treads mounted over the paddle wheels so that it could travel on dry land. Malvagio climbed aboard with Primo, his ratter captain and a dozen ratter soldiers, as the vehicle turned and ground away, out of the palace, crashing through the Paper Gate. The other ratter soldiers retreated as well, scurrying away after Malvagio.

Cosimo shot a burst of fire at the retreating ratters as the Gondoliers regrouped. Contessa and Uncle Gio approached down the main staircase as Joe and Eva joined Cosimo near the gate. "They are leaving," Joe called out victoriously.

"No," Contessa corrected, "they are getting away."

Cosimo looked about, assessing his gathered Gondoliers. "We cannot let Malvagio escape. We have to stop him now, before it is too late." Cosimo looked up to the second floor *loggia* and locked Enzo in a determined glance, flexing his fire fingers. "With Enzo's help, we have the advantage. So, we finish this, no matter the cost."

Enzo nodded, standing a bit taller. No matter the cost, he was ready.

The stone pavement of the *piazzetta San Marco* crumbled and cracked as the Scylla tore away, racing toward the quay. Guests poured out of the Ducal Palace courtyard as the ground shuddered again and pieces from the lace-like cornice broke and crashed to the ground.

Suddenly, a window on the second floor of the palace shattered outward. Enzo, pole-vaulting out at the top of a gondolier sweep, flew toward the Scylla as it sped off the boat landing and disappeared over the edge.

Uncle Gio, Contessa, Cosimo and the other Gondoliers rushed forward but stopped short as they peered out over the lagoon, stunned. It was empty, or, more accurately, drained of its water for as far as the eye could see. Only puddles and small pools remained, boats resting on their sides at the bottom. And speeding away across the muddy lagoon bed, were Malvagio and his massive ratter army, with Enzo clinging to the back of the Scylla.

Cosimo started forward, then tapped his earbud transmitter. "Enzo!" he called urgently. But before he got a response, a section of the walkway by the royal gardens eroded, collapsing into the empty lagoon. People leapt back, terrified.

Contessa stepped up beside Cosimo. She looked concerned, but certain. "Without water, Venice will crumble."

"We need more help," Cosimo acknowledged as he turned to Uncle Gio.

Uncle Gio suddenly paused, an uncertain look on his face. He looked about. "Where did Fantina go?"

CHAPTER TWENTY-EIGHT — HELP

The star-filled sky shimmered above the clock tower, as Fantina stepped carefully down onto the ledge near the top. A brisk wind whistled past, catching the bottom hem of her ball gown on the stone edge. Fantina tugged at it, ripping free of her top skirt but losing her balance and grip. She reached out as she stumbled, grabbing onto a stone shape moments before falling off the ledge. She paused. It was the statue of Leo. Fantina looked into his still and lifeless eyes, searching for some sign of his warmth and wisdom. "Wake up! You have to wake up," she pleaded. "Venice needs your help. The Gondoliers need your help."

It was an odd plea for Fantina. She felt that maybe she should ask for more, but asking for help was new to her. On her own, she had always been secure in herself. She remembered from early on, looking up into the eyes of her parents, both of them, and knowing that she would always be safe. Traveling the world with them she had felt the strength of their love—like a gentle, glowing wave within her. Her father had taught her to be strong, to be confident of her place in the world, wherever that place might be. But now, on the rim of the clock tower overlooking Venice below, she felt alone. Fantina leaned close to Leo, desperate...determined. "Please. You have to come back."

The Gondoliers, led by Cosimo, charged out onto the lagoon bed, moving as quickly as they could over the muddy terrain. They were a small force, fifty at best, heading toward the ratter army which flowed like a vast wave behind Malvagio's fleeing Scylla. Under the stars before the crumbling shoreline of the city, it would be an extraordinary clash on an epic, surreal battlefield.

On the Scylla, Primo spotted the charging Gondoliers and pointed out the challenge to Malvagio. "Boss, it no look like they are beyond all hope." Malvagio scoffed, maddened by their persistence.

Then suddenly, Enzo pulled himself up onto the deck. He rose to his feet and confidently flicked his stun guns into place with a spark. "Not at all," he confirmed.

A dozen ratters on deck lunged. Enzo advanced, spinning, stunning and clearing the deck. Primo shrank back as Enzo paused before Malvagio, a spark dancing at his fingertips. "The Gondoliers would like to have a word with you," he said.

Just then, Enzo's spark sputtered and fizzled out. Enzo considered awkwardly. "So, when you get a free moment maybe you could stop by."

Two ratters scampered up and seized Enzo from behind, as the ratter captain emerged from below deck. Her red eyes locked Enzo in a chilling stare and she prowled over to him raising a vicious claw toward his throat. She glanced at Malvagio, awaiting the order. Enzo stared at Malvagio defiantly. Malvagio nodded.

The ratter captain snarled then slashed, ripping Enzo's electrode power belt from around his waist and shoving Enzo to the deck at Malvagio's feet. Malvagio then waved her off. "Go, join the others. Make sure no one else follows."

The ratter captain nodded, backing away from Enzo reluctantly. She swept over the edge of the Scylla with her troops and scurried off to join the rest of the ratter army in the middle of the dry lagoon as they turned to face the approaching Gondoliers. The ratter captain looked out over the battlefield, her eyes fierce…and ready.

Cosimo eyed the ratter force warily. It would be his fifty Gondoliers versus over five hundred. Not the best odds, he admitted, but it would be a valiant last stand. He exchanged a determined nod with Joe and Eva, then tossed a final glance back toward Contessa and Uncle Gio watching from the crumbling quay. Venice was dying. They had to fight. There was no going back.

Exposed wooden pylons splintered as a huge section of the boat landing collapsed into the muddy lagoon basin. In *Piazza San Marco* a violent shudder shook the square. Paving stones buckled and ripped open at the base of the towering *campanile* before the basilica. People cowered as walls popped and settled, and then, the *campanile* collapsed in a cloud of dust.

Up above, on the clock tower, Fantina closed her eyes, still clinging tightly to Leo's neck. Venice was crumbling, and now, more than anything, she wanted to stand and protect it. It was…home. A single tear ran down Fantina's cheek and splashed on Leo's stone mane, as a peal of thunder rumbled in the distance. "Please," she whispered, "we need you. *I* need you."

Suddenly, Fantina paused. A glow, like a fine mist of flickering stardust, began circling gently around her. She looked out over the rooftops. A glistening wave slowly rose from the city below. It swirled up toward her, as a light drizzle began to fall from the sky above. Raindrops joined her tear on Leo's mane, washing the stone and mingling with the rising mist, the rising Glim.

Fantina stood, raising her arms as the Glim accelerated around her. Then suddenly, it flashed and flowed outward like a glowing shockwave across the sky, refracting through the rain from raindrop to raindrop in every direction, tracing an intricate pattern over the city like a delicate veil of lace. Fantina's eyes widened in awe. She moved her hands in the flow and directed it outward with her downturned palms as it pulsed and swept over the rooftops and beyond.

Glowing raindrops dotted the bronze backs of Nicos, Dimitris and the other two *Quadriga* horses on the basilica's balcony. Other sculptures throughout Venice were misted as well —every bronze in every alcove, every stone figure on every ornate cornice, every glass statuette in *Murano*.

The statues of Hercules and Atlas, flanking the doorway to the Golden Staircase, like those of Mars and Neptune at the top of the Giants' Staircase, stood motionless as waves of Glim flashed around them. Somehow, in the throbbing glow, their faces seemed changed, as if lit by feeling, stirred with hope.

In the ruined courtyard of the Gondolier headquarters, ravaged by the lagoon waters but now drained dry, the time-polished statues of the sentinels stood silently. Exposed to the night sky above, the bull, eagle, she-wolf…their finely-chiseled faces still covered in a sheen of seawater, were still as stone, but somehow their expressions seemed oddly aware. The air around them seemed to brighten with a mist of flickering stardust, reflected in their damp eyes. And then, Gen, the Griffin of Genoa, her stern gaze locked over centuries of time…blinked.

On the clock tower, the two Bronze Moor statues suddenly began to move, but this time, there was nothing mechanical about it. The first statue, Ding, set his hammer down, looking about blankly as if having just woken from a long nap. "Ah, nothing like a little beauty sleep," he yawned.

The second statue, Dong, trying to work out a crick in his neck, cast Ding a sideward glance. "Yes? Well you had better go back to sleep then. It did not work."

Ding paused, his eyes drooping, his expression still blank. "Huh?"

"Well at least it is raining," Dong continued. "I need a shower. I feel like I am covered in pigeon—"

"Shhhh—" Ding interrupted, alerted to someone's presence nearby. "Who goes there?"

Fantina popped her head up over the edge of the tower. "You're awake," she said, eyes wide with surprise.

Ding looked at Fantina suspiciously. "Yes. Your point is —?"

"Ding, do not be rude," Dong interjected. He leaned over to offer Fantina a hand. "You are needing some help?" Fantina took his hand and Dong lifted her effortlessly onto the top of the tower.

"Yes, we need a lot of help," Fantina explained. "Venice is under attack."

Ding leaned forward excitedly, "Again? It's that short French fellow, right?"

Dong swatted Ding on the head, ringing him like a bell, "Napoleon, Ding. His name was Napoleon. But you know, historically he actually was not as short as people say."

Ding groaned. "Boring! You have been talking to that horse again…" He turned to Fantina to elaborate. "I heard it was a very stressful time for him."

Dong raised a hand to argue, then shook his head instead. He turned back to Fantina. "So sorry. He is still a little groggy. I think we have been out for a while."

Just then, a familiar voice interrupted the moment. "Too long," the voice said. Fantina turned. Leo, golden mane flowing, wings spread wide, was poised at the tower's edge.

"Leo!" Fantina beamed. "You came back."

Ding scratched his bronze head. "Why, where did he go?"

Leo stepped close to Fantina. "We were lost in the ordinary ending of an ordinary tale. But now, the Glim has been raised again, and thanks to you Fantina, things are about to get fanticulous."

Ding and Dong exchanged a confused look. "Fanticu… Is that good?"

Fantina smiled, "Oh yeah."

"Boys," Leo directed, "ring it in. It is time." Ding and Dong paused uncertainly for a moment, but with a nod from Leo, they raised their hammers…and swung.

Chapter Twenty-Nine — turning the tide

A sonorous chime pealed in the distance, as the Gondoliers and the ratter army rushed at each other across the muddy lagoon bottom. The trampled trail of a thousand ratter feet pitted the battlefield between the two sides with a hammered, other-worldly appearance. Cosimo, leading his Gondoliers, raised his hands, ready to scorch a path through the enemy line. The ratter captain shrieked her commands, driving her troops onward.

They plowed into each other midway through the lagoon, mud spattering, flames bursting, water canons blasting, blades and claws slashing. The Gondoliers, though badly outnum-

311

bered, held their own for a while, wielding Enzo's arsenal of inventions with skilled precision, but the ratters pushed back like an unrelenting wave against their foe.

On the crumbling quay, Mayor Grimani stared out at the battle, surrounded by both guests from the ball and locals who had gathered on the scene. The Mayor slumped with shame in his costume, making himself seem even smaller than he was. He tugged the tips of his mustache glumly. "We are doomed," he fretted. "I have destroyed the magic of Venice." Contessa and Uncle Gio stepped up beside the Mayor, surveying the clash on the lagoon. They shared a worried look, wondering if the Mayor might be right.

Then, a sudden rumble drew everyone's attention back toward the *piazza.* They turned, and gasped in surprise.

Charging forth from *Piazza San Marco*, over the crumbled pavement and through the sky above, a spectacular force of every statue and creature in Venice, alive with the golden pulse of its Glim, moved to defend their city.

Nicos and Dimitris, their bronze manes now alive and flowing in the evening wind, galloped past, leading the *Quadriga* horses and an entire platoon of commando Frogmen into the lagoon. Romulus and Remus, astride the She-Wolf of

Rome, leapt over the crowd and raced out toward the battle. The Bull of Torino charged. The Double-Headed Eagle of Trieste launched itself toward the fray with a blood-curdling battle cry.

The Griffin of Genoa rushed forward as well, her sharp beak glinting in the night. The Mayor seemed stunned. "But, you are the sentinel of Genoa. You fought against us."

Gen paused and turned back to face the Mayor and the others gathered at the quay. "Yes," she said. "But tonight...we all fight for Venice." With that, Gen leapt up and soared out into battle.

Everyone looked up in amazement. The night was alive with a multitude of faeries, a flock of *fate* that nearly blocked out the star-filled sky. With them, a kaleidoscope of butterflies from *Murano* and a squadron of winged lions, some large, some small, from every building cornice and church steeple throughout Venice, swarmed out over the lagoon, all awakened by Fantina's call for help.

And astride Leo himself, bold and confident, was Fantina. Her torn gown flowed about her like a protective cloak, her pearl-studded bodice, shimmering armor. She was no longer just a girl looking to belong. She was a warrior, a leader with a spark of Glim flowing from within. She was there to defend

Venice, as every Gondolier including her father had done before her. It truly was a family thing, she thought to herself.

Leo landed on the edge of the shore before the astonished crowd, as Contessa and Uncle Gio stepped forward to welcome his return. "Well, it is about time," Contessa said. "I was wondering what it was going to take." She leaned close to Fantina, looking deeply into her eyes. "There *is* something about you."

Just then, Ding and Dong, their bell hammers slung over their massive, bronze shoulders, stepped up beside Contessa. Behind them, the now animated, stone, statues of Hercules and Atlas struck a heroic pose as well. The crowd stepped back uneasily before the giant foursome.

"Not to fear, Hercules is here," Hercules called out, hands on his hips, trying to put everyone at ease.

Atlas rolled his eyes. "Oh please. You are not a real demigod you know? And I am not a real titan. We are just statues."

"I know," Hercules said. "But if there is some Herculean task to perform, who is better suited?"

Just then, Mars and Neptune, from the Giants' Staircase, came tromping along to join the fray. "I will avenge the sea," Neptune bellowed.

"To war!" Mars thundered.

Leo turned to Contessa. "We will go after Malvagio. You and the boys should go and...turn the tide." Contessa smiled with a nod.

With Primo at the helm, the Scylla raced forward over the muddy lagoon bed. Enzo, still sprawled on the deck, edged backward as Malvagio advanced on him. "First Venice, then the world," Malvagio laughed wickedly as he aimed his silver-tipped walking stick at Enzo's throat. Enzo glanced over at his stun gun device, now a twisted scrap of metal. He was defense-less and alone. Malvagio sneered. "Did you really think that you could defeat me?"

Enzo hesitated, trapped against the back railing of the Scyl-la. He had no more tricks up his sleeve. Or did he? He shot Malvagio a suddenly confident look, and with a sweep of his hand, he pulled a small, compact, metallic item from the small of his back. With the flick of a spring-loaded button it extend-ed—a sleek and intimidating gondola bow iron scimitar with six razor-sharp, comb-like teeth that snapped into place along the cutting edge. "Yes, I thought I might," Enzo said as he spun the sword in his hand before him.

Malvagio's wicked laugh caught in his throat, his eyes dark and murderous. He unsheathed his rapier from his walking stick and lunged.

Back in the thick of the battle, Cosimo and the other Gondoliers tried to hold their ground, but were driven back. The ratter captain shrieked a command and her troops surged forward on each flank till they had the remaining gondoliers surrounded.

Cosimo's fire gauntlets began to sputter. He checked his fuel belt. A gauge arrow hovered near empty. Cosimo sighed, a resigned look in his eyes as he scanned the enemy forces, still numerous and ready to finish their assault. The ratter captain stared back at Cosimo with a pleased, wicked grin. Nose twitching, teeth gleaming, she prepared to issue the command, when suddenly…

Leaping over the ratter line, the Roman She-Wolf, her fur bristling, tore into the fight with a ferocious growl. The Torino Bull charged through as well, horns-first, plowing over a column of ratters. The sentinels and all of Venice had arrived, rushing in to join the battle. Cosimo looked to the sky, taking it all in, suddenly hopeful.

Faeries and *Murano* butterflies flew interference for the winged lion squadron from above while a herd of glass unicorn figurines stabbed at the ratters' feet from below. The Trieste Eagle, screeching through the night sky, soared to the aid of both Joe and Eva, its two heads picking off two ratters simultaneously. Nicos then galloped in to scoop Joe and Eva up onto his back. And from the direction of the 'cursed isle,' Luigi, Angela and a swarm of misty ghosts, ready for their moment of greatness, charged into the fray. "For destiny!" Luigi cheered.

Dimitris skidded to a halt beside Cosimo. "I am thinking perhaps, you could use lift."

Cosimo nodded and leapt up onto Dimitris' back. "We finish this."

The Adriatic pressed mightily against the outside of the iron sea wall at the *Lido* inlet, but the wall held fast. It was an impressive structure, reinforced with riveted iron bands across its seams—a wide dam holding out the water that Malvagio despised so much.

On the wall, peering through a spyglass, a ratter guard chattered nervously. He could see the skirmish off in the distance but couldn't make out how it was going.

A second ratter arrived and angrily snatched away the spyglass to have a look himself. Looking through, he could see the Gondoliers, now joined by the sentinels, surging against the ratter army. Then suddenly, a face rose into view. The ratter lowered the spyglass to find Ding standing directly before him.

"Time for beauty sleep!" Ding bellowed before smashing his bronze skull into the ratter's face. The ratter stumbled backward, out cold, and fell off the wall into the sea behind it.

The first ratter guard hesitated, its beady, black eyes going wide with surprise at the giant before him. He then shrieked an alarm. Mid shriek, however, a large, bronze hammer struck him full force across the chest. He went tumbling from the wall as well. Dong completed his swing and stepped up beside Ding with a grin. "This is so much better than ringing a bell every hour all day long."

Just then, the remainder of the ratter patrol emerged from Malvagio's Lido watchtower and rushed forward to attack. Ding and Dong exchanged a look and a nod, ready for battle.

They swung their hammers back and forth, sweeping the ratters from the wall as they charged, while Contessa adjusted the antenna of her earbud. "This is Bronze Team," she reported. "We have engaged. How is it going Greek Boy?"

At the second lagoon inlet, Hercules ripped the steam-powered water pump from its cement mount and tossed it aside like a toy, as ratter guards fled in terror. He tapped his earbud. "Hydra-pump is deactivated. My first labor is complete." He then

CHAPTER TWENTY-NINE

tossed a look toward Atlas, approaching the inlet. "It is up to you now, my titan friend."

Atlas shook his head, a bit irked. "Oh great. The weight of the world on my shoulders again…no pressure." Atlas shook off a dozen or so ratter guards as he advanced toward the *Malamocco* sea wall.

On the Scylla, the duel continued. Malvagio advanced mercilessly on Enzo, swinging his blade down hard and forcing Enzo back against the railing. "You cannot win, you know," Malvagio sneered. "The Murk in this world is more powerful than any Glim you might be able to muster." Malvagio laughed wickedly, "You are not even a true Gondolier." Malvagio raised his sword and swung down for a final blow.

Suddenly, Enzo spun his bow iron blade, catching Malvagio's rapier in the comb-like teeth of his weapon. With a twist, he disarmed Malvagio, sending the rapier flying over the edge of the boat. With another slash, Enzo sliced the bottom of Malvagio's breast pocket. The old skeleton key from *Poveglia* dropped out into Enzo's hand. "Maybe not yet, but I will be."

Just then, at the helm, Primo's face went pale. The boat was heading full steam toward the edge of a crater. "Boss, hold on!" he shouted as he throttled back and tried to turn. Malvagio and

Enzo were tossed to the deck, Enzo's sword jarred from his grip.

The Scylla spun, out of control and rumbled over the edge of a large, watery sinkhole in the middle of the Venetian lagoon. It slid toward the bottom where the half-buried ruins of a sunken monastery rose, battered stone walls that had been lost in time, now just visible above the sediment. The boat flipped onto its side near the tip of a buried, stone tower, tossing Malvagio, Primo and Enzo into the mud.

Malvagio eyed the ancient tower and rose slowly to his feet. "It is here," Malvagio beamed greedily. He took a step toward the ruins when suddenly…

A guttural, rasping noise rumbled through the ruins, and a low hiss, like a steaming boiler, swelled around them. Malvagio and Enzo looked about uncertainly, but Primo's eyes widened in fear.

Just then, an enormous reptile, the fiery, red dragon of Marco Polo came slithering around the sunken ruins, hugging the buried walls protectively. Malvagio considered his options quickly, then pushed Primo out in front of himself and dove away to take cover in the ruins.

"Wait," Primo called after him. "I am your right hand, no?" Primo, on his knees, betrayed and alone, looked up with a deluded stare as the dragon loomed over him, the glow of an impending fireball growing at its lips. "Oh no," Primo sighed.

Just as the dragon loosed its fire, Enzo leapt. He tackled Primo out of the way and pulled him to safety behind the shattered hull of the Scylla. They huddled together as the fire licked the hull, heating it bright orange and illuminating the night.

From high above, the burning glow shown like a beacon, reflecting off the sunken ruins, as the dragon slithered around to launch a second attack.

Enzo rose heroically, the metal hull of the Scylla melting around him, as Primo stared up at him in awe. "After all the wicked things I have done over the years," Primo said, "and the danger and trouble I have caused you and your friend...you saved me anyways."

"Well, sure," Enzo acknowledged. "I am—"

"—a Gondolier," Primo said gratefully.

Enzo considered with a nod. Yes, he was. He realized now that he had always been one. It was something that came from within. It was something he would be for the rest of his life.

The dragon suddenly appeared around the edge of the hull. It reared back preparing another blast of flame. Primo cowered;

Enzo braced himself. The 'rest of his life' sure did not last long, he thought.

Then, Fantina astride Leo, his mighty wings spread wide, soared down from above, landing between the dragon and Enzo.

The dragon's eyes flashed. His red scales rippled as he recoiled, then bowed submissively.

"Leo!" Enzo called out in amazement. "You are back, and just in time." Enzo eyed the dragon warily.

Leo shook his head. "It is not me he bows to." Leo cast a gentle gaze at Fantina. Fantina stared back at him, puzzled. "You have the same spark that I saw in your father's eyes many years ago," Leo said.

Enzo looked to Fantina clearly confused. "What?"

"Venice is a timeless city," Leo explained to Fantina. "And while your grandfather and father protected it...so were they." Fantina's eyes widened, a memory stirring within. Leo nodded, "Think back, to a different time. Think back, to the story beyond the ordinary."

Fantina considered, then closed her eyes, and suddenly, she saw a place, a glittering palace of red and gold, the great Emperor Kublai Khan smiling as a set of massive, vault doors opened before her. From within, a golden light brightened until it washed over her. Leo's voice continued. "A treasure can be more than gold."

Fantina crinkled her nose, closing her eyes tighter… She saw a sunset. Marco Polo, now in his fifties, and his father Niccolò sat astride Nicos and Dimitris, on the balcony of St. Mark's Basilica, surveying the *piazza* below as the golden pulse of twilight swept over them.

Leo's voice drifted in over the memory. "Glim flows through the city and through the lives of those who defend it."

"The Gondoliers." Fantina nodded as she saw Marco Polo before a row of newly enlisted Gondoliers in *Piazza San Marco,* standing at attention. And on the clock tower ledge above them was Leo, watching with an approving gaze.

Enzo interrupted. "Wait, you mean her father—"

"—lived a very long time," Leo completed the thought.

Fantina clenched her eyes tightly, searching her mind until she saw…a day not as long ago, a departure from the quay along the *Riva Degli Schiavoni,* a steam *vaporetto* ready to cast off. On board was a couple with a small child…a young girl no more than two. The father was Marco Polo, looking older, but nowhere near the 633 years he should have been. His father Niccolò stepped close, placing a chain and gold pendant around the young girl's neck with a smile. It was a coin actually, and the markings on it, though already timeworn and somewhat faded, looked a bit like Chinese characters. He touched a finger to her forehead as if placing a memory…

Fantina paused. Her closed eyes narrowed, thinking deeply, as if a stunning realization was taking shape in her mind. She reached up to touch the shape of her pendant beneath her shirt.

Leo continued. "But your father was an explorer at heart. And with you and your mother, he chose a different life…a mortal life."

An image swirled in Fantina's mind—a photograph in an oval, silver frame on an old chest of drawers in a dusty attic space. It was her frame, her father; it was Marco Polo.

Fantina gasped as a cloud of steam hissed over the image taking her mind back again to the quay as she looked up through the eyes of the little girl she once was. Her father and mother standing at the bow as the *vaporetto* chugged away from Venice toward a new horizon.

"He left the protection of Venice in the caring hands of his Gondoliers, and he ventured out so he could show you the world," Leo concluded. "He told you his story, though, so that one day you might find, here in Venice, that 'one thing' for which you are looking."

Fantina opened her eyes, bright and clear, remembering… "And locked in memory, of time long gone; You'll find the place where you belong."

Enzo looked at Fantina curiously, holding out the *Poveglia* key. "Another clue from the journal?" he asked.

Fantina hesitated, staring uncertainly at the key. She looked to Leo, then turned toward the sunken ruins. "This way."

Fantina and Leo led Enzo and Primo down a dark and damp stone corridor toward a heavy wooden door. Fantina took the skeleton key and turned it in the lock. The door clicked open. She shared an expectant look with Enzo…then pushed.

The door swung on its ancient, creaking hinges into a cavernous, domed chamber. Dim starlight reflected in from windows in a small cupola high above, as Fantina and Enzo entered. The room was empty and old, filled only with gloom, like a dark crypt that the lagoon had swallowed in time. The walls and ceiling were dingy and water-stained with vague fresco images fading in the plaster. Primo stepped in, a grim and weary look in his eyes. "Nothing. There is no gold. I knew it." Primo eyed Fantina suspiciously. "Lots of shoes, right?"

Leo crossed into the chamber, pacing the ancient stone floor. "There *is* a treasure here in Venice," he explained, "and it *is* golden."

Primo doubled back, then rushed to inspect every dark corner in the room. "Where, where...I no see it."

Fantina considered, wondering what treasure might be hidden in what seemed like an empty space. She looked up at the domed ceiling curiously, studying the faint images there until suddenly she paused. The room seemed to brighten. The dim frescoes became...familiar to her and began to swirl before her eyes.

Like a giant, domed, moving work of enchanted art, the ceiling images became clearer till they leapt from the plaster itself to reveal the wondrous story of places and familiar faces that Fantina had seen and met since her arrival in Venice: the *piazzas* and palaces, *Burano, Murano* and the stunning Grand Canal...Cosimo, Joe and Eva and the Gondoliers...Nicos, Dimitris, the sentinels, statues and creatures...the ghostly crew from *Poveglia*...all fighting side by side on the battlefield... On the shore, Mayor Grimani and the gathered people at the quay, cheering their champions, hope restored...and Uncle Gio smiling, as if in that very moment he was there, standing beside

Fantina as she discovered her part in the extraordinary adventure and story of Venice...

Fantina placed an arm around Leo's golden mane and took Enzo's hand in hers. Enzo looked down at his hand in Fantina's, somewhat surprised but quietly pleased. Fantina smiled. "Treasure found."

Enzo nodded and tapped his earbud. "We are done here. Finish up. We will fly out with Leo."

On the battlefield, Cosimo nodded as Dimitris spun about and smashed a ratter with a well-placed kick. He motioned to the Gondoliers. "We head back. Contessa...let the waters flow."

Contessa took out one last ratter with a solid punch to its pointed nose, then whistled to Ding and Dong. "All done, boys. Open it up."

Ding shot Dong a lively glance, then squared up to the sea wall. "This is fun. We have to be getting out more often."

Dong nodded in agreement as he heaved his hammer high. "Less sleep, more party." Ratters shrieked and scurried away as Dong swung. The wall buckled. Rivets at the seams popped and shot across the inlet, taking out a few more fleeing ratters.

Contessa smiled and tapped her earbud. "Everyone back," she ordered.

Cosimo reined Dimitris to a halt as the *Poveglia* ghosts swarmed over the remaining ratters. Luigi and Angela floated up beside him. "Is it time to go?" Angela asked.

Cosimo nodded. "You were all a great help," he said. "Venice is in your debt."

Luigi sighed happily. "Then it has been a most fulfilling evening. Thank you. Now you go quickly. We will hold them here for a while longer while you retreat to higher ground." Luigi looked to Angela with a wistful gaze. "Then," he said, "we will move on as well."

Cosimo nodded appreciatively then urged Dimitris onward toward the shore.

Back in the sunken chamber, Enzo motioned urgently toward the exit. "Time to fly."

Leo nodded and turned Fantina toward the exit when suddenly, a figure appeared in the doorway. It was Malvagio. Mud spattered and bedraggled, he stood, blocking the way out, staring coldly at Fantina and the empty room behind her. "All these years, for nothing," he muttered wearily. "It was all just a story." Malvagio raised his arm menacingly toward Fantina, Enzo's bow iron scimitar in hand.

Fantina retreated a step to stand beside Enzo and Leo, and eyed the door anxiously. There was no time to delay. Soon the sea walls would come down and the lagoon would flood back in and reclaim everything that had been exposed, including the empty chamber in which they were standing.

Primo stared at Malvagio disappointedly, the lustre of the Malvagio family name (and fake noble pedigree) clearly tarnished. He stepped forward, putting himself between Malvagio and Fantina. "It is no use. It is over. You have failed."

Malvagio looked stunned by Primo's insolence. Then his eyes flashed. "How dare you," he fumed. "I will show you and everyone what I am capable of."

Malvagio raised his sword overhead preparing to strike, but Primo didn't flinch. He stared back at him, unapologetic. "No. I think you have already shown all Venice what you are capable of," Primo said, shaking his head like a disapproving father. "And no one is impressed." Primo stood tall and spread his arms wide to shield Fantina and Enzo.

Malvagio froze—his anger quickly swelling to rage. "Maybe," Malvagio said, "but this fairy tale of yours does not get a happy ending." Malvagio slashed downward. The blade struck the rusted door handle, snapping it off. Malvagio then retreated from the room, slamming the door shut soundly.

Enzo rushed forward, trying to grip the door's edge with his fingertips, but it was no use. "We're trapped," he sighed.

The *Lido* sea wall was battered and weakened, water spraying in through every seam and at every edge. Ding and Dong braced themselves on either bank of the inlet and raised their hammers together for a final blow. With a nod, they swung. Iron buckled and gave way. The wall collapsed in a twisted heap, and the sea came rushing back into the lagoon.

At the *Malamocco* inlet, Atlas reached down and dug his fingers into the mud. He gripped the base of the sea wall and pulled. His muscles bulged and the steel bent in his grip as water began trickling in along the muddy bottom and sides of the inlet. Nearby, Hercules struck a heroic pose. "You need a little help?"

Atlas shook his head as he strained, "No, no, I got this."

"Are you sure? I am a demigod, after all."

Atlas groaned. "I told you, you are not a real— Oh, never mind." Atlas tightened his grip and heaved. The wall ripped from its foundation as Atlas lifted it high up onto his shoulders.

The tide poured in through the inlet swirling past him as he shot Hercules a triumphant look. "Titans rule."

The *Chioggia* sea wall warped inward as Mars pressed his giant, war spear into the side bank and pried. On the other bank, Neptune did the same with his mighty trident. The Adriatic Sea, pressing from the outside, began spraying in at the seams. Neptune smiled. "Flow, my beautiful *Adriatico*. Flow freely and come home to Venice." Finally, the wall bent inward and tore away from the inlet banks as the sea burst through.

The ratter captain grinned menacingly as she watched the Gondoliers and sentinels retreat back across the lagoon bed. Her ratter army, still fighting back the ghostly crew from *Poveglia*, noticed the retreat as well and paused to chatter victoriously.

The unsettling din, however, was quickly drowned out by a different noise—the sound of rushing water. The ratters hesitated, then turned toward the swelling roar. A tidal wave was raging toward them from the *Lido* inlet.

Luigi looked to Angela with a roguish grin. "This is what I call closure," he said. And with that, he and his ghostly crew quietly and quickly dissolved into mist and disappeared.

The ratter captain stood dumbstruck, her nose twitching helplessly, as ratters turned and fled. An instant later, the giant wave of water crashed down over them all, erasing them and the muddy battlefield from existence.

"Marco Polo," Malvagio grumbled as he trudged up the side of the muddy sinkhole away from the sunken ruins. "When I am through with this city, no one will even know he existed."

Malvagio scoffed, but then, suddenly paused. A rumbling noise was swelling above him. He looked up as a pair of large, red, intimidating claws appeared at the rim of the sinkhole followed by a pair of large, fiery eyes. Malvagio wilted in the dragon's stare, but as he did, the dragon changed. The dragon's red scales faded and became a bluish green, like the seawater itself that now rose behind him like a tsunami. The water and the dragon then poured over the edge, racing down toward Malvagio, its jaw opening wide. Malvagio's face drooped as he shook his head defeatedly. "I really hate water," he grumbled a moment before his world went dark.

Cosimo, astride Dimitris, leapt up onto the partially destroyed boat landing before the Ducal Palace. The other Gondoliers and sentinels followed, water lapping at their heels as it raced back into the lagoon bed. Uncle Gio rushed out to meet them. "Fantina?" he called. He turned to Cosimo. "Where are they?"

Cosimo paused, then scanned the sky over the rapidly filling lagoon with concern.

The Adriatic Sea flowed, rushing back in to fill the lagoon, washing away Malvagio and his threat for good. From *Lido* to *Malamocco* and from the inlet at *Chioggia,* the turbulent tide poured in and covered the muddy bottom, reclaiming whatever secrets might have been revealed along with the ruins of the sunken monastery…and everyone left inside.

The water crashed against the sidewalls of St. Mark's Basin, restoring the lagoon to its former depth. It splashed up onto the quay, spraying the pavement with a sheen of seawater that glistened in the starlight. Uncle Gio, Cosimo and Contessa stood silently on the landing, looking out uncertainly over the water as it stilled itself and the evening went quiet. "They are with Leo," Cosimo assured them. "They will be…safe."

"We should have waited a bit longer," Contessa said as she scanned the sky above.

"We could not," Cosimo explained. He looked along the ravaged shoreline, at the eroded walkways and damaged buildings. "Venice would not have survived." Cosimo hesitated, re-considering, then looked to Uncle Gio.

"You are right," Uncle Gio said. "That was the plan—to save Venice. It is what Fantina wanted...no matter the cost—" Uncle Gio paused, words caught in his throat as his eyes filled with tears. He wasn't quite used to the feeling. He had been alone in his work for so long, and certainly unprepared when Fantina had arrived, but as perplexing as he had found her, he knew now that without her he would feel...less hopeful. "A real...pain in the neck, that girl," he said as his tears over-flowed.

Chapter Thirty — secrets

Inside the sunken chamber, the starlight filtering down through the water and the windows of the cupola above began to fade. Soon the chamber would be dark and secret again, as it had been for centuries before. Fantina and Enzo stood beside Leo, as Primo took a tentative step closer. "I am sorry. I am to blame," he said quietly. "All I wanted was a little bit of treasure, to buy a little *trattoria,* serve every kind of *pasta* and the best *Fettucine al Pesto* in all of Italy." He considered. "Well, better than what they serve in Genoa anyhow. A little place to call my own."

Fantina considered. She shared a sympathetic look with Enzo and Leo...and understood. "I think that's what we're all looking for."

"Really?" Primo sounded surprised. "*Fettucine al Pesto?* Or you are just saying that because you are hungry and we are probably going to starve to death down here in this watery tomb. That is what you are thinking, right?"

Fantina frowned. "Well it is now."

"No," Enzo cut in, "She meant the part about finding a place, where we belong."

Primo paused. "Ah, right. Silly idea, *eh?*"

Leo shook his head. "No," he assured Fantina, Enzo and Primo as he spread his wings and gathered them in protectively, "it is never foolish to hope." Just then, the chamber went dark...

But not for long. A giant, undulating shadow passed directly over the cupola, blocking out the dim starlight for a moment before it swam past. Fantina and Enzo looked confused, but Primo, with one glance from Leo, knew the truth. "Dragon," Leo whispered.

The cupola above suddenly shattered as the dragon of Marco Polo, now blue as the sea, soared into the chamber. Water cascaded downward with a roar as the dragon landed in the room's center, its long, slender body coiling protectively around the group. It looked down at Fantina with a docile expression, motioning to its back with a tilt of its giant head. Fantina smiled.

Cosimo and the Gondoliers rushed along the quay preparing to launch a hastily assembled fleet of rescue boats—gondolas, steam *vaporetti* and water taxis—anything that hadn't been damaged beyond use. Bianca, in the meantime, marshalled her pigeon patrol of *fate* along with Gen and the Eagle of Trieste, to begin a search from the sky.

"You let us know if you see anything out of the ordinary from up there," Contessa called to Bianca.

Bianca cooed when suddenly...

The water just off the bows of the assembled boats exploded upward like a geyser, drenching everyone from head to toe. A massive form leapt through the spray and landed solidly on the shore. It was the dragon with Fantina and Enzo riding high on its back.

Faces froze in astonishment. Uncle Gio considered with a raised eyebrow. "I would say that is out of the ordinary."

Just then, the dragon flicked its tail out of the water. Primo, clinging desperately to the end of it, landed with a thump on the edge of the shore. He opened his eyes, astonished. "I am alive! Yes! Thank you!" He let go of the tail and kissed the ground gratefully, over and over.

Leo swooped down from above, landing on the *piazzetta* amongst the gathered guests from the ball and festive locals in costume. The people stared at Leo, the other sentinels, statues and creatures…and the dragon, speechless and uncertain.

Leo noted their apprehension and turned gently to face them. "Friends," he began, "never be afraid…to hope. It is the 'one thing' that makes all things better."

Fantina crinkled her nose, then nodded, as if hearing her father's voice again, reminding her to see with more than just her eyes, to feel that common thread of hope coursing through every story he had told her and in every place they had been, as tangible as the wind and water. Fantina rose, then slid down the side of the dragon to stand beside Leo.

Leo continued. "You must all be Gondoliers. Raise the Glim every day, and your *Venezia*, this wonderful city where hope springs eternal, will forever be saved." The gathered people nodded then cheered. Their city was now in their hands, and they would defend it with their whole hearts.

Enzo dismounted and stepped up behind Fantina. "Well, there it is, a happy ending—sunk, drowned, swallowed by the sea..." The dragon gurgled a gravelly but happy growl then burped up Malvagio's two service medallions, one bronze, one silver. They plunked down onto the pavement at the Mayor's feet. Primo patted the dragon on the head. "Good little poochy."

Leo turned to Fantina and bowed with grateful reverence. "You have a good heart, and Venice thanks you." The other sentinels and the dragon bowed low as well. The Mayor took note then bent down onto one knee, as did Enzo, Cosimo, the Gondoliers and every other person in the *piazza.*

Uncle Gio watched with pride as Fantina stood at the center in speechless modesty, surrounded by the gratitude of the entire city.

"Wonderful," Contessa chimed in. "What do you say we get this *Carnevale* back on track?" Ding and Dong stepped up behind Contessa excitedly. "Party time," Dong whooped as a heartfelt cheer swelled through the *piazza.*

Fantina smiled then ran over to give Uncle Gio a big hug. She had so much she needed to say. "Thanks, Uncle Gio. Thank you for everything," she began. "I know taking me in was a bit more than you were expecting, and I'm sure at some point you were probably kicking yourself for inviting me in the first place, but—"

Uncle Gio raised a hand. Fantina stopped. She was talking too much.

"You did well," Uncle Gio said with a nod. "Now, go celebrate…" Uncle Gio paused as he eyed Enzo across the *piazza*. "…a little," he added. "But stay out of trouble and be home by eleven, *eh?*"

Fantina considered with a smile, and whispered to herself… "Home."

The Paper Gate of the Ducal Palace was thrown open as costumed guests and locals alike joined in the last day of *Carnevale* festivities. The celebration spilled out from the formal palace ball into the streets of Venice where Ding and Dong drummed out a rhythm, and music drifted on air inviting everyone to dance.

Signora Sofia, from the *Cucina Segreta*, was hard at work, together now with Primo, serving her secret recipes and his *Fettucine al Pesto* (the best in all of Italy) to the gathered revelers.

Gondoliers were welcomed by the crowds, recognized as the heroes they were, while the sentinels gathered together to recount their own stories and adventures of years past.

Cosimo stood amid the merriment, pleased by the spirit now alive and well throughout the city. It would be a new era for Venice, a time when the progress and innovation of the new century would stand side-by-side with the traditions of the past.

"Congratulations," said Mayor Grimani as he stepped up beside Cosimo, tugging nervously on his mustache. "I was wrong. This may be a new time and a new world, but we will always need the Gondoliers. You have always been the true 'Protectors of Venice.'"

With that, he reached forward with the two regurgitated service medallions to pin them to Cosimo's pocket. Noting the dragon slobber dripping from them, he paused. "Maybe I should shine these up a bit first, *eh?*" Cosimo nodded gratefully. The Mayor offered a handshake instead, but when Cosimo raised his hand, he realized his fingertips were still smouldering a bit. The Mayor retreated a step with an awkward grin and patted Cosimo on the back. "Ah, well, good job. We will talk later," he chirped as he backed away cautiously.

Contessa, swishing her flounced, *Colombina* skirt flirtatiously, cozied up beside Uncle Gio in his *Arlecchino* costume with a smile. "I am thinking that you probably want to ask me to dance, no?"

"I…do?" Uncle Gio considered. He shrugged. "Yes, I think I do. How did you know?"

"*Beh*, I see what I see," Contessa winked.

Uncle Gio nodded. He offered Contessa his arm and led her away to join the dancers in the *piazza*.

Fantina stepped out through an archway at the front of the Ducal Palace and stood along the boat landing, looking out over the lagoon. The water was like glass, still and calm once again. The sky above was clear and cloudless, a canopy of stars twinkling brightly.

Just then, Enzo approached, hiding a trace of concern in his voice. "Hey, you are not leaving, are you?"

Fantina turned with a smile. "No, I think I might stay around for a while."

"Oh," Enzo nodded, trying to appear nonchalant, "good."

"Really…why is that?" Fantina played along.

"Because," Enzo thought quickly, "I have ideas, you know? To make my mark, fortune and glory and all that." He considered. "But I could really use a…partner."

Fantina laughed softly. "You don't say."

"I do say." Enzo hesitated then stepped closer. He looked into Fantina's eyes. "Because I think you are…fanticulous."

Fantina smiled. "And you're very Verne," she replied. Fantina leaned in and gave Enzo a quick kiss. It surprised her almost as much as it stunned him, and for a moment she felt like she was floating on air...or slipping on water.

"A little wobbly?" Enzo offered his hand to Fantina...to help her steady herself. Fantina laughed gently and took it.

Further up along the quay, Fantina spotted Leo, standing alone. He was rimmed in the dim light, almost a shadow in the mist, but somehow practically glowing from within. His golden mane flowed in the breeze off the sea, and his broad back and shoulders looked stronger than they ever had before, like he was...more alive.

Fantina and Enzo stepped close. Leo, still facing out into the breeze acknowledged them with a nod. "So, was the search worth the trip?" he asked.

Fantina paused, thinking back. She looked toward the celebration in the piazza—the light, the music...her 'one big family.' She nodded. "And the treasure was definitely worth the search," she said.

Leo looked pleased. He turned to face Fantina and Enzo. "Good. Then Venice is home," he stated.

Fantina smiled. "It is."

"Enzo, your *Nonna* Contessa said I should take you and Fantina on a little tour—the scenic route." Leo unfurled his wings and showed his back.

Enzo shared a look with Fantina and shrugged. "She does have a gift."

Fantina smiled, then climbed aboard. Enzo climbed on behind her, and Leo, with a mighty flap of his wings, leapt up into the air.

The thin sliver of the new moon shone against a black, velvet sky dotted with millions of stars, as high over the rooftops of Venice, Leo soared with Fantina and Enzo clinging tightly to his mane.

Fantina felt the wind on her face as it whistled past, sounding almost like a melody as they crossed the city, gliding over palaces and around towers, and swooping down to brush the glittering surface of the Grand Canal.

Then Leo spiraled upward again, higher than before till the city below and the surrounding lagoon became small, like a distant memory, a secret shimmering in the darkness.

"Look," Leo urged.

Fantina and Enzo gazed down in wonder. The magical city of Venice was laid out like a miniature model...or a map, the stars above, mirrored in the waters of the lagoon below. It was beautiful, Fantina thought to herself, and somehow...peculiar. She looked closer, as they soared onward, and the wind's melody became a voice, drifting on the breeze—words stirring from within her memory, words from an ancient journal...

"To find what is golden the journey must start, with an open mind and a worthy heart. Bring siren's gift and search awhile, where tolls the bell on a cursed isle. Beneath the pattern you will see, the key to solve this mystery. Then banished fires and dragon's bone, will point the way to traitor's home. Where Paradise before you lies, hidden beneath the starry skies."

Fantina stared downward curiously, her eyes widening as she noticed the reflection of the stars on the surface of the lagoon. She had never seen so many before. They formed a dotted pattern on the water, like constellations brought down from above. Stirred with the movement of the tide, a scene unfolded before her eyes—ships sailing the open sea, a Chinese dragon leading the way through the lagoon then swirling to a spot near the center. Fantina gasped, then heard the voice again.

"And locked in memory of time long gone, you'll find the place where you belong. For in darkest night, truth is revealed, the path to treasures yet concealed." Fantina crinkled her nose and hugged Leo tightly with a knowing smile.

Suddenly Leo threw back his wings and plunged downward toward the water. He dove past swirling clouds of mist and moisture and splashed through the mirrored surface of the lagoon, to reveal a world beneath. Flying, as if still through air but slowed in an altered form of space, Fantina and Enzo clung fast as Leo glided through a deep blue, luminescent flow toward the remains of a sunken ship, half buried in the muddy bottom of the lagoon. Huge and hidden, Fantina could read the name 'Paradise' written on the hull. Fantina smiled—'hidden beneath the stars,' she thought to herself.

Leo, Fantina and Enzo dove through a bulkhead opening, past the sweeping arched ribs of the hull that curved gracefully before them. Porthole windows glowed like crystal gems as they skimmed through the wooden corridors trimmed in golden accents and Far Eastern designs—lotus blossoms and orchids, peacock patterns and flowing koi motifs.

Up ahead, a sealed bulkhead door appeared. On it, the faint trace of faded symbols became visible—golden Chinese characters that suddenly began to glow. Fantina's pendant swung out from beneath her shirt. It was glowing as well as they soared straight for the door. The door flew open as they passed through into a dark and cavernous cargo hold.

A sudden spark, like flickering stardust, swirled through the space to reveal its contents—glittering gold, jewels of untold brilliance, chests of riches, treasures beyond counting—a breathtaking vision of past fortune and glory. And it was real.

Fantina smiled. Venice did indeed have a secret. But it wasn't just a golden treasure. It was a story, glimmering in the night and whispered in the evening air that would stir your hope and urge you to believe much more than simply what you saw. For when you truly open your eyes, search deeply and embrace all the wondrous people and places that swirl about you in an endless flow of possibility, you will discover more than you ever imagined.

Leo continued on toward an even brighter doorway, washing Fantina and Enzo in an otherworldly glow till they passed through, and disappeared in the light beyond.

EPILOGUE

"And that is how the magic of Venice was restored and the city was saved." Your gondolier smiles at you as your gondola ride coasts to its conclusion, through the mouth of the Grand Canal and into St. Mark's Basin. Above, the setting sun streaks the sky with a spectacular show of pink and orange as the water below reflects the colors across the surface and up onto the city itself.

"Of course," he continues, "that last part of the story is only a rumor. No one really knows if the treasure of Marco Polo was ever really found. Some say it is still out there, somewhere. Or maybe it really is something altogether different, a golden sun-set shared, a friend found...a family to be treasured."

With that, your gondola glides to the quay before the *piazzetta* where, in your mind, if you close your eyes and crinkle your nose, you can almost see Fantina arriving so many years ago. The gondolier steadies the vessel and offers you his hand to help you climb out onto the walkway.

As you pay him what now seems like much less than what the ride was actually worth, he nods gratefully. "There you go," he says, "back on the solid ground of reality, *eh?* Now you go, enjoy your visit. And remember, no matter where you find yourself in your life, no matter where you are coming from or where you are going...in Venice, the city where hope springs eternal...you will always belong."

With that, the gondolier pushes off with a wink and a smile, and for a moment, you'd swear that his eye twinkles gold, and looks...almost cat-like.

Then, the sound of a motor whirs. Two pontoon water skies descend from the gondola's sides and the gondola zips away into the Venetian sunset.

THE END

APPENDIX
TIMELINE OF VENETIAN HISTORY

421   Region along the Adriatic coast is settled.

539   The territory is claimed by the Byzantine Empire.

568   Germanic Barbarian Lombards invade from the north, forcing refugees to seek safety on the largely uninhabited islands off the coast.

697   Island settlements organize under a Byzantine governor (dux, later doge). They become a hub for seaborne trade.

810   Pepin the Short, the son of Frankish ruler Charles Martel, invades the region for the Frankish Empire. After an unsuccessful six-month siege, Pepin withdraws.

814   As a Byzantine territory under Emperor Nicephorus, the region is granted trading rights along the Adriatic coast and is named *La Republica Serenissima di Venezia* (The Most Serene Republic of Venice).

828   Venice acquires, from Alexandria in Egypt, the relics of St. Mark the Evangelist who is named the patron saint of Venice. His heraldic symbol, the winged lion, is incorporated into the city's architecture.

1000 Venice, now a naval power, defeats Narentine pirates of the Adriatic Sea and extends its commercial trading dominance in ports across the eastern Mediterranean.

1094 The first historical mention of a *gondola* is chronicled in a letter by a Venetian official.

1106 A great fire in Venice destroys many wooden homes and 24 churches, including the church of *San Lorenzo*. From that point on, building in stone becomes more common.

1162 The first *Carnevale* festivity is celebrated in honor of a Venetian victory against Ulrich II von Treven of Aquileia. Ulrich is forced to pay an annual tribute which includes 1 bull and 12 pigs which are butchered, thus the *carne-vale* or the farewell to meat.

1204 Doge Enrico Dandolo leads Venice in the Fourth Crusade. He secures additional ports and territories in the Ionian and Aegean Seas, and sacks Constantinople, returning to Venice with considerable plunder, including the bronze *Quadriga* horses which are placed on the facade balcony of the basilica of *San Marco*.

1254 Marco Polo is born.

1256 The first war between Venice and Genoa begins. It lasts 15 years. Venice triumphs, but loses the commercial dominance it won in Byzantium during the Crusades.

1260 Niccolò and Maffeo Polo (Marco's father and uncle) set sail on a trading journey to the East. They are welcomed in the court of Kublai, the khan of the Mongols. They return to Venice 9 years later.

1271 Marco Polo accompanies his father and uncle on a second journey to the East.

1275 Marco Polo is appointed as a special envoy of Kublai and travels throughout Asia on various missions for the khan.

1291 After a particularly disastrous string of fires in Venice, Doge Pietro Gradenigo orders that the large furnaces of all artisan glassmakers in Venice must be relocated to the island of *Murano*. The island becomes the main producer of glass in Europe through the 17th century.

1292 Kublai Khan sends the Polo's on their way with 14 ships loaded with gifts of untold riches. By the time they reach Persia, however, only one ship remains. No mention of the lost ships is recorded anywhere.

1294 The second war between Venice and Genoa begins. It lasts six years. The Genoese dominate.

1295 Marco Polo returns to Venice.

1298 Marco Polo is made a "gentleman commander" in the Venetian navy. In the battle of Curzola, he is taken prisoner. While imprisoned in Genoa, he recounts the story of his adventures in China to his cellmate, a writer from Pisa named Rustichello.

1299 Marco Polo is released from prison.

1300 Marco Polo marries a Venetian lady, Donata. They eventually have three daughters, Fantina, Bellela and Moreta. The book of Polo's travels, *Il Milione,* becomes popular throughout Europe, although no authoritative version exists. Early copies of the manuscript vary significantly.

1324 Marco Polo dies in Venice and is buried in the Church of *San Lorenzo*. The body, however, goes missing, and after a 16th century rebuilding of the church, no one is sure where it is.

1340 Redesign and rebuilding of the Ducal Palace begins under the direction of architect Filippo Calendario.

1348 The population of Venice is halved by an outbreak of the Bubonic plague. As the death toll rises, authorities forcibly remove Venetians who show any sign of the disease and confine them to the island of *Poveglia*.

1350 The third war between Venice and Genoa over commercial dominance begins. After six years, the outcome is inconclusive.

1355   Doge Marino Faliero plots to assume lordship over all of Venice. He is found guilty of treason and executed on the Giants' Staircase of the new Ducal Palace. His architect, Filippo Calendario, is also executed as a co-conspirator.

1355   Artist Guariento di Arpo is invited by Venetian authorities to paint on the walls of the great council hall of the Ducal Palace. Guariento's painting is called "Paradise." It is painted over in subsequent renovations.

1377   The fourth war between Venice and Genoa begins, this time over the island of Tenedos which is situated squarely within the trade route to the Black Sea. After a crushing loss in the battle of Pola, Venetian Admiral Vettor Pisani is removed from command and thrown in Venetian prison.

1380   The Battle of Chioggia. Admiral Pisani is released from prison when Genoa enters the Venetian lagoon at Chioggia and is poised to storm the city of Venice. Pisani and Admiral Carlo Zeno brilliantly blockade the Genoese fleet in the shallows of Chioggia, and force a surrender with the first-ever use of ship-borne cannons.

1575   Another plague outbreak kills 25% of Venice's population.

1600   Gondolas reach the peak of their popularity, numbering about 10,000.

1630   The plague returns, killing 50,000 (one third of remaining population).

1797   French forces, led by Napoleon Bonaparte, sack the Venetian Republic and depose the last Venetian Doge, Ludovico Manin. Works of art (including the four *Quadriga* horses) are plundered and taken to Paris. Napoleon signs Venice over to the Austrian Hapsburg Empire in the Treaty of *Campo Formio.*

1797   Venetian *Carnevale* celebration is outlawed under Austrian rule. The use of masks is forbidden. The tradition gradually and sporadically returns in the latter half of the 19th century.

1848   Venetians, led by Daniele Manin, rebel against Austria and establish the Republic of *San Marco.* They then join the Kingdom of *Sadinia* to unify against the threat from Austria and France.

1849   In the First Italian War of Independence, Austria defeats the Kingdom of *Sadinia* and retakes the Republic of *San Marco.*

1861   The Kingdom of Italy is created under Vittorio Emanuele II of the House of Savoy.

1866   Austro-Prussian War results in Austria ceding Venice and its surrounding territories to France, which in turn cedes it to the Kingdom of Italy as per the Treaty of Vienna. With a vote that is largely regarded as a formality, Venice is annexed by Italy.

1872   Through the patronage of Princess (and future Queen) Margherita *di Savoia*, the Lace School of *Burano* is established.

1872   First public transportation system in Italy, the *vaporetto* water bus, is introduced in Venice. Service throughout the Grand Canal begins in 1881.

1878   Umberto I ascends to the throne upon the death of his father, Emanuele II, and becomes King of Italy.

1894   The first *Esposizione Internazionale d'Arte* (International Art Exhibit of the City of Venice) is held. Attending the opening is Italian King Umberto I and Queen Margherita *di Savoia*.

1895   Guglielmo Marconi sends the first long-range radio transmission.

1895   Filippo Grimani becomes the mayor of Venice and serves through 1919.

1900   King Umberto I is assassinated by anarchist Gaetano Breschi, who is captured and convicted. Bresci is later found dead in his prison cell.

1900   The hydrofoil is invented by Enrico Forlanini.

1902   The *campanile* (bell tower) of St. Mark's collapses. It is rebuilt in 1912.

1979   *Carnevale* officially returns as an annual festival promoted by the Italian government to celebrate the history and culture of Venice.

2003   Construction begins on the *Mosè* (Moses) Project to install 78 mobile flood gates at the inlets of Lido, Malamocco and Chioggia to protect Venice from high tides and the rising sea level. Plagued by delays, cost overruns and charges of political corruption, the project remains unfinished to date.

2009   Venetian tradition receives an update with the first ever female gondolier.

2019   There are currently about 400 gondolas operating in Venice, licensed under the auspices of their guild...the Gondoliers.

AUTHOR'S NOTE

The inspiration for "The Gondoliers" sprang from my many
trips with my family to Venice, Italy, when I was a child, and
again years later when I returned as an adult with my own children. Wandering through the labyrinth of narrow alleyways and
canals as the sun was quickly fading, the story of a mysterious,
hidden world that came to life at that magical moment between
sunset and dusk mingled with the actual history of the city, and
I found myself creating a world layered with "fanticulous" possibilities.

Paolo Mazzucato

BEPIBOOKS

CPSIA information can be obtained
at www.ICGtesting.com
Printed in the USA
BVHW031929080419
544943BV00003B/10/P